SHADOW LEGION

J.E. GURLEY

SHADOW LEGION

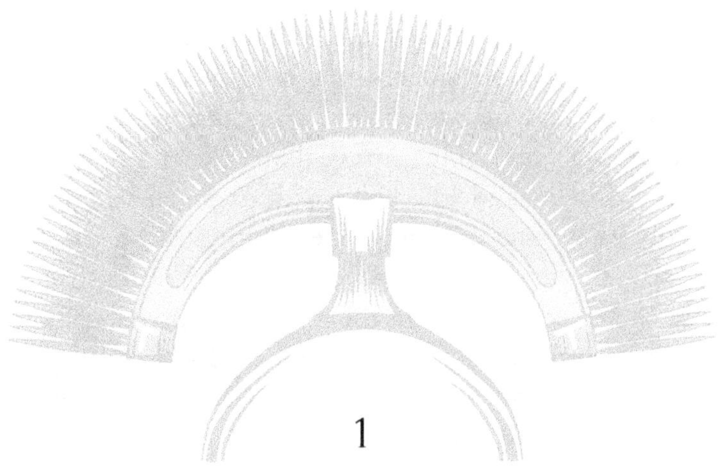

1

The blistering wind pried sharp grains of sand from the desert floor and hurled them into Gaius Marcus Linneus' face. Each tiny particle became a ravenous, silicate creature whose dagger-sharp teeth gnawed hungrily at the tender flesh around his fierce steel-gray eyes. He lifted higher the dirty, red focale covering his nose and mouth to protect it from the onslaught. Flinty dust sifted through the loosely woven linen scarf, souring his parched throat and leaving the taste of mighty mountains ground to dust by centuries of perpetually scouring winds. Thc odor of sun-baked earth plugged his dust-coated nostrils.

He snorted to clear his nose. "This accursed sand seeks to kill me even before I reach my new post."

Gaius was no stranger to deserts. Armenia and Mesopotamia had been his home for four years, but the deserts there had been the cradle of civilization, harsh and desolate but livable. Mesopotamian civilizations had arisen, thrived, and fallen over the centuries. The Sahara was unyielding, unconquerable. Man survived in the Sahara, but he did not thrive.

Gaius glanced up at the sun, a burning yellow ember perched in the dirty sky. He had cooked beneath its onslaught for weeks. Today, however, instead of broiling him, the searing wind sent a cold, foreboding chill crawling up Gaius' spine, as he surveyed the ragged collection of sun-bleached, brown leather tents that would be his new home. *For how long? If Emperor Marcus Aurelius has anything to say about it, until my death.*

Perched atop a rocky spine lifting like a skeletal finger beckoning from a sea of golden sand, the hovel of leather tents more resembled a double row of weathered tombstones than it did a proper Roman *castra,* or fort. The tents crouched behind a low, unfinished rock wall constructed to protect them from the winds that periodically flayed the bones of the earth upon which the camp rested. Two of the *papilia* sagged in the middle like worn saddles or a resting butterfly from which the name derived. The rough outline of a stacked-stone building formed one corner of the bleak compound.

The sight of the makeshift fort drew a deprecating scowl from Gaius. Like any proper Roman commander, he abhorred sloppiness, and the condition of the fort spoke of lethargy and neglect. *Yes, Marcus Aurellius has chosen my punishment well.*

He turned his attention to the surrounding sea of sand, scanning it, as would a sailor gazing out at the endless expanse of water from the prow of his ship. The stark landscape, barren and lifeless to the beholder, bore no trees save for the three withered date palms swaying above the fort, and no shrubs. Not a single blade of green grass broke the bleak, monotonous view extending to the distant, knife-edge horizon. No birds soared above it. No lizards, vipers, or scorpions patrolled the wasteland in search of scarce prey. It was a dry, parched, desolate land – a dead land.

White, wind-chased wispy clouds sped across the burnt sky, offering a tantalizing hope of rain that would never come. Like the Emperor's false promise of redemption, the pitiful camp reminded Gaius of just how far from the Emperor's grace he had fallen. A gust of wind sent particles of sand and dust around the edge of his focale and into his mouth. He moved it aside and spat out the bitter dust.

"Is it always this windy?" he asked Flavius Cirrus, his new Optio, his second in command. "This pervasive dust is unbearable."

"This day is calm compared to most. You will get used to it – eventually." Flavius reined in his mount. "Castra-Augustus," he announced with a wave of his naked, hirsute arm, indicating the sparse collection of ragged tents comprising the fortified camp. His forced smile barely creased his weathered face darkened by the sun, and his dark brown eyes betrayed no hint of amusement.

Flavius had ridden out from the encampment a few hours earlier to meet him along the way, a thoughtful gesture Gaius appreciated from a subordinate, but the entire ride back had been a constant barrage of questions Gaius preferred not to answer until he had taken proper stock of his new post. He nodded perfunctorily, his mind absorbing the implications of what he saw. He quickly realized that the *centuria* that the Emperor had assigned him to command lacked proper Roman discipline – no watchtower guarded the encampment, no gate barred the unfinished wall, and no Legion standard flew above the tents.

He raised the wooden cudgel lying across his saddle and pointed toward the camp. "I count but five tents, Optio," he said. "Normally, a *contubernium* of eight men is assigned to each tent. That means just forty men, Optio Flavius, not the eighty men of the full *centuria* I was promised."

"We have had ... casualties," Flavius offered before becoming strangely silent, as if reluctant to explain further.

Gaius raised an eyebrow and scowled, irritated that he must probe deeper. *Gods! Must everyone and everything in this place hold secrets like the cursed sand?*

"Casualties?" he asked.

Flavius shrugged his shoulders and sighed, the sound of a dry desert breeze escaping his parched lips. "Five men have deserted, though Jove knows where they thought they were going in this hell hole. Six more have died of poisonous bites or stings, disease, or of sun fever. A dozen are simply ... missing, vanished in the night." He glanced away. "Centurion Lucius Agrippa was one of the vanished." He wet his lips with his tongue and swallowed before continuing. "A foot patrol of five men failed to return six days ago. A second mounted patrol sent to search for them is two days late in reporting back."

Gaius fought to control his temper. The stifling desert heat sufficed without adding the heat of anger to the mix and only increased the churning in his restless stomach. His magnificent Andalusian warhorse, Apollo, as white as the snow atop the distant mountains of his home, detected his master's agitation and snickered uneasily. Gaius reached down to pat the horse's neck reassuringly.

"Missing men? Lost patrols? Vanished Centurions? Why did they not inform me of this in Leptis Magna?" he snapped.

"*Praetor* Augustus thought it best not to make the populace aware of our, er, difficulties. There is much dissent here in Tripolitania, especially after the recent revolts in Egypt."

Flavius did not meet his commander's eyes. Gaius took this to indicate he didn't agree with the Governor's actions. Gaius glanced back at the remaining ten of the twelve men who had accompanied him, three of which were non-combatants, the two wagonloads of supplies, and the ten native bearers driving the wagons and leading heavily laden packhorses. Two men had vanished without a trace during the night along the way. He had suspected that they had deserted, but now he had doubts. The accursed land, fit perhaps for the barbarian Berbers, offered only a living death for one born and reared in the forests and mountains of Northern Italy.

"Difficulties," he repeated. "If I had but known, I would have demanded more men from the garrison commander at Marzuq."

Flavius scowled. "I know the commander, *Praefectus castorum* Sunio Atticus." He spit in the sand, a gesture of contempt made even more significant in such a dry land. "He would not have given you any more men. He is jealous of his position and does not welcome your arrival in Tripolitania."

Gaius snorted. "Jealous! Emperor Marcus Aurelius Antonius Augustus personally banished me to this lost land with my tail between my legs. The sands of the Sahara are to be my grave. What does the Praefectus have to fear from me?"

Flavius sat up straight in the saddle and in a stern voice said, "You were once the finest *Legate* in the Third Legion; still are. It was not your fault your men failed you."

Gaius noticed the sparkle of admiration in Flavius' eyes and felt a raw wound open in his chest. It would be to dash his optio's hopes early. He didn't need a hero-blinded worshipper. "Yes, it was," he countered sharply, his voice filled with the vile taste of somber memories. "They trusted me, and I did not question my orders though I believed it a foolhardy plan of attack. I allowed my men to walk into an ambush, slaughtered to save my honor." He could not hide the rancor in his voice, the tone of self-recrimination that had grown stronger during the past four months of exile.

"*They* ran. Not you. You stood your ground, sword in hand, and faced your enemies. You were willing to die with honor."

Gaius rubbed the still vivid scar on his left leg just above the knee, another reminder of the battle. The long ride from the coast had intensified the constant ache with which he had grown accustomed. The pain served as a bitter reminder of his failure. "Better if I had."

"Here we are," Flavius said as they entered the camp, quickly changing the subject.

"Indeed," Gaius agreed, not attempting to hide the disdain in his voice.

Most of the men huddled uncomfortably under the sparse shade in the lee of tents or beneath the three, half-dead date palms that huddled like frightened virgins surrounded by sex-starved men in one corner of the compound. Three others, stripped to the waist, carried large rocks from a pile of stones in the center of the compound to reinforce the walls. They moved with the lassitude of galley slaves or condemned prisoners confined to the sulfur mines.

Gaius eyed the pitifully small stack of firewood beside the stone wall, gathered from ancient dead trees almost fossilized by the desert heat. Considering the three date palms in the camp were the only trees he had seen in over three weeks, he understood the lack of firewood. One of the wagons he had brought was half-filled with stacked wood and charcoal for the ovens and campfires.

The aroma of baking bread drifted on the light breeze from two dome-shaped beehive ovens beside the kitchen tent. A cook, his filthy red tunic hiked up until it barely covered his hairy, naked ass, glanced up at the approaching men, waved casually, and then continued stirring the contents of a large black kettle over an open fire. Beads of sweat dripped from his arms into the contents of the pot, turning Gaius' already uneasy stomach. The cook's helper, a dull-eyed youth holding a box of herbs and seasonings, stood behind the cook looking vapid and lost in time.

The chill that had enveloped him upon first seeing the encampment evaporated in a flash, as a blast of heat from the bare bone-colored rock swept up his legs and smothered him. His horse, struck by the sudden heat, reared. Gaius soothed the horse by gently speaking to it and patting its broad neck. "Calm, Apollo, calm. It is only the wind." He glanced at Flavius. "Get used to it."

Mistaking the dour expression on Gaius' face as a result of lack of proper respect for the new commander, Flavius called to a young man sitting cross-legged outside one of the tents. A curved brass horn lay across his lap.

"*Cornicen*, blow your horn."

The young man leapt to his feet, licked his dry, parched lips, and blew the Call to Order. Men awoke from their stupors and stared about them in confusion. Others stumbled from the tents half-dressed, weapons in hand, believing they were under attack. One old veteran began verbally haranguing the men as he lined them up in some semblance of order.

"Don't you recognize the Call to Order, you dogs? Are you *tirones* fresh from the fields? Get in line and at least look like legionnaires for our new commander."

"Sir!" the veteran called out stiffly as Gaius approached. "Acting *Tesserarius* Marcellus Qintilus at your command."

Gaius stared down at his temporary third in command. The man bore many battle scars on his arms and legs, including a leather patch over his left eye. *He, at least, has seen battle,* Gaius thought with approval. He was an *evocati*, a veteran who, after serving his term of enlistment, had reenlisted. *What perfidy has he caused to wind up here in this hellhole?* Swiftly surveying the men stumbling to ranks, fumbling to fasten their armor, he doubted that any of the others had seen action. Many looked too young to leave their mother's side, the *tirones*, freshly recruited from Roman families living in Tripolitania.

"Your men seem bored, *Tesserarius*."

Marcellus flinched under Gaius' hard gaze but didn't back down. He eyed the heavy cudgel Gaius held in his right hand, absentmindedly slapping it into the palm of his left hand, as if he had seen such symbols of office used on recalcitrant officers.

"Begging your pardon, sir," he replied, "but the heat is unbearable during mid-afternoon. We barely survived a sandstorm that blew for two days and two nights in which we lost two men and a tent." He paused, glanced at the gathered troops, and continued, "Sir, the men are exhausted." He relaxed his stance slightly as if to emphasize the point of his fatigue.

Gaius silently cursed his haste in judging the veteran warrior. He now noticed two sand-covered heaps that had been tents and another knocked-down tent inside the framework of the stone building. The sandstorm explained the disarray of the tents and the lassitude of the men. He pointedly slid the cudgel beneath the edge of his saddle to empty his hands.

"Very well, Marcellus," he said in a more gentle tone. "You are now full Tesserarius. You will take orders only from Optio Flavius Cirrus and me. I trust you know who I am."

The man smiled, revealing two missing teeth beneath an upper lip bearing a sword scar. "Of course, sir. You are Legate Gaius Marcus Linneus."

"I am *Centurion* Gaius Marcus Linneus," Gaius corrected promptly, cringing inwardly as he spoke aloud his new rank. "I am no longer in the Emperor's favor."

"Pardon, sir, but I have heard of the Battle at White Rock Pass."

Gaius managed a smirk. *Word travels fast.* "I lost over three hundred men in Armenia, Tesserarius. Does that not frighten you?"

"You saved eight hundred, sir. That encourages me."

Gaius smiled. The man either knew how to suck up to officers or genuinely meant what he said. "Thank you, Marcellus. Choose four men to help the bearers unload the supplies we have brought, and allow the remainder to rest through the heat of the day as you suggest. Recall the men at the wall until the sun has set. We will continue the repairs at night when it is cooler."

Marcellus cast a disparaging sneer toward the men at the wall. "They are on punishment detail for speaking of desertion."

Gaius wiped his hot, sweaty brow with his hand, cursing the feverish heat. "Is being here not punishment enough? Warn them that if I hear of such talk again, I will stake them out for the scorpions to feast upon their eyes. Let them consider that."

Marcellus smiled. "Yes, sir." He glanced toward the wagons. "I hope our supplies include wine, sir."

Gaius eyed the livestock huddled around the wagons with disdain. "Herding six oxen and two dozen goats cost me four extra days travel time on the journey here. The wagons are laden with crates of chickens – most survived – wood, charcoal, barrels of water, casks of salted meat, flour, dried fish, flasks of garum fish sauce, honey, wheels of cheese, baskets of carrots, leeks, beans, onions, fresh fruit and dried fruit, and, yes, casks of wine … I know not what else."

"I hope the food is not rotten, though with our cook's dismal skills it would matter little." He ran off barking orders.

"Welcome to your new home," Flavius said. His lips quivered slightly, as if he were suppressing a smile or a smirk.

Gaius couldn't decide if Flavius meant his remark as one of acquiescence or merely offered in jest. He had not yet learned to read his optio. That would soon change. "I will find a way back into the Emperor's favor somehow," he replied.

Flavius acknowledged the hint of bitterness in Gaius' voice with a slight nod of his head. "Here? Here there is nothing but sand and scorpions, as you just noted. I have become used to my prison."

"There is always an enemy, Flavius, someone chaffing against the rule of Rome. The Empire produces them as a sow produces litters of piglets. We just need to find them and escape our prison." Gaius surveyed the desert as if searching for his longed-for enemy.

Flavius also eyed the surrounding desert, but saw nothing in the vast emptiness surrounding them. "An enemy could be anywhere in this dead expanse."

"Then we will draw our enemy to us."

Flavius looked at the troops standing uncomfortably at attention in the broiling sun and scowled. "These men are mostly *milites*, untrained and undisciplined, outcasts from a dozen legions. The only thing uniting them is the crippling fear the Emperor has consigned here to this wasteland to die. Many are flat-footed *tirones*; raw recruits from the gods' only know what remote villages, farms, and whorehouses throughout the Roman Empire. They will hardly make a reputable centuria, much less a Shadow Legion."

Gaius detected acrimony in Flavius' pronunciation of the derogatory term, Shadow Legion. An undermanned centuria pretending they were part of a larger fighting unit, using a ranking system ordinarily reserved for full legions, had been the ultimate insult of the Emperor, as was his new rank of Centurion.

Flavius eyed the ten men who had accompanied Gaius and the native bearers. "If I know the *Praefectus castrorum* of Castra-Quietus in Leptis Magna, the men he sent with you are no prizes. They are doubtless thieving, slacking, drunken, libertine louts Sunio Atticus sought to rid himself of."

Gaius had ascertained the same thing of the new men on his three-week-long journey from the coastal city of Leptis Magna. He hardened his face as he stared at his optio. "Train them, Flavius. Train them hard. Fear will toughen them. Exhaustion will silence their grumblings. A common enemy will band them together into an effective fighting force. We will offer them a choice – Die fighting the enemy or die of old age or disease in this desolate desert. Only the victorious will leave these cursed sands with me."

Flavius saluted Gaius with his clenched right fist crossed over his chest. "Done, Centurion."

Gaius detected lingering doubt in his second's voice but dismissed it. He knew Flavius would do his job. The optio longed for a way out of his desert confinement and knew his best hope lay in his commander's success. All that remained was for their unknown enemy to play its part.

"Now, let us inspect my troops and see if I should thank our Emperor, or curse him."

That choice will be an easy one. I have been cursing him since leaving Rome.

"Tell me of this as yet invisible enemy, Marcellus."

Gaius and his two senior officers dined in his tent. In front of Gaius, amid the flagons of wine and plates of meat and cheese, lay a crude map of the region drawn on vellum – A dot representing Leptis Magna on the coast, a second dot representing the city of Marzuq to their north, and a third indicating Castra-Augustus. South lay only leagues of empty space. The map bore no other discernible features except a row of squiggly lines representing as series of low ridges a dozen leagues to the south.

Marcellus brushed his hand across the top of the parchment map to remove a few grains of the pervasive sand. "This area contains mostly Berbers driven from the west. They resist our rule as they resisted the Carthaginians before us, but they are few in number and not well organized. Lately, an unseen enemy has appeared." He stabbed the dot signifying Castra-Augustus with his finger. "He comes at night, taking one or two men, and then retreating into the darkness of the desert. At first, we followed but found nothing – no bodies and no tracks."

"This is a desert," Gaius reminded him. "Winds blow the sand, erasing tracks quickly. You sent out scouts, patrols?"

Marcellus shot a withering glance at him for asking such a question of a veteran soldier. "Aye. They found nothing. The last two patrols have not returned."

"How long have they been gone?" Gaius asked, taking a sip of warm wine and wincing at the sour taste.

"Six days for the first patrol, two days for the second, but the storm may have delayed them."

Marcellus' tone implied he had given up hope for the first patrol's return and feared for the second. Water was the determining factor. If the first patrol had not located an oasis, they would have exhausted their water supply by now. Gaius' concern for the men of his new command urged him to set out immediately to rescue them, but caution was required. The camp was in shambles and the men, especially the men who had accompanied him from Leptis Magna, were exhausted.

"After a day's rest, we will search for them," Gaius said. He pushed his meal, largely untouched, aside. The oppressive heat and his unsettled stomach dampened his appetite. "Inform the men. I will need ten volunteers, well armed. Pick them yourself if they hesitate. In addition, two packhorses for supplies. Take men of this country only, even if they are fuzzy-cheeked tirones. The new men I brought with me are unused to the desert." *As am I*, he thought wryly. *This accursed desert is a furnace compared to the deserts of Mesopotamia.*

"How long will we be gone?" Marcellus asked.

Gaius stared at Marcellus, surprised by the audacity of the question. "Until we find the patrols or their sun-bleached corpses, of course."

Properly chastised, Marcellus saluted and exited the tent.

With Marcellus gone, Gaius removed his heavy *galea,* and allowed a stream of sweat to pour down his forehead. The rounded metal helmet with its rear neck guard, topped by its transverse red plume of rank, had been sitting heavily on his head the entire day. It had felt as if the sun were cooking his brain. Then, he loosened his *Lorca hamata,* the bronze chainmail armor protecting his upper torso.

"Damn this abominable heat," he snarled. "I would rather fight the Germans or even the damned blue-painted Brits as endure this heat. Is there no succor from it?"

Flavius, who had remained silent during Gaius' exchange with Marcellus, smiled. He wore a short tunic and no armor with his sword thrust through his leather *balteus* cinched around his waist. "You need not impress this lot. Remove your armor; wear your tunic only. The heat will kill you as surely as the thrust of a *hasta,* though not as cleanly as a good, sharp spear."

Heeding Flavius' advice, he removed his chainmail armor, the *manica* protecting his arms, the *greaves* from his legs, and the leather tunic over his cloth inner tunic. The absence of the heavy, smothering armor had an immediate cooling effect. His skin breathed a sigh of relief, even as he damned himself for giving in to the desert. He would make many such concessions in the coming days, he wagered.

"You heard my orders to Marcellus?"

Flavius raked the heel of his sandal across the sand. Without looking up, he answered, "I heard."

"Do you approve?"

"It is risky. Ten men are too few if attacked."

"This unseen enemy poses an opportunity, Flavius, but we must give him a name."

Flavius scratched his head with the greasy bone of a roasted pork chop. "The Berbers are a handy scapegoat, but they believe this region is haunted. The *Sea of Lost Souls*, they call it. They seldom venture here. The Jews that fled Judea after the revolt that Lusius Quietus put down live in the wastes farther east, but they have caused no problems in years."

Gaius shook his head, slinging droplets of sweat from his curly, brown locks. "I cannot deliver stories of ghosts to the Emperor. I must deliver bodies, live ones if possible, to parade before the Senate, be they Berber, Jew," he paused, "or legionnaire deserters."

This last barb he aimed at Flavius. His optio flinched slightly but held his tongue. "First, we must find them."

Gaius smiled. "For that, we will need bait. I have played this part before. In one day's time, you will follow my trail with thirty men. I will draw out the enemy, and we will smash them between us." He slammed a fist into his palm with a smacking sound. "You will be the hammer against my anvil."

Flavius cocked a bushy eyebrow at Gaius. "You play the devil's game. What if they find you first?"

"In that case, march fast." Gaius allowed the briefest flicker of a half-smile to crease his lips. After a few minutes of awkward silence during which both men studied each other, Flavius moving his empty cup from hand to hand as if unsure what to do with it, and Gaius rubbing his aching leg, Gaius asked, "How long have you been posted to this place?" Seeing Flavius' hesitation, he added, "I mean no disrespect. Your circumstances for being here are of no importance to me. No doubt, we have all displeased someone in our careers. I need only know if you are familiar with this region, with these men."

Flavius cleared his throat before answering. "I have been here fourteen months, Centurion, though each day and each season flows smoothly into the next with little to mark the changes in this foul place."

"And Marcellus?"

"More than two years. I do not know exactly how long. We seldom speak of our former lives."

"What do you think happened to Agrippa?"

The sudden change of topic caught Flavius off guard. "I, er, I cannot …"

"Speak freely, Flavius."

Flavius sighed heavily. "Centurion Agrippa, though a good man, was not well suited for the desert or the solitude. He was too soft and given to deep contemplation. He had difficulty sleeping, which made him seem confused at times, indecisive. He often walked alone into the desert at night to think in spite of the dangers. One night, he did not return."

Gaius waited for Flavius to continue.

"Did he desert, you may ask? No, I do not think so. Did he continue to walk into the wastes until he died?" He nodded. "Perhaps. He was a good man, but as I said, not suited to the desert."

It was an honest answer, if not revealing. Some men chose a scented warm bath and a blade across the wrists to end their pain. Others made do with what was available. Gaius did not believe men simply disappeared in the night. No, someone took them.

"You will find that I am not indecisive. This fort is a holdover from the Jewish *Bar Kokhba* revolt is it not?"

"Yes, but it has been manned, abandoned, and re-manned many times in those 30 years. The Berbers called this place *tautult agbalu*, Spring of the Hare, an oasis." He waved the empty cup in the air and chuckled.

"I have yet to see a single hare in all the time I've been here." Becoming more serious, he said, "The well is almost dry. In the dry months, we ration the water or sometimes bring in barrels from Marzuq, as you did. Soon, the spring will die and this oasis will look like the rest of this weary land – Sand and dust, dust and sand."

"Then we must be gone before that day arrives, Flavius. With your help, we will return in triumph. Now, leave me. I wish to rest after my unpleasant journey. See that the men are given extra rations of the fresh fruit and vegetables we brought and a little wine." He stopped Flavius as the optio turned to leave. "Only a little wine, Flavius. I want them sober tomorrow."

Alone in the privacy of his tent, Gaius followed Flavius' advice and stripped down to his woolen *subligaria* girding his loins. He sat almost naked on his cot wishing he could take a bath, but such luxuries were behind him. In the desert, water was for drinking. He settled for a sip of lukewarm wine. He picked up a piece of dried licorice root and began chewing it. Despite its medicinal properties for soothing troubled stomachs, Gaius' guts remained in turmoil. The heat, the unaccustomed food, and the anxiety of the past few months had taken a bitter toll on his digestive system.

His new optio still withheld dark secrets from him. He sensed their heavy weight on Flavius' bearing. Perhaps he wanted to learn more of his new commander before revealing all, or possibly, he suspected Gaius would think him crazy from the heat. Given the sense of evil that lay over the land, Gaius decided to give Flavius a bit of latitude.

Giving up on his recalcitrant stomach, he wet a cloth in his water basin and draped it over his face. Lying on his cot, he ignored the rumblings in his gut and listened to the men eating and talking among themselves, occasionally punctuated by Marcellus' deep voice barking orders. The supplies of fresh fruit and the wine had eased their tensions somewhat, but he sensed an undercurrent of uncertainty flowing through the camp. He would give them direction and certainty over the coming weeks. He was not sure how they would like it, but they had little choice in the matter.

He was sure the Emperor would take hidden delight in the fact his centuria was reduced by almost half. The safe thing would be to keep all men in camp and simply survive, but playing it safe won no rewards. He was taking a gamble marching exhausted men into the desert in search of lost patrols, but he feared conditions and morale would not improve over time. They would act as bait to draw the unseen enemy to them, allowing Flavius to strike. It was a bold move, but one that could end the threat. *If any of us survive.* He did not worry about surviving. A return to Rome was his only concern.

He felt he had betrayed his family by accepting the Emperor's offer of a new post in Africa. He could have retired in disgrace and remained with his wife and child, idled away his life. He had been absent from their lives for over a year, and they deserved at least a small portion of his time for the sacrifices they had made. However, once a legionnaire, always a legionnaire. As long as a remote chance existed to overcome his banishment and once again rise in rank, his ego would allow him to take no other course. Better if he died in the desert and freed them of the burden of his disgrace.

Closing his eyes, exhaustion soon lulled Gaius to sleep.

He awoke amid a cacophony of confusion and screams, the familiar sounds of conflict. He leapt from his cot and grabbed his *gladius* from its scabbard draped over his stool. The leather-bound haft of the short sword felt reassuring in his hand. His fingers fell naturally into the depressions in the leather formed from tightly gripping the *gladius* in many battles. He glanced longingly at the chain mail armor he had discarded at the foot of his bed, but decided to dispense with it.

With time of the essence, he raced barefoot from his tent clad only in his underwear, hoping no scorpion sting found his bare heel. The muscle beneath the wound in his left thigh had tightened as he slept. He fought down the pain as he limped across the rocky space between his tent and the center of the camp. As he searched for an enemy, he praised the gods for answering his prayers. *I will return to Rome yet,* he promised himself.

His heart pounded with excitement and his blood raced in anticipation. *By the gods, this is how a man should live.*

The sickly jaundiced glow of the dying campfires revealed men dashing about wildly. Most were half-dressed and unarmed, their faces frozen into masks of fear. Marcellus stood atop a boulder amid the turmoil yelling uselessly for order. Gaius grabbed the young cornicen standing dazed and trembling beside a tent.

"Call them to order," he yelled.

The boy just stared at him. Gaius slapped him hard across the face with the back of his hand. The bugler reeled from the blow, but his frightened eyes focused on Gaius. He nodded, lifted the horn dangling from the cord around his shoulder, and pressed it to his lips. Its metallic blare pierced the night and the din of confusion like a peal of thunder. Men stopped running and looked toward the sound of the horn. Gaius grabbed a soldier by the shoulder as he rushed by and spun the man around to face him.

"What has happened?" he demanded.

"They came out of the darkness," the man said, gasping for breath, his face ashen. His eyes darted about wildly in fear.

Gaius pressed the man further. "What do you mean?"

"I was speaking with Vincennes as we stood our watch. I turned away, and then back again, and he was gone. I heard a gurgling sound and saw shadows moving swiftly across the ground, shadows cast by no one or thing I could see. I pursued, but found nothing. Something brushed me in the darkness, but when I turned, nothing was there. I ran," he added sheepishly.

Overhearing his comrade, another soldier spoke up. "I saw them by the light of the fire, four of them, dark like ebony cloaks. They fell like shadows upon poor Vincennes. He stabbed one with his spear, but it did not fall. They overwhelmed him and dragged him away screaming into the night."

Gaius glanced at the clear night sky. The stars were out, but no moon, nothing to cast shadows but the dying embers of the campfires. "Find weapons," he ordered. "Take torches. Search for him."

The man nodded and called several others to join him. They lit torches and began scouring the perimeter of the camp just outside the wall. Flavius appeared from the darkness, wearing unlaced *caligae* and nothing else, but he gripped his sword as if ready to use it. His nakedness didn't seem to bother him as much as wearing only his subligaria did Gaius, but then Flavius had never been a Legate. Gaius noted that Flavius had taken time to don his sandals. He wished he had. The sand hoarded the heat of the day and scorched the soles of his feet.

"These men are jumpy," Flavius said, "seeing ghosts."

"Ghosts don't snatch men in the night," Gaius reminded him.

"They probably …"

"Over here!" someone yelled.

He and Gaius ran to the crowd of soldiers staring down at a pile of cloth, the remains of a Roman soldier's tunic, shredded and blood soaked. Beside it lay a solitary sandal, its leather fastening torn.

"It's Vincennes' sandal, all right," one soldier commented, pointing at the sandal. "I recognize the patch on the heel."

"Demons," a second groaned. "Demons took him."

"Berbers," Gaius spat, stopping their wild speculation, "not demons, and Berbers can be killed with a thrust of a gladius or spear." He grabbed a spear from one of the soldiers and hurled it at a date palm thirty yards away. It struck the center of the tree with a loud thud. "In a day's time we search for those responsible and kill them. Tonight, we sleep."

The men returned his gaze as if he were jesting.

"Double the guard if you must," he yelled in irritation, "but get some sleep. Weary soldiers are easy prey. I'll have no soldier under my command die for lack of sleep."

Taking him aside, Flavius said quietly, "I saw no footprints in the sand. There is no wind to fill them in with sand, and there was not time to erase them."

"Speak of this to no one but me," Gaius warned. "The men are too jumpy to contemplate what may be of no consequence."

"Aye," Flavius replied, but without conviction.

Gaius returned to his tent, sat on a stool, and massaged his leg, forcing the cramped muscle to relax. After a few minutes, the pain subsided. He took a long swig from a wine bottle sitting on a nearby table, careful to take only one to follow his own advice. Outside his tent, the camp still stirred. He doubted many men would sleep that night in spite of his order. He knew he wouldn't.

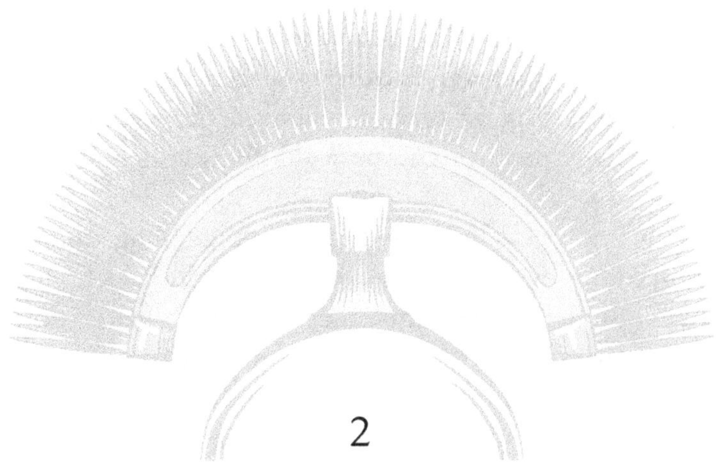

2

Dawn slunk into the camp like a whipped cur, silent and afraid as it dispelled the last vestiges of the night's clinging shadows. The sun, a searing, bloodstained orb, lifted from the desert sands as a fanned flame rises from banked embers. Though newborn, it already cast an invisible pall of heat that swept across the little rocky knoll, raising both the temperature and the level of the men's frustration and dread. After a hot breakfast of wheat porridge, bacon, bread, and honey, they assembled bleary-eyed with little talking among their ranks. The unnatural quietness of the still desert air mirrored their dour mood.

No one spoke of the sentry's disappearance, as if mention of it invited a repetition of the previous night's horror. Gaius had dismissed Flavius' explanations for the other missing men as just an excuse for his failures. Now, he knew he had judged his optio too hastily. He had personally searched the area around the camp at dawn's first light. No blood or footprints other than those made by the sandals of the previous searchers marked the sand. The enemy had boldly slipped into camp, unseen and unheard, and then exited with the sentry. Such an enemy would be a worthy opponent to a well-trained, disciplined legion. To a ragtag band of misfit legionnaires, they must seem supernatural, wraiths.

Gaius did not believe in ghosts. Their enemy was flesh and blood, whatever language he spoke. To catch their enemy, he would have to be bold and cunning. His plan, however well conceived, had risks, most concerning of all relying on Flavius, whom he did not know, to follow his orders exactly. One error and he would be sacrificing more men to the desert.

Gaius might have easily ignored the men's ramblings about shadows if it were not for his own observations. The desert to which the Emperor had exiled him differed from any other posting he had endured in his long career, even the deserts of Mesopotamia. Men scurrying through the Sahara did not impinge upon its timelessness or register on its consciousness, if one could imbue such a place with human qualities. Its vast emptiness bore no ruins of great cities, ancient temples, or well-trodden roadways. It reduced any temporary occupant, even a Roman Legion, to grains of sand blown by the incessant wind. Its constantly shifting surface gave men no place in which to put down roots. They, too, became transient, insecure, and unsure of themselves. He would have to adapt his thinking to these new circumstances.

Gaius felt undressed walking the camp only in a short tunic with subligaria beneath, a belt to hold his sword, and sandals. He wore his focale around his neck to catch the perspiration that poured from his face in torrents. The sun had not yet cleared the horizon and the heat was unbearable. Later, it would be abusive.

Flavius wasted no time learning the skills of the new men, milites with little training, tirones with none, and veteran triarii with training but a deep contempt of officers. They were men from different countries, nationalities, and legions. The only thing they had in common was their resentment at that abandonment in the desert. Flavius put them through their paces, drawing deprecating stares from some and grumbles of discontentment from others, but none dared challenge the optio or test his skills.

The camp resembled so many others Gaius had called home over the years – a cook tent, beehive ovens for baking, open fires for roasting and boiling, a supply area inside the fallen walls of some ancient abandoned structure, a corral for the horses, a valetudunarium for injured or sick, and a double row of tents for the men. A low breeze brought with it the stench of the latrine located at the far end of the camp.

The immunes, the skilled workers, such as cooks, butchers, grooms, tailors, musicians, leather craftsmen, and blacksmiths worked with the lassitude of men waiting for death. The Tebu natives who had accompanied him from Leptis Magna maintained their distance from the others. They remained near the empty wagons, sitting in a group and watching the Roman activities with amusement. When they had rested from their journey and consumed all the Roman food and wine they wanted, they would return to Leptis Magna.

Gaius patrolled the camp, allowing the men to see him, while he surreptitiously rated their skill with sword and lance, which he judged mediocre at best. Few had seen battle. Only three men proved adept at using the long bow, a very small Sagittarii. Flavius drove them hard, but Marcellus went from man to man, showing him the proper stance to deflect sword bows or to thrust a lance. The veteran's patience amazed Gaius. He would have made a fitting addition to any legion. Gaius wondered why he was wasting away in such a hellhole.

By midday, the heat beat down on them like a tempest, and the sand scorched their feet through the leather. Gaius' focale and tunic were soaked, but at least he had stopped perspiring. The thought troubled him, but he could not remember why. The horizon danced as he stared at it. The stark line tilted first one way, and then the other. It became difficult to orient himself.

"You must find shade, Centurion."

Gaius looked up into the blurry face of Flavius trying to make sense of his optio's words. "What?"

"You are sun sick. You must remember to drink more water to remain hydrated." Flavius took his arm. "I will help you back to your tent."

Gaius struggled to clear his mind. He closed his eyes to quell the illusion of motion and shook off Flavius' hand. "No. I will not let my men see me weak." He straightened. "I can make it to my tent."

It required all his concentration, but he managed the short distance to the privacy of his tent. He collapsed onto his cot, exhausted by the effort.

Flavius poured a goblet of water from the skin hanging by the entrance and handed it to him. "Her, drink this, slowly," he added, as Gaius gulped down a few sips, his hands trembling. The water, though lukewarm, tasted like chilled ambrosia to his parched lips and throat. Flavius handed him a piece of salt. "Swallow this. Remember to take salt daily. This is not Mesopotamia. The Sahara is a murderous bitch searching for a victim. She is indiscriminant and vicious."

Gaius swallowed the salt and leaned back against the tent wall. "Thank you Flavius. I forgot where I was."

Flavius grinned. "I doubt that, but you forgot for a moment that you are but a man."

"What do you think of the troops?"

Flavius squinted at Gaius with one eye. "A practical question. You saw them. They have some skill at weapons, but believe skill will not save them. The disappearance of Vincennes is fresh on their minds. This is a battle of minds."

The water and salt refreshed Gaius. He had learned a valuable lesson. Against the heat and the desert, he was nothing. He would not forget. The fog faded from his mind, but his body was still weak.

"Let them rest."

"As you wish."

"Inform them that as soon as the sun sets we will add two more layers to the unfinished wall. Perhaps that will give them a stronger sense of security."

When Flavius had gone, Gaius stretched out on his cot. His body had betrayed him. He felt like a fool for underestimating the deep desert. He was no novice to deserts, but the Sahara seemed the most inimical of them all. It was larger, hotter, and drier than the deserts of Mesopotamia or Arabia Petraea. It could swallow entire armies and leave no bones. In Mesopotamia, a caravan could find watering holes or streams every few days. It had taken him three weeks to reach Castro Augustus from the coast, and though no Roman had ever ventured as far, natives swore the desert continued south for three times that distance. The enormity of the sandy expanse was overwhelming.

He stifled a yawn. He had not slept after the incident during the night. He needed rest. A short nap while the others were sleeping would revitalize him, allowing him to remain active later in the day. Sleep took him as soon as he had closed his eyes.

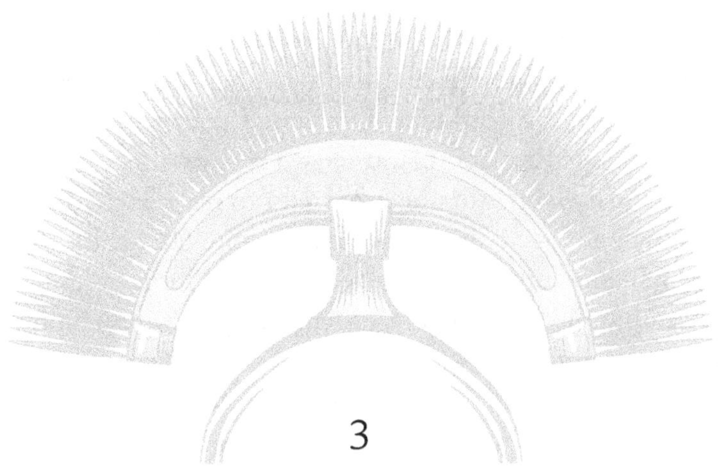

3

The next morning, the ten men chosen for the patrol fell silently into a ragged double line behind their commander sitting atop his white steed, while those who remained behind watched on in uncomfortable gratitude at not being among them. Gaius rode Apollo with his back held straight to present a scene of dignity to his men. Following Flavius' advice, he wore only a tunic, his Lorca hamata to ward off Berber arrows, and his helmet. The rest of his armor he left behind. He would not be fighting trained soldiers in hand-to-hand combat, but desert rats who preferred killing under the cover of darkness. Two pack animals followed the small column, tethered together and led by one of the soldiers.

As he passed the stone wall with its newly placed double layer of stones, he gazed back at the camp and at Flavius with a touch of jealousy. The camp, as pitiful as it was, represented a degree of safety, an oasis against the unknown. Ahead, lay many leagues of burning sand, empty except for their unseen enemy. He badly needed an enemy to battle. Confinement to the deserts of North Africa demeaned any Roman officer. The road to Rome and to redemption lay in victory.

He thought back to the ill-fated campaign in Parthia. At stake were Armenia and Mesopotamia, both recently invaded by the Parthians. After the bitter defeat of Attidus Cornelliaus, he had followed General

Martius Verus' *III Legio Parthica* and crossed the Euphrates River into lower Mesopotamia. The fighting had been hard and bloody, but they had finally taken the city of Duras-Europos. The Parthians fled in defeat. Martius Verus tasked his command of two *cohorts* of five hundred men, plus an additional *maniple* of one-hundred-seventy men with routing the retreating Parthians at White Rock Pass. In spite of credible reports of a much larger enemy force than believed, Martius Verus ordered him into the pass. Fearing the worst, Gaius ordered all but two maniples to hang back in case of ambush.

As he had feared, the Parthians were waiting for them. The mid-morning sky grew dark with Parthian arrows as his men died all around him. He rallied them to his side, but a charge from the Parthian heavy cavalry broke their ranks. Faced with death from above or death from their beleaguered flanks many of his men fled. He remained with those who had not. By late afternoon, three hundred of his men lay dead around him. By the time his cohorts arrived, only he and fifteen men remained standing.

Enraged by his failure and his men's cowardice, Imperator Martius Verus had ordered his cohorts *decimated*; executing one of every ten men, and stripped him of his rank. He then sent Gaius back to Rome in disgrace to face the wrath of the Emperor. Rather than a quick death, Marcus Aurelius had decided to make an example of him. Now, forgotten in a desert wasteland, he led a band of equally forgotten soldiers against an unseen enemy, bringing the *Pax Romana* to an empty land.

After the Jewish Bar Kokbha Revolt in 132 A.D. and the Egyptian Revolt of 139 A.D., Rome had decided that a firmer hand in her outlying provinces would prevent a repeat of such rebellions, establishing a series of small fortifications, *Limes*, between Judea in the east and Mauritania in western Africa. Castra-Augustus was technically part of *Limes Arabiscus* and *Limes Tripolitanus* protecting Roman interests along the coast from the dangers of the deep Sahara. That nothing lived in the deep Sahara made little difference to the methodical Roman military planners. Their models called for a fort south of Marzuq, and thus one came into existence.

Saharan Africa had once been a lush, fertile land. Petroglyphs found in caves and canyon walls depicted giraffes, crocodiles, hippopotami, and lakes and rivers of fresh water where now only sand rock and prevailed. Too vast to cross from the south, the Sahara itself became a vast *lime* dividing Africa. Renegade Jews, Tauregs, Berbers, Egyptians, and Nubians called the desert home, but even they avoided the heart of the desert. If an enemy existed, he would find them and redeem himself in the eyes of the Emperor.

Within a day's march, they came upon the remains of the first patrol on the leeward side of a large, curved dune. Tattered, bloodstained clothing, a few pieces of armor, and discarded weapons lay scattered around the cold ashes of a several-day's old campfire half-covered by the blowing sand. A pair of dice and several copper coins lay on a soldier's *focale,* the scarf he wore around his neck to prevent his armor from chaffing. Gaius bent down and picked up a sword, thinking it odd that their attackers had not taken the weapons. In disgust, he thrust the sword into the sand, the only monument the dead men would receive and better than they deserved.

"The fools," he muttered. "They didn't even post a guard."

He spent little time mourning their loss. His time in Rome awaiting the Emperor's pronouncement of his fate had greatly diminished his tolerance for fools and their folly. Plebeians, Patricians, Senators, and common citizens had all demanded war with the Parthians, but none had insisted on proper rations or clothing for the troops or additional legions when the Parthians proved formidable opponents. Their frenzied mob zeal for revenge and wild-eyed fanaticism had turned them into fools, but he had been a bigger fool for obeying orders.

It would have been far better to have slit Martius Verus' throat with his *pugio*, and then face the punishment for killing an officer. His fingers caressed the pommel of the dagger thrust through his belt, as his mind replayed the image of Verus' imagined death for the hundredth time.

When Gaius ordered the men to camp in the same spot on which the patrol had died, they became nervous but remained vigilant, just as he hoped they would. The ghosts of their dead comrades kept them awake.

He did not make the mistake of the patrol. He posted two sentries on the crest of the sand dune and another at its base.

Their first night in the open proved uneventful. The men seemed in better spirits as the sun rose to dispel the last shadows of the night. They resumed their march south toward the low hills that lay like a dark smudge across the distant horizon. The soft crunch of sandaled feet on the burning sand and the quiet rustle of their uniforms were the only sounds of their passing. The wind sliding down the faces of the dunes hissed at them like thousands of unseen serpents.

Gaius feared that the occasional flash of a burnished shield in the sunlight might alert their enemy, but he could do little about that. Relieving them of the burden of the heavy, 22-pound *scutum* by having the already overburdened pack animals carry them would leave the men vulnerable in case of a surprise attack. In a tight formation, shields interlocked, a phalanx of Roman soldiers could withstand a mounted cavalry assault or force back a determined enemy on foot. A man without his shield was of no use to his companions in battle and of little use to himself.

As they neared their destination, the row of low hills resolved into deceivingly high bluffs riddled with numerous caves, some with ornate carvings framing their dark openings. The ruins of an ancient city, half-swallowed by the encroaching sands, sat at the foot of the bluffs. *No, not swallowed by the sands*, he decided looking at the uninviting ruins, *emerging from them, as if a corpse rising from a grave.*

"Tombs," Gaius said aloud, noting the caverns' appearance, but regretted it immediately. The men overheard his comment and began to mutter among themselves. He turned on them quickly. "The dead cannot harm you. Best be warier of live Berbers than of dead ghosts."

The ruins were neither Carthaginian nor Egyptian, nor were they Greek, Roman, Persian, Mesopotamian, or of any other architectural style that he recognized. Rather than built of blocks of stone or of brick, the buildings had been carved directly from an outcropping of the same chalky, blood red rock comprising the cliffs. Wind-etched fluted columns fronted open entrances. The windows were mere slits set high in the walls. The symmetry of the single doorway in each building seemed oddly out of proportion to the buildings, being singularly tall and narrow. No windows adorned the featureless lower walls, giving the buildings the appearance more of fortresses than domiciles.

Gaius stopped his horse before one such building, the largest structure still standing, and gazed at the grotesque beast carved above the door lintel. The eroded head slightly resembled that of a human, but the eyes were narrow slits, and short, truncated tentacles surrounded a wide mouth lined with multiple rows of needle-thin teeth. The elongated head possessed no ears, just a tuft of skin where ears might have been. As he stared at the anthropomorphic figure, a sense of trepidation overcame him. Why a thing carved of stone should unnerve him more than a live enemy, he could not fathom.

"What manner of creature did these people worship?" he asked no one in particular.

"Demon worshipers," one soldier suggested.

Gaius rebuked him with a stern look but said nothing. With no answer of his own to offer, he could not admonish a man for saying aloud what he himself thought.

"Scout around by twos. Find a suitable building in which to make camp, a well-defended position with a clear field of view."

He watched them go, saw their fear in the way they walked, not with the self-assured saunter of a Roman soldier, but cautious and uncertain, peering around each corner and into every opening. Perhaps caution and uncertainty were called for, he thought. He dismounted, grabbed a torch from a packhorse, and entered the structure with the carving, which he assumed was a temple. Inside, the building proved darker than he thought possible. More than the mere absence of light, it seemed as if the walls exuded darkness as a suppurating wound oozed puss, cloying and putrid. The room smelled of death and decay.

Smudges of light dotted the fuliginous walls entering from slits high in the ceiling, but cast little light on the stone floor below. He ignited the torch with flint and steel, and by flickering torchlight, explored the room. Sand blown in by the ceaseless winds filled one entire corner, blocking a door he presumed led to another room. The torch did not illuminate the large room's entirety. He scanned the walls first, examining them for more carvings or writing, but found them all oddly bereft of ornamentation save one.

Near the center of that wall, beneath a duplicate of the outside carving, a large block of dark stone rose from the floor of a different material from the soft stone of the building. Cursive writing decorated its smooth, glass-like sides. The script flowed like a serpent around the stone and like a serpent, repelled him. He loathed touching it. The top of the stone bore a shallow bowl-like depression. As he drew closer, he noticed the depression stained darker than the surrounding stone. Holding the torch forward, he saw to his horror that the stain was blood, some still glistening and wet, not quite congealed.

A chill breeze brushed past him, startling him, and he knew that he was not alone. Hand on sword, he swept the torch around him, but saw nothing. Examining the floor, he detected no footprints other than his own. Still, he did not relax. His senses had never failed him, and they warned him danger lurked.

Puzzled, he asked aloud, "What manner of creature leaves no footprints in fine dust?"

With a feeling of dread, he hurried from the building. The light of the sun, only moments before so despised for its accursed heat, felt like the reassuring touch of a mother to a troubled boy. He stood for a moment to allow it to burn away the last lingering traces of unnatural darkness that clung to his flesh like a pox.

The others, finding no tracks or sign of the enemy, were equally uneasy in the dead city. Some spoke of shadows watching them, others of voices that whispered their names. They muttered unhappily among themselves wishing to leave the city.

Gaius admonished them. "Are you legionnaires or whipped curs? The enemy is killing your comrades under your very noses. Do you not want to avenge them? Is your fear of the unknown so compelling to make you forget you are men? The Emperor believes you not worthy of your salt, that you are poor specimens of the Legion. He has sent you here and forgotten you. I think you are better than that. I will not wither away in this desert. If you wish to leave it with me, steady your spines and curb your tongues."

His words had the effect he sought. They straightened their postures and stood like Roman soldiers, proud and determined. He had shamed them into remembering who they were. He knew though that their wills would melt away with the next attack.

They had located one building near the city's center that could serve as a temporary camp, having an intact roof, a single, easily defended door, with two rooms on the lower floor and with narrow second-floor windows from which a sentry could keep watch on the surrounding sand-filled streets and crumbled buildings.

Gaius had seen a few dead trees in what once may have been a garden within the crumbling walls of the city. A blazing fire would abate the men's fears somewhat. "Gather wood for a fire," he told them.

The city mystified him. Ancient beyond any Grecian or Egyptian influences, yet unrecorded in any ancient scrolls that he had read. For what purpose had the city's inhabitants constructed such narrow doorways and windows? What repugnant god or gods did its people worship, and what had become of them? He knew from ancient Greek writings that the desert had once been wet and fertile before the Sahara's blowing sands encroached upon it many centuries ago. A civilization could thrive in such a place, but why no record of its existence? The thought that an army capable of bringing down such an empire could then itself disappear into history dismayed him. It held dark portents for Rome's future.

Gaius shook his head to focus his thoughts. The past was not the problem, but the future. If the Berbers were using the city or the caves above it as a base of operations, they could expect an attack after dark. He thought to reveal his suspicions to his men but saw that they were already wary. They sat alert near the fire, casting furtive glances toward the door. Sentries patrolled the upper floor and stood flanking the single entrance. An air of expectation pervaded the room like a chill night air. The fire radiated its flickering light but yielded no warmth, casting curious moving shadows upon the walls, cruel parodies of the objects around them. Men appeared headless or with horns. The shadow of javelins writhed like serpents. Shadows of smoke rising from the fire became dancing *Querquetulanae*, spirits of oak wood, swirling around men's heads, as if beguiling them.

There is no oak in this desert, Gaius mused to dispel his own unease.

The pack animals and Apollo, secured in the adjoining room, seemed more attuned to their surroundings than did their human masters. The building made them nervous. They snickered uneasily and dug at the stone floor with their hooves. If not for the confining walls and Apollo's commanding equine presence, the frightened packhorses would have bolted.

As they ate a hot meal of stewed pork with vegetables, bread with honey, and sour wine, the ground shook, lightly at first, but soon the building shuddered as the tremors grew in magnitude. Buildings made of stone or brick would have crumbled, but the city's enduring structures, carved from native rock, withstood the violence of the earth. Dust and stone chips cascaded from the ceiling, but the building stood. The ground groaned like an angry giant. Gaius had experienced quakes in Neapolis. They had been common in Persia as well, but most of his men had never felt the earth move. The event frightened them.

"The gods are angry!" one man cried.

"We are doomed," another added.

"Silence!" Gaius shouted, trying to head off a full-blown panic. "It is the earth moving. Nothing more. There are no gods in the desert, only scorpions and lizards."

He stood erect, swaying with the floor to show he was unafraid. His example steadied them. The tremors subsided. With the ground once again firm beneath their sandals, most of the men regained their composure, chastised by Gaius' example. However, one young soldier, his face pale from fear, sat beside the fire hugging his knees.

"It is an omen," he moaned. "We are marked."

Gaius stood over him, grabbed him by his tunic, and pulled him to his feet. "It is no omen, soldier. It is an act of nature. Do you not remember Vesuvius? The ground trembles around it."

"I remember Pompeii," the youth replied almost in tears. "It was destroyed by the gods."

"There is no volcano here, only the echoes of the earth moving." He released the youth and looked around the room. Some were convinced. Others remained skeptical. "Get some sleep. Tomorrow we continue our march."

Before they could comply, one of the sentries called out, "I see someone!"

Gaius raced to the doorway. A figure stood outside just within the shadows, barely visible in the darkness. The sentry prepared to hurl his aclis, but Gaius stayed his hand.

"Come forward into the light," he called out to the visitor.

A man shambled forward. His Berber robes were torn and filthy, and his blue upon blue eyes unfocused. His bare head revealed short, curly black hair. He eyed the men around him cautiously, but said nothing, as he swayed unsteadily on his feet, one hand resting on the door lintel for support.

"Fetch him in," Gaius ordered.

The guards handled the man roughly, but he paid them no heed. His eyes sought the light of the fire as if hypnotized by it.

"Who are you?" Gaius demanded. The stranger didn't answer. He continued to stare into the blaze. Gaius strode briskly to his side and slapped him lightly on his cheek. The man turned slowly to face him, his eyes blinking rapidly. "Who are you?" Gaius repeated.

Slowly, the man's mouth formed words. "I am Rashid Ahmed Abdullah."

He spoke the words in rough Latin, but in a whisper forced out painfully through blistered lips in his sun-parched face.

"Give him water," Gaius ordered.

Rashid Abdullah sipped slowly from the proffered water gourd, wincing as the gourd brushed his tender lips. His hands shook. Water spilled and dripped from his tangled black beard. Born of the desert, he took only a little water, swished it around in his mouth, and spat it out before drinking more and then swallowing. Then, his legs refused to support him any longer, and he collapsed to his knees.

"Are you one of the men killing my soldiers?" Gaius demanded.

Rashid shook his head. "I am a Berber of the Meshwesh tribe many leagues east of here. We do not war with you Romans."

"You speak our language well for a barbarian."

Rashid smiled. "It is wise to understand your masters."

"Your people claim no masters. Where are the rest of your men?"

Rashid's smile faded. "Dead," he moaned, "all dead. Slaughtered like lambs for sacrifice."

Gaius' men exchanged glances and began whispering among themselves. Gaius ignored them. "Dead? How?"

"The *tabyni* came alive and took them."

"What is *tabyni*?" Gaius asked.

"The darkness. The night came alive and took them." When no one laughed at his explanation, he continued, "We were camped two days ride from here on our way to the *chott*, the salt flats. My people depend on salt for life and for trade. My men were leery of camping so close to the dead city of Hamad Rus, but I dispelled the rumors as a child's tale." He shook his head and whimpered, "I wish upon my forbearers that I had not."

"Hamad Rus? You call this place Hamad Rus?"

Rashid nodded. His right hand clasped an amulet hanging from his neck on a gold chain. The metal amulet, a misshapen five-pointed star, looked melted by heat. A bright blue stone graced the center of the amulet, unlike *lapis lazuli* or any jewel Gaius had ever seen. It glowed softly from within. He stared at it mesmerized by its beauty as the Berber spoke.

"It is an ancient place, as old as *Jannah*, which you call Eden. Its people were *Kashites*. They appeared different from us, taller, thinner." He nodded toward the narrow door. "It is said they entered their homes sideways so they that did not turn their backs to their enemies."

"Who were their enemies?"

Rashid shuddered. "The *Inyosh*, children of Lilith, first wife of Adam cast out of Eden for her wicked ways. It is said the people of Hamad Rus, the *Kashites*, once lived in *Havilah*, a land east of Eden rich with gold and jewels, but were driven west by the Inyosh, the Dark Ones."

As Rashid spoke the word Inyosh, the flames seemed to recede into themselves, growing dimmer. The flickering shadows froze, as if imprinted upon the walls like a dark frieze. The room grew chilly. Then, as suddenly as it had come, the flames soared higher and the room returned to normal. No one spoke of it. Gaius wasn't sure if it had been real or just his imagination.

He had heard of Eden from the teachings of the Jews in Palestine and of their promised Messiah. He dismissed both stories as the hopes and dreams of all conquered people. Why yearn for a mythical Eden when the world had Rome to look to as an example of majesty?

"Nonsense," he snapped. "You or your people are murdering my men. You are in league with Jewish rebels from Judea. Confess or die."

Rashid meekly lowered his head to expose the back of his neck to Gaius' blade. "Then I must die."

Gaius removed his sword and touched it to the Berber's neck, but something held him back from delivering a fatal blow. The man appeared more victim than perpetrator. He decided the stranger would better serve as a source of information than as an example. He replaced his sword. Rashid visibly relaxed at the sound of metal sliding into metal.

"You may live. For now," Gaius added. "I need information. Provide it and you might live longer still."

Rashid tucked the amulet inside his tunic and opened his arms wide. "All I know will be yours freely given."

They gave their visitor water and food. As he devoured the bread and meat, he recounted his story.

"After my men were killed and our camels fled, I could not reach my village on foot. Instead, I journeyed for two days to reach a spring near here, only to find its waters tainted and unfit to drink. I saw firelight flickering on the horizon. I feared to enter the city, but knew only Romans would be foolish enough build a fire in dreaded Hamad Rus. Without food and water, I would have soon perished. Better you Romans than Tauregs. They would have slit my throat immediately for sport."

Gaius dismissed Rashid's comparison of Romans to bloodthirsty Tauregs. "What do you know of this city?" he demanded.

Rashid took a drink of water, wiped his mouth with his sleeve, and shrugged. "Only what I gleamed from tales from my childhood. The *Kashites* disappeared long before my people moved into the desert from the west. It is said that they fought great battles with the children of Lilith who had pursued them westward from Havilah. The Inyosh worshipped *Nergal.* They were creatures of the night, drinkers of blood. It is further purported that the sages of Hamad Rus, in an act of desperation, cast an incantation that killed the creatures, but being without souls, the creatures did not die. They instead became wraiths, shadows haunting the night, eternal and invincible. The people of Hamad Rus finally succumbed to their onslaught and were no more. Their ghosts are visible from time to time, stalking the city. It is for this reason we avoid it. It is not good to have dealings with the dead."

Gaius shook his head. *Fairy tales and fantasies.* For all he knew, the man before him was responsible for the deaths of his men. He glanced at his men, who had been unnaturally silent and attentive as the Berber spoke. He could see in their eyes that they believed the Berber's wild tales. Perhaps that was Rashid's purpose, to instill fear in his men. Fear was like a plague. It spread quickly from man to man, but its scars were not visible to the naked eye. It did not kill. It lay dormant within a man's flesh, growing stronger; weakening a soldier until he was worthless to himself and his comrades. Gaius dismissed such tales. Stories of ghosts and demons of the night would not return him to Rome, but a living, breathing, defeated enemy might.

"I think you are responsible for the deaths," he said. "Your knowledge of the Jewish writings seems too complete for a Berber not in league with Jewish rebels. Tomorrow, you will take me to your village. I will have your comrades also."

Rashid looked at him and slowly shook his head. "The desert is full of exiled Jews forced from Jerusalem after its destruction by Roman hands. We trade with Jews and with Romans alike. My *aduar* is many days from here. It is the time of the moonless nights and the ghouls gather. I fear we will not live to reach my village."

"Did you feel the earth tremble?"

"The earth had been quaking for many months. The tremors

grow more frequent. It is said giant demons stir in their underground labyrinths." He shrugged. "I do not know. Once, I did not believe in demons."

Gaius stared at his prisoner, debating torturing him to learn the truth. A scream from upstairs split the night, postponing his decision.

"Watch him!" he ordered, shoving Rashid toward two soldiers; then ran upstairs.

The room was empty save for a broken Roman longbow and a leather quiver with its iron-tipped arrows spilled across the floor. Both sentries, the only *sagittarii* in his small expeditionary command proficient in the use of the *arcus* recurve longbow, were gone. He had placed them in the upper room to allow them greater range with their arrows. Marks in the dust indicated a scuffle had occurred. Blood, still glistening crimson in the torchlight, marred the sills of one of the windows and dotted the dusty floor beneath it. They found no sign of the two archers or of their assailant, and discovered no means of escape through the window slits too narrow to admit a man.

Peering down through one of the windows, Gaius noticed a shadow on the ground below. When it turned to stare up at him with two eyes glowing fiery red deep within the formless darkness, his heart quickened. He had faced Brits, Huns, Celts, Parthians, and Visigoths without fear, but the twin baleful orbs froze him in place for several seconds before releasing him, as the shadow turned and melted away into the darkness. The deep sense of hunger he felt emanating from the shadow terrified him.

He shook his head to clear it of the impossible image, quickly deciding his overeager mind had conjured his fear. The enemy was flesh and blood. He could contemplate no other explanation. "A trick of the light," he muttered to himself. He rushed back down the stairs, drew his sword, and pressed it to Rashid's throat. The Berber made no sound as he stared up at Gaius. His eyes widened, but he betrayed no other sign of fear. A trickle of blood ran down his neck.

"You were sent here as a distraction while your men attacked my sentries. What did your men do with them?" Gaius demanded.

Rashid ignored the sharp point breaking the skin of his neck and offered a little smirk. "What men do you know who can scale a sheer wall and enter a room through such narrow slits?" he asked, mocking Gaius's observations.

"They must have been taken out those windows. There is no other exit."

Rashid shook his head. "Not alive. It was so with my men."

Gaius pressed the sword deeper, drawing more blood. Still Rashid did not flinch.

"Use it," Rashid spat at him. "We will all be dead soon enough if we do not leave this accursed place."

Gaius quavered; then lowered his sword. "Bind him tightly," he told the two men under whose charge he had left the Berber. "Watch him." Rashid swiped at the blood running down his neck before the men grabbed his arms and twisted them behind his back. "The rest of you, follow me."

No one moved. His eyes bored into them, one-by-one, staring them down. "I do not repeat orders," he growled, barely suppressing his anger. As he left the room, Gaius heard feet scuffing the floor as the others rushed to follow him.

Outside the building, they found splatters of blood, strips of cloth, and shreds of leather below the upper-story windows, but no footprints or bodies. They examined the perimeter of the building and found nothing more of the missing men. The strange temple drew Gaius' gaze, looming over the dead city like a massive shadow in the dark night. He led the way through the empty streets, entering the building carefully. The darkness pressing against his face felt like the dry, dead skin of a mummified body. The fetid air tasted of death. His fear rose like bile in his throat. Only the flickering torchlight held it in check. He focused on the blaze of the torch, trying to ignore the surreal shadows the light cast.

As he suspected, fresh blood pooled in the altar bowl, black, shiny, and obscene by torchlight, but again, no footprints in the undisturbed dust on the floor. He was too late to save his missing men. By their mutterings and grumbling, he knew the men were frightened.

"Back to the camp," he ordered. "We will search for them at first sunlight."

As Gaius entered the building, Rashid looked up at him with pity in his eyes. "I cared for my men as you do yours," he said. "One was my nephew, the only son of my sister. It was his first journey to the salt flat. Now, I must tell my sister that I killed her only son. Do you think I fear death at your hands more than that, Roman?" He shook his head. "What can you do but kill my body? My spirit is dead already.'

Gaius believed the Berber, but decided to keep him bound through the night. He did so to prevent the Berber's escape, but mostly to discourage the frightened soldiers from slitting his throat in the night. In spite of his conviction that the Berber did not lie, he felt Rashid withheld vital information, perhaps to protect the real murderers.

"Tomorrow, we march to your village. If I find anything Roman there, even a scrap of Roman cloth," he warned, "I will slaughter your people."

"If they are not slaughtered already," Rashid added.

The men were restless and huddled around the fires as if wrapping themselves in the feeble light they cast like a blanket. Javelins and swords remained close within reach. No one removed sandals or armor, fearing another attack.

Gaius ordered two more men upstairs. They unashamedly quaked in their sandals as they climbed the stairs, their eyes frozen on their sympathetic comrades. One of the men glanced at him hoping for a reprieve, but Gaius remained steadfast. He didn't blame them for their reluctance, but someone had to remain on guard. He ordered the fires strengthened and the open doorway barricaded with shields. The increased blaze only lengthened the eerie shadows along the walls, which danced with a life of their own. Men huddled in twos and threes, grumbling. Gaius, fearing mutiny, removed his sword from its scabbard and hid it beneath the folds of his blanket. He laid awake, eyes open, watching the strange shadows until sleep crept over him.

Dawn came at last, seeping from the earth like a blood-tinged miasma, clinging long to the horizon, reluctant to loosen its tenuous grasp on the land. Gaius awoke with a start, his neck aching from sleeping leaning against the wall. His mind shuddered with snippets of a half-remembered nightmare. An image, dark and dire, rose as a specter to haunt his memory. The aftertaste of the blurred image's power left him cold and afraid, though the dream itself had vanished from his mind upon awakening. He had experienced nightmares before, but this one differed from any previous bad dreams. Bizarre and haunting, it felt more real than such a sinister dream should be.

He did a quick head count – No one lost; no one deserted. The men breakfasted quickly but unenthusiastically on bread and dried beef. The stale bread had no taste, and the cold meat tasted of blood. After the meal, they made a second cursory search around the building for their lost comrades but found only a second shattered longbow, a few spots of dried blood, and nothing of their enemy.

As Gaius assembled his exhausted men in the dusty street for the march from the city, he tried to ignore the tricks of the light and sudden susurrations of the wind that conveyed a feeling of being under observation. Each darkened window and doorway held stirring shadows the sun did not erase. The center of his back itched with the expectation of an enemy arrow or javelin, though his enemy used no weapons and came and went like an unseen breeze.

The light of day did nothing to diminish the sense of dread that oozed from the mysterious structures like the pall of death rising from the blood-drenched soil of an ancient battlefield. The countryside around Rome teemed with old and abandoned buildings – Etruscan, Sabine, Celt, and Umbrian – but none approached the advanced age of Hamad Ras, not even the Greek ruins of Italy's boot heel. Nor did they convey such a mood of erstwhile abandonment, as if the inhabitants of Hamad Rus had not fully left their homes or had died and returned as specters, shades of their former selves.

The men felt it too, a fear that leapt from man to man like the ubiquitous sand fleas infesting their clothing. They carefully scrutinized their surroundings, paying scant attention to their commander as he spoke to them rallying them for the coming journey deeper into the terrifying desert. As much as they feared what the desert sands might conceal, they loathed remaining in Hamad Rus more. Facing the rising sun, they filed from the city and marched past the hollow-eyed cliffs moaning mournfully as the wind blew across the openings, as if flutes carved from dead men's bones. Shadows within the caverns writhed like nests of vipers. No amount of curiosity, Legionnaire loyalty, or promise of worldly wealth could have forced any one of them to enter the dark opening in search of their missing comrades.

Gaius, too, scanned the caves, but with the gaze of a professional soldier. His concern lay not in forcing his men into the uninviting caverns but in what might be lurking just inside the shadows to emerge as they passed. Astute Apollo noticed his master's unease, prancing and snorting as if to flush the stench of Hamad Rus from his nostrils.

The men forced the pace, eager to be away from the dead city and its aura of primordial evil. Gaius did nothing to slow their march. He, too, would feel better with some distance between him and the ruins.

Beyond the city, crescent-shaped dunes thrust skyward twice the height of the date palms at Castor-Augustus, marching endlessly across the sere landscape. The column wound serpentine between the one-hundred-fifty-foot hillocks, meandering like a line of ants in search of food. Miniature avalanches of sand slid down the steep slopes with the soft whispers of unseen voices. The men were uneasy. Gaius was as well, wondering if the Berber's tales were lies and his companions waited among the dunes to ambush them from the concealing mountains of sand.

At one point, amid a series of dunes that appeared no different from any of the others dunes they had passed, Rashid called out to him. "We must turn north here," he said.

Gaius glanced at the sun and saw they were still traveling due east. "You said your village lay east of Hamad Rus." He suspected the Berber of treachery.

"Beyond this point the sand gives way to a wide *hamada*. Travel across the pitted, rocky plain is difficult for men and dangerous for horses. The heat is unbearable, even for a Berber. Turning north to skirt its edge is longer but safer."

Gaius saw little reason to trust the Berber. Any delay gave the villagers time to flee. "We continue this way," he said.

Rashid held his arms wide in supplication. "As you wish, Roman, but you were warned."

Travel became easier by late midmorning when the encroaching dunes gave way to smaller dunes and sandy ridges. He increased the pace of the march to make up for time lost in the maze of dunes. As they passed over the crest of one ridge, the dunes yielded to a vast, endless plain of gray, windswept rock pockmarked with deep holes etched by sand and wind, just as the Berber had predicted. Across this dangerous terrain, Gaius dismounted and led Apollo.

The hamada reflected the sun's fury upon them like the cooking stones of an oven. It wavered as a translucent veil through which they plunged ever deeper, its folds enveloping them in suffocating folds of heat. The scuffing sound of the men's metal-shod leather *caligae* on the stony surface and the rhythmic clatter of the horse's hooves echoed loudly in the desert silence, punctuated by the curses of weary soldiers as they stumbled into holes.

After a time, the plain became narrow stone fingers barely wide enough to accommodate the men and horses in a single file. Each ridge ran as straight as a knife's edge into the heart of the desert. On either side of the fingers, lay flat expanses of hard-crusted sand that that produced clouds of fine choking alkali dust when their weight broke through the thin crust.

Gaius noticed the Berber slowing, carefully testing each footstep, and rode back to order him to move faster. Moments later, the first man in the column disappeared from view. The sand sucked him down so quickly he barely had time to cry out. Only the fact that he retained his hold on his aclis saved him. His comrades formed a human chain to reach the shaft of the javelin protruding from the sand and pulled him to safety.

"You were warned, Roman," Rashid said. "The sand here is filled with such dry mires as deadly as quicksand found near the coast. Amazigh and Tauregs alike avoid this area."

"From now on, you march at the head of the column," Gaius told him; and then ordered the men to stay on the stony fingers of rock.

Spirits lifted when they reached another *erg* of dunes and basins in late afternoon. A short time later, a scout waved from atop a nearby dune. Gaius rode ahead and joined him. In an oasis below the dune, a camp of a half dozen tents lay scattered around a small pool of water. The water reminded Gaius just how thirsty he was. The hamada had leached the moisture from his body like a wick. He licked his raspy tongue over parched lips, as he lay on the dune crest on his belly watching the camp. After several minutes, he hadn't detected any movement within the camp. The eerie silence and lack of movement seemed strange. He motioned for Rashid to join him.

"Are these your people?" Gaius asked.

Rashid frowned as he surveyed the empty camp. "Of my tribe," he answered, "but not my kin. Perhaps they, too, are en route to the salt flats from farther south." He paused for a moment, biting his lower lip as he craned his neck to see beyond the small copse of palm trees. "I see no camels, and where are the guards? Even if they were resting through the heat of the day, they would post guards in this dangerous country."

"I thought you said there were no oases here."

"No, Roman, I said the spring near Hamad Rus was foul. This spring is far south of my route. Hamad Rus was much closer."

Gaius quietly motioned his men forward. They converged on the camp from two sides, weapons at ready. He soon realized that stealth was not necessary. The stench of death hung heavy over the camp. Clouds of black flies buzzed around pools of dried blood. Black scorpions and ants scavenged tidbits of food from the remains of the occupants' last meal, while small lizards concentrated on the scorpions and ants, their sticky tongues snatching scuttling insects. Vultures circled warily at a distance, as if fearing to land. A search of the tents revealed no corpses, only tattered robes. Again, no possessions were missing.

"Where are the bodies?" Gaius asked.

Rashid stared at him. "The devils took them, perhaps back to the evil city."

Gaius pointed to the sand. "There are no tracks."

"Does the wind leave tracks? Does the morning mist leave footsteps? Death does not walk on the feet of men."

Gaius ignored Rashid's rhetorical questions. The atmosphere of evil that lay over the oasis matched that of Hamad Rus, the spore of a predator that had developed a taste for human flesh. *Or a demon*, he thought; then, quickly dismissed the idea as too preposterous to consider in spite of the Berber's suggestion.

"How far to your village?" he demanded of Rashid.

Rashid bit his lower lip in thought. "Perhaps a day and a half farther, but I fear it will be the same. A newly awakened evil stalks the land, and none are immune to these horrors."

Gaius considered his options. So far, he had already lost two men and almost lost a third. He had encountered no enemy against which he could draw his sword. Even if he located Rashid's village, he knew he would need more than eight soldiers to subdue it. His first foray into the desert had been a dismal failure except for his captive.

"We return north and meet Flavius," he announced.

The remaining men met this news with much enthusiasm. They were not eager to continue their fruitless trek through the desert or to face an unseen enemy.

"What of me?" Rashid asked. "May I return to my people?"

"You will remain my prisoner until I deem otherwise."

Rashid lowered his head but said nothing. Gaius had a second reason for intercepting Flavius. He wanted to stop him before he reached Hamad Rus. If an enemy existed, Gaius suspected he skulked at Hamad Rus and was no ghost. The time for battle had not yet arrived. His troops needed more training. As he scanned the empty waste spread out before them, he hoped his prisoner didn't attempt to escape and force his men to kill him. He suspected the Berber had more answers than he wished to reveal. Later, if he refused to talk, he would personally slit the Berber's throat.

Ignoring the stench of death, Gaius stripped naked and plunged his body into the tepid pool of water, allowing the water to refresh his drained body. By closing his eyes, he could imagine himself floating in the Mediterranean. Soon, his men joined him. For a few moments, they forgot their weariness and set aside their fear, frolicking in the water like schoolboys, splashing and laughing. Only Rashid refused to join in. No amount of washing could remove the smell of death.

As he floated on his back staring up at the sky, the water rippled, as if struck a blow from beneath. The second occurrence a few seconds later was stronger. Water sloshed onto the banks. The palm trees swayed drunkenly. A stack of spears, their butts thrust into the sand toppled. Men rushed from the pool to don uniforms, yelling to one another in fright. To maintain discipline, Gaius strode from the pool slowly and made a show of donning his uniform, taking his time fastening straps. His actions calmed many of the men, but a few stared at the desert in fear. More than a few glared at the Berber, as if he were somehow to blame.

Gaius mounted Apollo and announced, "It is time we continue our journey."

They marched until sunset and camped in the open. By the redness in their eyes and their quiet demeanor as they roused to break camp the next morning, Gaius knew few had slept soundly. He had slept but a few hours himself the last three nights and badly needed sleep, but nightmares had disturbed any snatches of sleep he had managed. He could not remember them, but felt they had been prophetic.

No one had deserted during the night, too frightened by the bloody scene at the Berber camp to risk straying too far into the desert. Like him, they were overjoyed at the prospect of returning to their own ramshackle encampment at Castra-Augustus.

"We will never make it in time," Rashid said as Gaius checked the bonds on his prisoner's wrists.

"What do you mean?"

Rashid pointed to the southeast with his bound hands. Gaius followed the Berber's gaze. As he watched, the dried-blood red horizon toward sunrise edged closer. A few grains of windblown sand struck him in the face. He swiped them away.

"It is a *tignut*, a sandstorm, a very bad one," Rashid warned. "We have no cover here. Your men must lash themselves together or they will be scattered and lost."

Gaius stared with mounting apprehension at the increasing fury of the approaching storm. The roar of the wind grew louder, a terrible tempest bearing a burden of sand before it like the hand of a god swiped across the desert. He had never witnessed a sandstorm of such magnitude. He decided to follow Rashid's suggestion.

"Use rope," he told them. "Each man must secure himself to the man in front and behind him. Cover your mouth and nose with your focale."

As the men hurriedly lashed themselves together, Gaius made certain Rashid took the spot in front of him where he could watch him. Apollo and the two pack animals trailed the line of men. By the time they had completed the task of securing themselves together, they choked on the fine dust filling the air.

The sandstorm, when it hit, showed them no mercy. It slammed down on top of them like a collapsing wall. The sharp grains of sand rubbed exposed flesh raw, and the incessant wind insured that the fine dust invaded every orifice, no matter how well covered. Fists of wind battered men to the ground. When they rose, it slapped them down again. They made little progress. The sky grew as dark as night, and the wind howled like a living creature. Only the constant tug on the rope by stumbling men before and behind him eased Gaius' fear that he was alone in the storm.

It was therefore great cause for alarm when the rope behind him suddenly slackened. He called out, but the banshee scream of the wind swept away his voice. All he managed was to fill his mouth with sand. He tugged on the rope in front of him until Rashid's face appeared from the sand.

He shouted into the Berber's ear. "The line broke!"

Rashid reached behind Gaius and examined the end of the rope.

"No," he said. "It has been slashed. Here is blood."

Though almost blinded by sand, Gaius saw that Rashid was correct. The rope had been cleanly cut, and blood dampened the end.

"We must find them," he shouted against the wind.

"Impossible," Rashid warned. "We will die. Three men remain in front of me. Will you kill them in a hopeless venture to find the others in this?"

Gaius gritted his teeth in anger, but he knew that Rashid was right. Finding anyone in the sandstorm would be impossible. "We wait here."

The five remaining men sat in a tight huddle, cowering as best they could beneath shields and blankets to wait out the storm's fury.

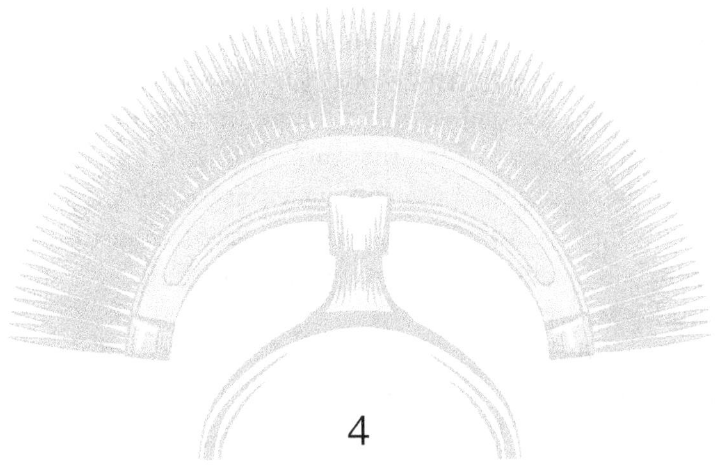

4

Gaius awoke beneath his blanket pressed down by a heavy layer of sand. Once again, images of a creature so nightmarish only a deeply disturbed mind could have conjured it assaulted his sleep. Did the desert weave a mad spell over him? Did the Berber have some arcane power at his disposal to tamper with his mind? At the thought of the Berber, he noticed the severed rope that had secured him to Rashid dangling at his waist. The Berber was gone.

He burrowed from beneath the heavy burden of sand, wiped away the dust that coated his face, and stared around him. The outlines of his men's bodies were barely visible beneath the sand.

"Get up!" he yelled, brushing the sand from his clothing.

Slowly, the other three men pushed back their blankets and shields and shook off the sand entombing them. They stood around bewildered.

"Find the Berber," he ordered.

"There is no need," Rashid said, walking from behind a hillock of sand. "I was simply relieving myself."

The Berber's reappearance surprised him. "Why did you not escape?" Gaius asked. He held out the cut rope.

Rashid shrugged. "You slept soundly, and my morning ritual would not wait." He swept his arms around him. "Where would I go on foot with no food or water?"

Gaius flinched at the implication of Rashid's comment. In spite of the danger, he had slept soundly as the storm raged. By the present position of the sun, he had slept for hours, leaving his remaining men unguarded and exposed to both the storm and their unseen enemy. The days of pent up tension had drained away the fatigue as he lay beneath the sand, allowing his mind to succumb to sleep's irresistible allure. He was as guilty of breaking his personal sense of duty as a soldier who abandoned his sentry post.

"We must find the others."

"I have searched the area. There is no sign of them." He stared at Gaius with sympathy in his eyes. "They are gone, Roman. The desert has taken them, or something far worse."

He felt the truth of Rashid's words. The rope securing them had been bloody and cleanly cut, not broken. They had not wandered away in the sandstorm. The five soldiers had suffered the same unknown fate as the others. What kind of enemy could seize men in a blinding sandstorm? And horses. Apollo was gone, as well as both packhorses and most of their supplies. He felt a momentary twinge of guilt that the loss of Apollo struck him more deeply than the deaths of his troops. He would have to walk out of the desert, a sign of weakness for a Centurion.

The ordeal of the sandstorm had shaken their nerves and shattered their confidence. After coaxing by Gaius, they built a small fire for their meager breakfast, but no one possessed an appetite for the roasting meat. They stared into the flames lost in thought. Some brooded over the lost supplies; others over missing companions.

Rashid did not share their reluctance to eat. He sliced a piece of beef from the spit and chewed it slowly, savoring the moisture from the meat. They had lost most of their water supply with the packhorses. Among them, they had only two partially filled water skins, not enough to see them back to camp. If they missed Flavius, they would be very thirsty by the time they returned.

Gaius felt the blazing heat of the sun on his back and realized the day would only grow hotter.

"Okay, men," he said. "We must march now."

They eyed him with suspicion but moved to obey.

"Quench your thirst now, but drink sparingly. What little we have must sustain us until we reach camp."

Wearily, they packed their few remaining supplies, picked up their weapons, and began their long hike across the dunes. Gaius looked at them and sighed. Three men, he, and a Berber prisoner remained from a patrol of eleven. His command dwindled rapidly. They no longer marched as Roman Legionnaires. They trudged along, beaten and without hope, their dragging javelins leaving furrows in the sand behind them, like farmers plowing a field. If they did not cross Flavius' path soon, they might not make it back to Castra-Augustus.

In the middle of the afternoon, they rested. With no escape from the sweltering heat of the blazing sun directly overhead, Rashid showed them how to dig shallow holes in the sand to reach cooler earth deeper in the ground and how to use their blankets and javelins to erect temporary awnings to ward off the sun. Gaius forbade them to drink too deeply from their rapidly shrinking water skins, though his own mouth ached and his lips swollen and parched. One sip in the morning, one at midday, and two at night would have to suffice until they encountered Flavius or they reached camp.

He had difficulty rousing them from their brief respite. He understood their lack of enthusiasm. Dehydration, the oppressive heat, and the leagues of marching had drained him of most of his reserve of strength. He now continued on sheer determination, using the anger of his failure to drive his steps.

By late afternoon, they stumbled along blindly, having traveled less than two leagues since their brief rest. Gaius' old wound troubled him like an itch he couldn't scratch. He limped along, each step sending fingers of agony shooting through his thigh. The only positive aspect of his misery was that he had no time to contemplate his stomach problems, which seemed to plague him doubly with nothing in his stomach. He considered calling another time-consuming halt when, squinting against the sun, he noticed what he at first thought a mirage dancing above the wavering sands; then he saw it was a troop of men.

His anxiety did not lift. They could be Berbers or Tauregs. If so, he and the fate of his remaining men would be uncertain at best. Then, he saw the flapping banner and the glint of a gold eagle above it. *Flavius!* He would have cried tears of joy if his desiccated body could spare the precious moisture. Cries of, "*Eaux!*" erupted from the weary men hurrahing the arrival of their comrades. Flavius spotted Gaius and rode out to meet him. The joyous reunion faded when Gaius observed that nearly a quarter of Flavius' men were missing.

"Ho, Flavius," he called out in dismay. "What dire fate has befallen you?"

Flavius hung his head in shame. "Demons. They struck during the sandstorm. We saw shapes darting among us but could not catch them. When the storm passed, nine men were missing. We searched but found no one."

Gaius nodded. "The same fate befell us, I fear."

Flavius scowled at Rashid and pointed his finger. "Who is he?"

"A Berber. He claims his men are dead also. We did discover a deserted camp and signs of a struggle."

"Do you trust him?"

Gaius stared at Rashid. "Not entirely."

"Do we continue?" The tone of his voice made known his thoughts on the idea.

Gaius' gaze took in Flavius' men, and then his. "We must return to camp. We need supplies. Then we return to Hamad Rus."

"Hamad Rus?"

Gaius patted Flavius on the back. "I will tell you of Hamad Rus on our return journey." He turned to his men. "Bind our Berber friend." Rashid had not escaped during the storm, but Gaius still did not trust him. He withheld something, some bit of information that might prove the difference between life and death. Rashid scowled at him, as he held out his hands for the soldiers to secure them with leather thongs.

Gaius accepted a horse from one of the men and mounted. Until that moment, he did not realize how debilitating his wound was. It had been over four months and still he could walk no more than half a league without enduring excruciating agony. He decided he needed to exercise his leg more often. *But not just yet*, he thought. It felt good to sit astride a horse once more although he felt none of the connection between rider and horse as he did with Apollo.

They turned their backs to the deep desert and headed north, following the tracks Flavius had made on his southbound trek, traveling slowly for the sake of the exhausted men. Later that day, just before sunset, they encountered the second lost patrol, all five men alive and well. Their welcomed appearance offered small recompense for the men he had lost, but their safe return signaled the gods might yet be smiling on him. He spoke with the *sesquiplecarus* of the patrol, a corporal named Dracus Armis.

"We thought you all dead," he said.

Dracus Armis replied, "We, too, thought we were lost, especially during the second sand storm we have suffered in six days. I regret that we did not find the earlier patrol, Centurion Linneus."

"We located their empty camp, but I don't think we will find them alive."

The officer glanced back at his men; then nodded. "It is as I suspected. We heard ominous sounds in the night. I feel we have been watched. We crossed the tracks of men and horses and decided to follow. We are glad it was legionnaires." He looked at the bedraggled appearance of Gaius' few men and at the Berber captive. "Did you encounter much trouble?"

Gaius resisted the urge to laugh at the absurdity of the sesquiplecarus' question. "An unseen enemy. We now return to camp for supplies and reinforcements."

The hour neared midnight when they entered Castra-Augustus the second day after joining with Flavius. The men, footsore and weary from their five-day forced march, threw themselves on the ground as soon as they passed the wall. Gaius noted the men left in the camp by Flavius had added only a single layer of stones to the wall along one side of the compound.

They did not expect us to return alive. He would have to remind them, forcefully if necessary, that their lives might depend on the wall.

Marcellus rushed up to greet them.

"Thank the gods you are well." He took in the missing men and frowned. "You encountered trouble, I see."

"Later, Marcellus." Gaius was too tired to reprimand Marcellus or the men left in camp. He noticed a soldier, stripped to the waist, strapped to a makeshift rack, his back red and blood-scabbed from flogging. "What is his story?"

Marcellus scowled and spat on the ground. "He tried to inspire the others to desert. They did not." He looked apologetically at Gaius. "I would have waited for your order, but the men needed an example."

Punishment by *flagrum*, a short leather whip with bits of metal braided into the multiple leather cords, was a grisly sight. In the hands of a practiced *lictor*, the tips could peel flesh from bones. The minimal ten lashes left a man bruised, bleeding, and in agony. Scourging served two purposes: to punish an offender and to serve as a warning to others.

Gaius waved his hand in dismissal. "You did right."

A half-smile creased Marcellus' lips. "Do we leave him for the scorpions?"

"Release him in the morning. A night hanging stretched between posts will drive deeper the point. He will serve us better as a sentry than as a corpse."

Marcellus stroked his chin and frowned. "You trust him to stand guard?"

"His screams when our enemy takes him will serve as a warning to the others."

Marcellus nodded. "He will serve better in death than he did in life."

A familiar whinny from the corral lifted Gaius' spirits. Apollo had found his way home.

"Your horse is safe," Marcellus said. "*Fortuna te favet.* Luck favors you. The gods think you worthy of their consideration."

As he stared out at the remains of his small garrison, Gaius muttered, "Perhaps the gods are instead toying with me as gods often do."

After building fires, the men collapsed in the shade of their tents, or on the bare sand near the fires. He set no guards. In spite of his fatigue, he would personally remain awake to watch over them.

Gaius decided to damn the lack of water and rescind his abnegation of a hot bath. "Heat water," he told his aide. "Set up my tub and fill it one-quarter full." The aide stared at him for a moment before rushing off to carry out Gaius' order. Gaius made a rapid mental calculation and concluded that the amount of water he ordered would equal what the seven men lost on his patrol would consume in two days.

He detested bathing in such primitive conditions, but as a soldier, he had long ago resigned himself to such squalor. A small, portable leather tub, supported by wooden poles and filled with a few pails of hot water was a poor substitute for the luxurious sunken *balneum* in his family home in Rome. From the bath, he had an unobstructed view of the River Tiber and the magnificent Aqua Claudia aqueduct bringing water to Rome. Here, he had no *capsarii*, or bath slaves, to aid him in his bathing ritual, and he would allow no soldier to attend him. That would be undignified.

After soaking and then rubbing his body briskly in the tepid water with his hands, he used his prized curved bone *strigil* to remove dirt and body oils. Once out of the tub, clad only in a towel, he anointed his legs, arms, and shoulders with scented oil, a parting gift from a female admirer. He longed for a slave to massage his aching muscles, but slaves required food and water, and both were far too precious in the desert to waste on slaves.

A low cough outside his tent alerted him that Flavius wished to speak with him. *At least he was courteous enough to wait until I completed my ablutions.* "Enter, Flavius," he said.

"Your pardon, sir. What of the bearers who accompanied you from the coast?"

Gaius realized he had forgotten about them. Originally, he had intended to send them back. He had half-expected them to flee during his absence, but now, with the loss of so many soldiers ... "Perhaps recruiting them would be best."

"Recruiting them? You mean as *munifex*."

Gaius smiled inwardly at Flavius' skepticism, but fatigue workers were not what he had in mind. "Why not?" he asked, as he donned his tunic and sandals. "They are strong, relatively healthy, and more importantly, they are already here. Promise them full Roman citizenship, gold … I don't care what you promise them, just don't allow them to leave."

Flavius said nothing, but his scowl revealed much.

"You disagree?"

"It is not my place," he growled.

Gaius sighed. "No, it is not, but I must depend on you, Flavius. You are right. It is unorthodox, but we have lost far too many men. We face a seemingly invisible enemy. Teach them the use of the *hasta*. They are familiar with spears. The short sword requires too much training. Most have knives and scimitars with which they are more familiar and are equally effective. Train them with those."

Flavius nodded as he scratched his stubbled chin. "Aye, they could learn the proper use of the *hasta* quickly enough. We could use them as sentries or to rebuild the wall."

Gaius smiled and held his arms out wide. "See. Already you have found a use for them."

Flavius returned Gaius' smile. "With this unseen enemy, I may have to pair each with a tirone to keep them both from fleeing in the night."

Gaius shuddered, as he thought of the darkness and the unseen dangers within. "I doubt they will move very far from the campfires at night."

Flavius nodded in agreement. "I find the flames more comforting than in times past."

Gaius clenched his right fist. "We will find this enemy, and we will defeat him. I will not die forgotten in this sandy waste. I will return to Rome in triumph. I swear it." He turned to Flavius. "With you by side, eh, noble warrior?"

Flavius drew his sword. "I swear my allegiance," he said with a solemnity that touched Gaius deeply. He suddenly felt a stronger bond with his optio. He reached out and grasped Flavius' sword with his hand, allowing the sharp blade to draw a few drops of blood that splattered on the sand.

"I pledge my favor for that loyalty. Now, tell me, Optio. What secret do you harbor you have not yet decided to tell me? I must know all."

Flavius rubbed his chin. "I told you Centurion Agrippa was quiet and moody. He ... he revealed to me he had troubling nightmares."

Gaius shuddered, remembering his own dreams. "Nightmares?"

Flavius nodded. "Dark dreams of shadows with teeth and eyes. They spoke to him with voices he could not understand but knew their message was dire. It drove him insane. I believe he went in search of them that night, perhaps to learn their secret."

With his glimpse of the red eyes of the shadow in Hamad Rus, Gaius hoped Agrippa had not found them. "Five days ago, I would have doubted you. Now ... Now, see to the men before you sleep. In two days time, we return to Hamad Rus."

"They will be ready," Flavius promised, and then turned on his heel and exited the tent. Gaius smiled at his second-in-command. Although now only a Centurion, Flavius treated him as if he still commanded a Legion.

"With a dozen like him, I would conquer these shadows of the night."

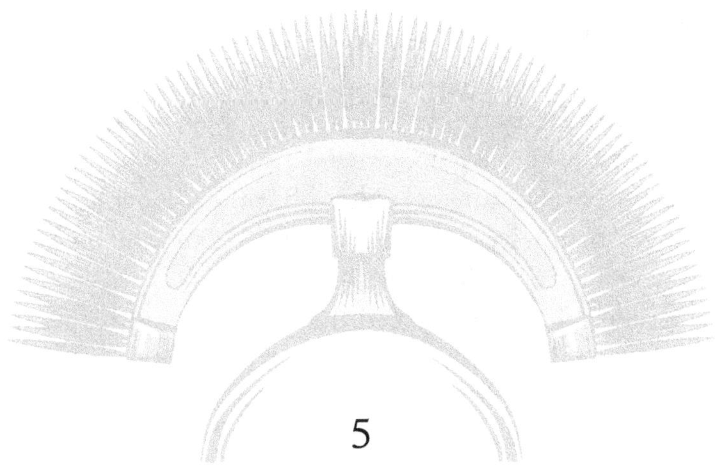

5

Gaius declared the following day one of rest for his exhausted men, but Flavius heeded his advice and began training the newly conscripted native bearers early. Most seemed pleased by the promise of Roman citizenship and Roman gold, but a few balked and attempted to leave. Flogging one of them as an example to the others squelched further objections. Gaius detested such harsh methods of discipline, but he had witnessed many men's objections wither under the well-placed blows of a leather *flagrum*. The wounds were painful and the scars became a reminder to all that saw them.

All morning, Flavius instructed the new recruits in the proper use of the aclis and the hasta. The Roman javelin, with its long wooden handle ending in an iron point, proved a formidable weapon in trained hands. The *hasta,* with its heavier, broad point, excelled as a close-fighting weapon used to protect the ranks and required only basic training to be effective. He had no time to teach them finesse, but demonstrated to them the fundamentals of thrusting and parrying singly and in tightly formed ranks, drawing a little blood and bruising a few hands in the process. There were no extra shields for them, but as they would unlikely be opposing an armored enemy, the long spear would suffice. Their very lack of armor and shield gave them a speed advantage over the heavily armored troops.

By midday, the extreme heat had taken its toll on even Flavius' boundless enthusiasm. He dismissed the men and returned to Gaius dripping with perspiration. He accepted a goblet of wine from Gaius' hand and drained it in one gulp.

"They will never be Roman soldiers, but they know how to kill and how to protect themselves." He chuckled. "I dare not push them too hard, or they will harm each other."

Gaius nodded. He had watched the training from his tent, pleased by Flavius' dogged determination. "Choose one of the more adept and promote him to *decanus*. Be sure he can speak at least some Latin. They will follow one of their own more readily than they will a Roman."

"*Decanus*," Flavius scoffed. "We have milites that will never advance to private. They will not like a foreigner outranking them."

"He will be decanus in name only. He will command only the auxilia. I would not have a Roman subordinate to a Tebu or a Berber."

Flavius nodded and offered his goblet for a refill. Gaius poured more wine, and Flavius seated himself on a gilded wooden trunk, sipping more slowly this time. "As you wish. Their food is horrendous – spicy, and smelly. It turns my stomach. I will billet them together, and they can cook their own mess downwind of the camp. Perhaps the stench of the latrine can mask it."

Gaius stared out at the sea of sand surrounding them, recalling his visits as a young boy to the island of Ischia off the coast of Napoli, a green, mountainous island jutting from the Tyrrhenian Sea, surrounded by blue water, not flat, dry, featureless desert. His uncle's villa perched like an eagle's aerie on a high cliff facing west toward the wide Mediterranean, *Mare Nostrum*. Each evening as the sun set, it transformed the tranquil blue waters to blood crimson, the same color he had seen so many times on battlefields since, almost as if an omen of his future life. He remembered meals at his uncle's villa, sumptuous affairs with dozens of slaves and servants and food from all of Italy and the lands beyond. He picked up a dried fig from the tray of fruit beside him and stared at it.

"I ate my first fig as a boy in Ischia, Flavius. Will I taste my last one here in this dead place?"

Flavius sat up straighter. "Not as long as I have my sword," he growled.

"Good Flavius, I fear our weapons might be no match for our enemy."

Flavius' screwed up his face as if Gaius' words had offended him. "Good Roman iron is a match for any blade."

Gaius nodded. "Yes, for an enemy we can see. What good against these wraiths?"

"Wraith, witch, ghost, or goblin, we will defeat them."

Gaius took a bite of the fig, letting the sweet juice fill his mouth. As he swallowed, he shuddered. *Will I ever again see Rome?* "Yes, yes, I grow maudlin. We will find our enemy and slay him." He raised his goblet to Flavius. "Victory."

Flavius held out his goblet, splashing a little of its dark red contents on the sand. "Victory," he repeated.

Gaius looked at the stained sand at Flavius' feet, the color of the sea at Ischia. He shuddered again and pulled his tunic tighter against a sudden chill only he felt.

"How many men accompany us to this dead city?" Flavius asked as he raised his goblet.

"We will strike camp. All will go."

Flavius stopped his goblet before it touched his lips. "All?" he asked.

"We number but 64. We would risk losing the few we leave behind. The temptation to desert would be strong. We are safer together."

"Yes." The tone of Flavius' voice indicated hesitation.

Gaius glared at his second-in-command, irked by Flavius' reluctance to spit out what he wanted to say. "You disagree?"

"No. These walls have proven no defense, no matter how high we build them. The walls of a city, even a dead one, should be easier to defend."

Gaius suspected Flavius of leaving something unsaid. "You wish to say more?" he prompted.

Flavius shuffled his feet nervously. "We were ordered to establish this fortification here at this location. Abandoning it and moving deeper into the desert might be construed as desertion."

Gaius understood Flavius' reasoning. An order, even the order to establish a punishment camp in the middle of nowhere, was one to obey. In Rome's long history, more than one Praetor had formed his own personal legion, sometimes using it to oppose Rome's power. Rome moved swiftly to quash rebellion and punish commanders who overreached their authority.

"We can wait here on this useless piece of rock for our enemy to attack us, or we can seek him out. I prefer offense to defense."

Flavius nodded his head. Gaius saw a flicker of anticipation in his eyes. "A legionnaire is useless behind a stockade or stone wall." He slapped his sword. "Attack is the only way to defeat an enemy."

"We will return to Rome together or die here, our bones bleaching in the desert. There can be no alternative."

"With the sound of swords clashing in our ears," Flavius added.

Flavius suddenly stood, set his empty wine goblet aside, and walked away, surprising Gaius.

"Where are you going?"

Over his shoulder, Flavius replied, "These Tebu require more training if we are to depend on them in battle. They will soon learn to hate me."

Gaius smiled at Flavius' back. *My optio pushes hard. That is good.* "Let them hate you, so long as they fear you," he said.

A stomach spasm wrenched Gaius' guts, as if someone had jabbed the butt end of a gladius into his midsection. He doubled over in intense pain, grasping the edge of the tent flap to keep from falling. He called out to his aide, standing just outside his tent. "Bring me the *medicus,*" he gasped.

The aide rushed off to fetch the physician. Gaius clasped his stomach with both hands trying to quell the rushes of agony. He struggled across the tent to his cot and lay down. The pain now sliced him open from the inside out. He looked down expecting to see a blood-smeared blade protruding from his belly.

The physician, a gruff looking, dark-complexioned man whose stony face appeared to never have produced a smile, entered without announcing himself. He took one look at Gaius, frowned, and crossed over to his cot. If the troops were outcasts, Gaius wondered what twist of fate had brought the physician to such a lonely outpost.

"My stomach pains me," he told the physician. "I have chewed dried licorice root, but it no longer works. Have you some herb or ointment that can ease this discomfort?"

The physician used a dirty finger to pull up Gaius' eyelids and examined his eyes, and then his tongue. He took two steps back and studied the prostrate Centurion. "How long has your stomach bothered you?"

Gaius couldn't remember exactly when the pains had begun, sometime after leaving Syria Palaestina. "Three or four months."

"Do they grow steadily worse?"

"Yes," Gaius answered grimacing as another bolt of pain shot through him.

The physician nodded. "I have seen this condition before, Centurion. It is a cancer of the stomach."

"Give me a balm," Gaius said.

The physician pulled a small vial from his satchel. "I have henbane powder for when the pain becomes too severe." He also handed Gaius a packet of herbs. "This is dried rhubarb and yarrow root. They will soothe minor pains, much like the licorice you chew, but soon the pain will become more than you can bear."

Gaius wondered how it could become more severe. "What can you do?"

The physician stared at him. "Do? I can do nothing. The cancer is eating at you, and you will eventually die."

The physician's diagnosis, delivered in such a cold, matter of fact manner, stunned Gaius, forcing him to face his own mortality. "Your bedside manner needs improving, physician. How long?"

The physician shrugged. "I cannot say with certainty, only guess. Perhaps a year longer with proper care, but here in this hellhole, who can say? Less, I would venture."

He stood there as Gaius' mind raced through possibilities, but came up with nothing. "Tell no one, physician."

A brief flicker of anguish crossed the physician's face. "The men allow me to treat their blisters and their ills, but they do not talk to me. It is unlikely any will ask. Do you know why I am here, Centurion?"

Gaius shook his head, not interested, but the physician seemed determined to speak. "I know not."

The physician glanced out the tent to the men outside. "They do. I killed a man, an officer." He held out his hands. "Once, these hands could perform fine surgeries. I saved the lives of many men after battles. My demon was wine. I attempted to remove an arrow from a Legate's side while I was in my cups." He raised his hands and frowned. "These unsteady hands slipped and he died. He went to his Hades, and the Emperor sent me sent to mine. I envy the man I killed. His death was mercifully quick." As the physician stared at him, Gaius saw pity in his eyes. "Call on me when you need more medicine." He looked upward. "Call on the gods if you want mercy. I do not believe they can hear you from this desolate place, but you can try."

When he left, Gaius sprinkled some of the henbane powder in his goblet and poured wine over it. He downed the draft in one gulp. The medicine tasted as sour as vinegar, but not as bitter as the physician's pronouncement of doom. It would be better to die in battle. He waited half an hour for the sedative to ease the pain, and then summoned the Berber to him.

When Rashid arrived a few minutes later, he bore a vivid purple bruise on his right cheek, and the eye above it was swollen and almost closed. He stood at the entrance to Gaius' tent, his hands bound tightly in front of him. Gaius slipped his pugio from his belt and used the dagger's keen edge to slice Rashid's bonds. The Berber rubbed his raw wrists as he examined the furnishings of Gaius' tent.

"You Romans believe in your comfort," he said after his survey.

Rashid's observations surprised Gaius. He had always believed his personal belongings sparse and utilitarian. Too much comfort distanced him from the men under his command. By eating and sleeping as they did, he earned their respect and better understood their limitations. Each *libra* of weight of personal belongings the pack animals or wagons carried meant that much less food, weapons, or water. As a soldier lifted from the ranks, he preferred extra weapons to extra clothing. Then he remembered the leather tub in the back of the tent. Though lightweight, to a desert dweller, such a contrivance would seem extravagant.

"We are unused to this desert heat."

Rashid smiled. "Perhaps you Romans should return to more favorable climes."

Gaius scowled but ignored the taunt. "Any soil beneath a Roman Eagle is a favorable clime." He pointed to Rashid's face. "I see my men treated you roughly. I did not order it."

Rashid touched the bruise above his eye and winced. "It is nothing, a disagreement over my *iharz*."

His hand went to his neck and Gaius saw that the blue-jeweled amulet no longer hung from around his neck. "I will see that it is returned. Sit."

Rashid ignored the stool Gaius offered and instead sat cross-legged on the sand facing Gaius. He continued to rub his wrists.

"We are returning to Hamad Rus." Gaius didn't know why he bothered announcing his plans to Rashid, but he felt that he somehow needed the Berber's presence with him.

Rashid nodded. "So I suspected. You will all die."

"You will die before us if you do not tell me all you know of this unseen enemy," Gaius growled.

Rashid stared at Gaius as if judging him. "They are the Dark Ones, invisible, deadly shadows that kill silently. Your weapons will not protect you." He raised his hands and spread them wide. "What more is there to know? Flee this place while you can."

Gaius ignored Rashid's advice. "I saw fresh blood on an altar in the temple at Hamad Rus. Why was it there?"

Rashid sighed. "The Inyosh worship an even darker god they name *Nergal*, ruler of the underworld. The people of Hamad Rus built the temple in an attempt to appease *Nergal*." He shrugged. "They failed."

The wild tale Rashid wove intrigued him. The Berber believed his words to be true, but Gaius listened with increasing skepticism. *Lies and half lies*, he thought; then, wondered why he shuddered at the name Nergal. He had heard more believable tales for a few copper *denarii* from *fakirs* wandering the deserts of Mesopotamia, but the Berber's conviction was undeniable.

"And the blood?"

"The creatures offer the blood to *Nergal*. What they do with the flesh and bones of their victims I do not know."

"How did you learn of these … Dark Ones?"

"From my grandfather. He learned from an Egyptian, a priest of Thoth in the temple of Gz-eh near Karnack. The priest fled Egypt during a religious purge by the Roman Governor Marcus Sempronius Liberalis. He gave my father the amulet your men took from me. Upon his death, it became mine."

Gaius remembered the hypnotic lure of the stone of the amulet, like liquid *lapis lazuli,* which glowed softly as if smoldering from a flame within, but it was a pretty bauble and nothing more. He lost his temper at Rashid's ridiculous ramblings, meant no doubt to elevate his position from that of a lowly expendable hostage to an expert of their invisible enemy.

"*Di Omnes*! By the gods do not lie to me," he snarled. "If these Dark Ones have been here in this desert for centuries as you claim, why have they not wiped out your people?"

"Once they were content to haunt the old city and the nearby caverns, preying only on the unwary or the unlucky. Something has disturbed them." He turned his head toward Gaius and smirked. "Perhaps it is the presence of you Romans. You enjoy stirring ant nests."

Gaius felt a fleeting moment of sympathy for his captive, but let if pass. Hating Romans was the world's pastime, the fate of the conquered. "You hate us so much?"

Rashid shrugged. "Greeks, Persians, Carthaginians, Romans, Parthians, and Egyptians – You are all the same. You claim to worship your gods, but you conveniently ignore your own religious beliefs if they conflict with your desires. My people have lived in these deserts for millennia, yet you try to enslave us and take from us land you do not want or know how to use. Now, you drive us deeper into the desert, and we face the same creatures you now seek out. I will take you to them in hopes that your bones and blood will satiate them, perhaps saving my people."

"If you attempt to deceive me …." Gaius warned.

Rashid laughed and shrugged. "Yes, yes. You will kill me. So be it. We are all dead men if we return to Hamad Rus."

Gaius pointed to the wine flagon. "Do you wish wine?"

"I drink no wine while mourning the deaths of my friends and kin. If you offer water, I will take it."

Gaius picked up the goblet Flavius had drunk from and poured water from a goatskin water bag. He handed it to Rashid. The Berber's eyes fell to the dagger in Gaius' belt well within his reach, but he ignored it and accepted the water. Draining it, he held the empty goblet in his hands, staring at it, rubbing his fingers over the etched floral design around its base. Gaius wondered if Rashid thought he might use the heavy goblet as a weapon.

"My thanks. I tell you this. If I thought you could defeat these creatures, I would welcome your weapons, but you cannot. Your deaths will only bring more Romans into this country seeking revenge on my people. I implore you. Leave this place."

"I cannot."

Rashid sighed and nodded. "So I feared. I overheard your men speaking of you. You displeased your Emperor, and he sent you here to my country as punishment. You are a warrior and believe a victory will carry you back to Rome with honors." He shook his head. "There can be no victory over that which has existed since the dawn of time. You and your men will die here and become a legion of the dead."

"You read omens now in an empty water flagon?"

Rashid set the empty goblet on the ground in front of him. "I read your death in the blood of my murdered kin and in the eyes of your frightened men. Death awaits you in Hamad Rus, and you go to meet it in typical Roman fashion, eagle held aloft, shields and swords glinting in the sun, trumpets blaring." He shook his head. "You cannot fight shadows as you would fight a living foe. You cannot win this battle, Roman."

"We will see."

Smiling, Rashid said, "You are brave but foolish."

Rashid's smile angered Gaius. He rose quickly and stood looming over him. Rashid didn't flinch. "I have fought many men of many lands and have defeated them. I have also extracted information from recalcitrant captives. Do not force me to turn you over to men who would take pleasure from your pain."

Rashid threw his arms wide and bowed his head until it brushed the sand. "All I know I will tell. I will accompany you to our deaths to prove the truth of my words. In the end, it will make no difference."

A strong compulsion to strike the Berber gripped Gaius, but he resisted. Pain inflicted for no purpose other than from anger served no purpose. He didn't claim to be a truthsayer able to discern the sincerity of men's words, but he felt the Berber prisoner had spoken truthfully. He couldn't punish him simply for hating Romans. Half the civilized world hated Rome, even some countries who called her friend and ally. He called out to his aide waiting patiently outside the tent.

"Take the prisoner back to his tent. Do not bind him but watch him closely. Treat his wound and see that he has proper food and water. Warn his guards that if they strike him again, I will duplicate his wounds on their backs twofold with a *flagrum*. Have them return his amulet."

The aide blanched at the mention of the *flagrum*. He had seen the savaged back of the legionnaire bound to the rack. He swallowed hard, nodded, and followed Rashid back to his place of confinement. Gaius noted that the Berber strode across the compound with a confidence uncommon to a prisoner, especially a lowly salt merchant as he claimed to be. It looked as if he were escorting the aide instead of vice versa.

Gaius poured more wine into his cup and brought it to his lips, but didn't drink. He wondered if he made a mistake by not executing the Berber now and rid himself of his insufferable presence. However, something inside, a small voice that had kept him alive through many heated battles, warned him that Rashid's life now inexorably intertwined with his.

A shudder of disgust passed through him at the thought of some intangible bond with a member of an inferior race. He had seen many Berbers, as well as Carthaginians, Jews, and Numidians on the slave blocks in Leptis Magna. As a Roman by birth and one of the ruling class, to give a Berber equal standing for any reason demeaned him.

He tossed the untouched wine outside his tent and dropped the empty cup beside his cot. "This country and its people vex me," he said.

He collapsed on his cot and flung his arm over his eyes in a fit of annoyance, an attempt to erase from his vision the pitifully small encampment in the middle of a vast emptiness, as far removed from the pleasures of Rome as the sky from the earth. He lay there for a considerable time, letting the memories of the sound of the waves crashing on the rocks below his uncle's villa wash away the dull, boring sounds of camp life. Not until he heard the call for the evening meal did he reluctantly emerge from his stupor.

Darkness often came to the desert with a swiftness with which those unfamiliar with such barren vistas are not accustomed, sometimes as completely as a drape pulled over the land, cloaking it in mystery and shadows. The brief span of time between complete darkness and the rising of the moon or the appearance of the stars was a time of uncertainty. Would the night be pitch black, impenetrable, and frightening, or illuminated by the heavens?

The night fell so suddenly and so completely, that Gaius, who had campaigned in several such deserts, found himself briefly confused by his surroundings. He attributed it to the aftereffects of the henbane. The gloom brought an unnatural stillness to the camp but no relief from the oppressive heat. Men ate their meals in silence, staring into the night and waiting. Sentries gripped their weapons tightly in their hands, as if eager to use them. Even the native Tebu bearers, now fledgling Roman auxilia, refrained from their usual singing after their meal. Men huddled in groups near the blazing fires, ignoring the sweltering heat for the illusory comfort of the light.

Gaius, too, ate his meal in silence, apart from his comrades. The salted meat was necessary in the desert where men sweated away their salt, but the preserved meat had none of the flavor of fresh beef. The cheese tasted rancid in his mouth, but he knew its vileness only represented the foulness of his present predicament. His stomach knotted itself like the coils of a serpent around his middle. The wine tasted of piss and vinegar. Only water slaked his thirst, as only victory could sate his appetite. He debated pouring another dose of henbane but refrained for fear he would grow too accustomed to its soothing qualities. He would have to learn to live with the pain. He laughed. According to the physician, living with the pain might be a short undertaking.

In an attempt to exorcise the demons of despondency that had descended over him, he roamed the perimeter of the camp, inspecting the sentries, warning them to remain alert. They took heart from his presence though his heart was little in it. He offered them a few words of encouragement that he himself did not feel.

He stopped at the corral and rejoiced at the sight of the white ghost prancing alongside the wooden rails. He gently rubbed Apollo's stout neck, soothing the horse's unease. Gaius had always felt more comfortable in the presence of horses than in men. His love of horses had led to his choice of a cavalry officer as his career. Storming the enemy from atop his steed, slashing downward at his opponent with his *spatha*, the heavy long sword that could cleave enemy armor, thundering into the enemy's lines – Those were the moments that paid for the tedium, the endless waiting between battles.

Now, he faced more waiting. The night would be long, but with the dawn, they would break camp and move on Hamad Rus to confront their unseen adversary. He sensed Apollo's eagerness to attack, gleaned somehow from his master's touch. The eager horse pawed at the earth with its massive hooves, snickering his agreement to carry Gaius to victory.

Satisfied, Gaius returned to his tent for sleep.

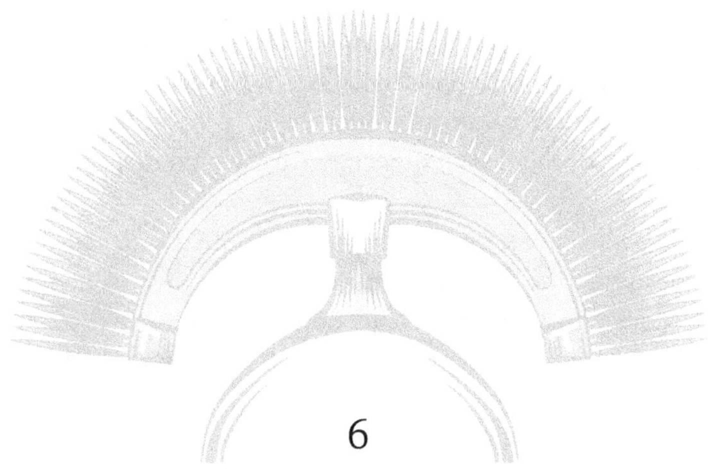

6

Marcellus shook him awake the next morning just after dawn. Startled, he groped for his sword, fearing another attack.

"No, Centurion," Marcellus said, staying his hand, "there is no attack. Two men on horseback approach the camp."

Gaius splashed water on his face, strapped on his sandals and belt with his sword. "Are they Berbers?" he asked, wondering if Rashid's men had come to barter for his release?

"No, they are Roman."

Had he heard right? The last thing he expected were Roman visitors arriving at Castra Augustus. Marcellus' war-weary, deadpan face betrayed no chance of mistake, but Gaius detected a slight tremor in his jaw. "Romans? Here?" he asked.

"So it seems."

"And only two?" To Gaius, that was more curious than the fact they were Romans.

Marcellus nodded.

Gaius strode from his tent and stared north. Indeed, two men rode toward the camp on horseback. Both wore Roman armor that gleamed like burnished brass in the early morning sun. One wore a *paludamentum* draped around his shoulders. The red cloak billowed in the morning breeze. What would bring two Romans alone into the desert so far from civilization?

Flavius stood near the rock wall waiting for him. Gaius joined his optio and the dozen curious men standing around watching. As he recognized the cudgel one of the men held in his hand, he turned to Marcellus. "One of them is an officer. Have the men turn out to properly greet him."

Marcellus's deep voice broke the morning quiet ordering the men to turn out for inspection. The camp came suddenly alive, as men rushed to don armor and find weapons. Gaius noted his own sweat-stained, dirty tunic, but now he had no time in which to change. The strangers had already entered the camp.

The leader, a thin, blond-haired young man with cold, close-set blue eyes, glared down at him from his horse with a hawkish stare. "I am Tribune Sevilius Antonius Livinius, second in command of the garrison at Marzuq. My companion is Quintus Cantos, my aide."

Gaius noted the *torc* around the tribune's neck. He wore the gold necklace military decoration as if on parade. "I am Gaius Marcus Linneus," he replied.

"I know who you are, *Centurion*." Sevilius spat his rank at him, and then stared at the camp and the men pouring out of the tents for inspection. "I was informed that rejects from other companies comprised this motley centuria, but I expected better than this." He scowled when he saw the new native recruits carrying Roman *hastas*. "You arm these dogs? Have you lost your mind?"

Gaius fumed but held his temper. "We have been under attack and on the march. I armed everyone who could carry a weapon."

Sevilius stared at him. "Under attack? From whom, sand fleas?"

At Sevilius' laugh, from the corner of his eye, Gaius saw Flavius' hand reach for his sword at the insult. He shook his head. He would have no Roman blood on his hands.

"Our enemy is unseen, but nonetheless deadly, as you can see from our reduced ranks. Why are you here, Tribune?" He glanced behind the pair. "Did you cross the desert alone just to fling insults?"

Sevilius bridled at Gaius' tone, but withheld comment. "I lead two centuriae to track and apprehend a band of Berbers that attacked a patrol near Marzuq and killed ten soldiers. I left my troops at a deserted village last night while my aide and I rode ahead to arrange billeting here. I preferred riding in the relative coolness of the early morning. Have you seen any Berbers?"

"Just one. He is my prisoner."

"Deliver him to me."

Gaius bridled at the Tribune's deprecatory tone. "No."

Sevilius fumed. "I am an officer. I demand to question him."

"You may question him in my presence, but I will not hand him over to you for rough handling."

Sevilius raised his cudgel and pointed it at Gaius. "I'll have you flogged." His aide's face paled at the threat.

Gaius kept his voice steady, as he replied, "Do not equate my demotion with fear, Tribune Sevilius Livinius. I do not fear you. I command here. You are my guest."

"You have not learned your place."

"It will take more than an unruly child to show it to me. Come, Tribune, rest and dine. Then I will bring the Berber to you." He held out his arm in welcome. "You may refresh yourself in my tent."

He coughed to hide Flavius' snicker. Sevilius said nothing as he dismounted his horse. His aide followed him. Clearly, the exchange between the two bewildered the aide. He stared at Gaius with undisguised contempt. Gaius did not flinch. He motioned for a soldier to deliver the two horses to the corral. Sevilius stopped to count the men lined up for inspection.

"I count but fifty three men and officers. Where are the others?"

Gaius noted that the Tribune had summarily dismissed the new recruits as unworthy of mentioning. "Dead," he replied, "as I informed you. We have been under attack."

"How many Berbers have you slain?"

"We have slain no one. We have seen no one, except for our guest, and he delivered himself to us after his men were attacked."

"By this unseen enemy?" Sevilius asked. His tone was haughty and mocking.

"Yes, I fear your men might not be safe. Perhaps I can send riders to bring them here. Together, we would be safer."

Sevilius scowled. "My men do not need your protection. They will arrive by nightfall once they have rounded up and dealt with the accursed Berbers."

"As you wish."

As Sevilius and his aide stalked away, Flavius came to Gaius' side. "I have heard of young Sevilius. He is a friend of the Emperor. That is why he made Tribune at such an early age. *Praefectus castrorum* Atticus defers to him. They say the Emperor will soon call him to Rome. Emperor Marcus Aurelius himself placed the torc he wears so proudly about his neck with his own hands. It might not be wise to anger him."

"What more can the Emperor do to me?"

"He could order your death."

Gaius laughed. It seemed his death was now out of the hands of the Emperor. "Death would be preferable to this exile, but that would not suit the Emperor's purpose. No, young Sevilius is no threat to me. He is not worth his own piss. However, until he recognizes the danger we face, he can be a problem."

"He and his aide could vanish mysteriously," Flavius replied. "Then his men will be yours to command. The shifting sands can hide much."

Gaius smiled. "Flavius, you are a bloodthirsty old man. Your solution has some merit, but we are not yet reduced to killing fellow officers."

"Oh, well. Perhaps the shadows will take him."

Gaius wondered if the shadows would not take them all. "We need him. When he has faced these dark creatures, his word to the Emperor will be weightier than that of a disgraced former commander who has suffered *militae mutatio* and *gradus dejectio*."

Noting the bitterness in Gaius' voice, Flavius replied, "The Emperor can relegate you to an inferior service, such as is our pitiful sandbox fort, and reduce your rank, but he cannot take from you your dignity or your honor unless you allow him. Your skill, your knowledge, and your sword are as keen as they were before Parthia. I am an old war dog, long in the tooth and too free with my words to rise any further in the ranks than I have. For me, this is my last post. Though we are few in number and a poor excuse for a Desert Legion, you name me optio, and I hear no ridicule in your voice. I will be worthy of your trust, if you will be worthy of your name. Do not allow this place to defeat you, Gaius Marcus Linneus."

Flavius' heartfelt oratory shamed Gaius for doubting himself. Giving in to self-pity now when he had resisted succumbing to it under much more difficult circumstances in Rome would be beneath him.

"You are right, Flavius. Only the dead have no hope for tomorrow."

As Flavius walked away, Gaius silently thanked the old veteran for the swift kick to his behind. Despite the physician's dark prognosis, death would not find him cowering in fear.

After allowing Sevilius time to refresh himself after his long journey, Gaius ordered Rashid brought to him beside the perimeter wall. The Berber eyed the Centurion's tent, now housing the newcomer.

"Another officer wishes to question you. He is not as forgiving as I am. Do not anger him."

Rashid shrugged. "It is difficult not to anger a Roman. You are offended by anything not Roman."

Gaius ignored the barb. He escorted Rashid to face Sevilius. The Tribune sat, still fully dressed in spite of the oppressive heat, sipping from a goblet of wine. He eyed Rashid with contempt as he entered. The look of derision did not fade as his gaze drifted to Gaius. In fact, the corners of his lips curled slightly higher. It seemed the Tribune had a special scorn for him.

"Who are you?" Sevilius demanded of Rashid.

Rashid bowed. "I am Rashid Ahmed Abdullah, a humble salt merchant."

"Salt merchant indeed. Rebel more likely."

"My people, the Meshwesh, live humbly and respect all travelers in this land, even Romans."

"We are not travelers. This is our land."

Rashid shrugged. "We are all travelers. Is life not a journey?"

Sevilius didn't wish to discuss philosophy. "Where are the Berbers who killed the soldiers at Wadi Ashar?"

"We Berbers do not kill Romans. Perhaps you seek Tauregs. They kill all interlopers into their domain, even Berbers."

Sevilius glanced at Gaius. "Where did you find him?"

"Near a ruined city he calls Hamad Rus some leagues south of here. Two of my men died there, but we could find no bodies."

"And him?" Sevilius pointed his cudgel at Rashid.

"He was with us."

Sevilius slapped the cudgel on his knee. "Then his men killed them."

"Perhaps, but we found no tracks or any other signs of people."

"My men will find them when they arrive."

Rashid spoke up. "Wadi Ashar is northeast of here, near *aduar* Ishiri."

"Yes, we visited the village of Ishiri seeking the murderers and found it deserted."

Rashid wailed aloud and fell to his knees, grief-stricken. "The people of Ishiri were blood kin."

"Silence!" Sevilius snapped.

Rashid ignored the command. "Deserted? You found no one?"

Sevilius smiled. "Nothing but bloody rags. Perhaps some of the dogs were wounded while killing my men."

Rashid didn't answer. He rocked back and forth on his knees.

"Take this sniveling coward outside and execute him. He was probably involved in the ambush."

"This man has been with us for five days and could not be involved. We came across a small camp at an oasis and saw the same thing you saw – bloody clothing and no people. The same for a lost patrol."

Sevilius glared at Gaius. "You waste your time with this cur. He should be executed. When my men arrive, we will scour this country until we find the culprits. What of this Hamad Rus?"

"The city is empty, long abandoned, but there are caverns nearby. Our enemy may be hiding within." He decided not to mention the temple or the blood in the altar bowl. He doubted Sevilius would believe him. "I believe he Berber may prove useful when we go there."

Sevilius stroked his chin. "Yes. Perhaps we do need a hostage. Very well. My men will march to the caverns and vanquish this enemy." He pointed to Rashid. "He will show us the way. You and your men will remain here and await our return."

"I will not remain here."

Sevilius sat forward in his chair. "What, Centurion? I gave you an order."

"You do not know this enemy, Tribune. You will need as many men as we can muster."

"I do not need this rabble of yours. They are cowards, like your men at White Rock Pass."

Before Sevilius could react, Gaius strode forward, grabbed the startled Tribune by the neck with one hand, and squeezed. Startled, the Tribune's eyes opened wide, and a stifled gasp creased his lips, which now trembled in fear.

"My men were battle-hardened veterans of many campaigns. They won Duras-Europos for the Emperor at a heavy cost. At White Rock Pass, an officer like you, cocksure and foolhardy, ordered us forward into an ambush. Three hundred of my men died around me, and I paid the price for their failure." He grabbed the gold medallion around Sevilius' neck and yanked on it, as if he were going to rip it away. Instead, he let it drop. "What battle did you fight for such an honor," he scoffed. "I have three pair of *amillae* in my trunk, one golden armband for each of my victories in Gaul and Parthia. These men here are under my command. You will not slander them or the men at White Rock Pass in my presence."

He released his grip. Sevilius fought for breath, his face red. "You dare lay a hand on me?" he gasped. "I will have you killed."

Gaius smiled. "If any of us survive the next few days, you may try, Tribune." He motioned to Rashid. "Leave." Rashid bowed and left the tent. Gaius faced Sevilius. "We do not face a few Berbers or Tauregs, or even rebellious exiled Jews. There is another enemy here, deadly and unseen. They are like shadows in the night. They will not bow before the sword. We must work together, or we will all die."

Sevilius rubbed his throat. The red imprint of Gaius' hand still marked it. "We will locate this unseen enemy you fear so much and destroy him. Then, I will deal with you."

Gaius nodded his head and grinned. "As I said, you may try. I will have a tent made ready for you." As he turned to leave, he said, "There is no Emperor here, no Rome. There is only sand and the things that thrive in such desolate places. We must rely on our wits more than our swords."

As he exited the tent, he heard the Tribune's curse and the sound of the thrown goblet as it struck the side of the tent.

Night fell with still no sign of Sevilius' men. Sevilius showed little concern, but Gaius feared for their safety. After the evening meal, Marcellus posted sentries and built the fires high to serve as beacons. By the night sentries' second watch, even Sevilius began to show signs of worry. Several times his head popped out of the tent, which he had not left all day, to scan the desert. At midnight, he sent Quintus Cantos to the wall to watch. The aide, a sallow-faced man whose soft features made him look more like a eunuch than a legionnaire, paced along the wall for a time; then sidled up to Gaius, who made no pretense of his concern for Sevilius' two past due centuriae.

Quintus spotted a crude drawing of a man with an enlarged penis scratched onto a rock in the wall, such graffiti as bored soldiers scribble. "Is he boasting or wishing," he asked, his voice unnaturally high-pitched for a man, reinforcing Gaius' earlier opinion that he was a eunuch or a *castrato*, though they were rare.

"Perhaps he's advertising for companionship," Gaius suggested.

If Gaius' evocative comment distressed the aide, he didn't show it. "If true, he would be the delight of many a Patrician's wife and the envy of any Equestrian's *delicati,* though more money can be made in a *lupanarium.*"

"None here is youthful enough or of well-formed features to be an Equestrian's plaything, and most are more likely to spend their hard-earned pay in a brothel than profit from one."

Quintus glanced at the drawing once more. "Pity, such a man is wasted here in this awful place."

Before Gaius could reply, one of the sentries called out. Then, like ghosts, a group of men appeared from the darkness, shuffling silently but for the sound of their sandals in the sand.

"Ho!" one called out to the sentry's challenge. "We are Roman soldiers."

"As are we," Gaius answered. "Come forward and be recognized."

Sevilius emerged from his tent and brushed past Gaius. He stood at the edge of the camp as his men marched in, each one weary and in shock. Several wore bloodstained uniforms. After thirty-one men passed him, the Tribune's eyes searched the darkness for the rest of his troops. He grabbed a soldier and shook him. The soldier looked up at him with glazed eyes.

"Where are the others?" Sevilius demanded. "I had eight score men and officers."

"Gone," the soldier said. "All gone."

"Did Berbers attack you?"

The man croaked out a hysterical laugh. "Berbers? No, they were demons, shadows of demons. My sword cut cleanly through one to no effect. They fell upon us as we marched in the night. Men vanished before our eyes with bloodcurdling screams, leaving no trace. We fought, but they were invisible. We formed ranks, fought shield-to-shield, but it did no good. They slipped through our ranks as easily as the wind." He laughed again. "Demons, I say, black, evil demons."

Sevilius released him, and the dazed soldier stumbled away. Flavius directed the men to the fires and ordered food and wine for them.

"It is as I feared," Gaius said.

"How?" Sevilius asked. His mouth worked, as if he wanted to ask more but could not form the proper questions.

"I don't know. It was the same with my men both before and after I arrived; no one saw anything." He didn't mention his brief glimpse of the shadow creature with baleful red eyes beneath the window at Hamad Rus. The Tribune held him in low enough esteem already.

Sevilius now no longer looked as sure of himself. His troubled brow belied his youthful face. His eyes darted to the darkness and back to the light. "A hundred and twenty-nine men, gone." He looked at Gaius. The first traces of panic had crept into his eyes. "We must leave this accursed place. Now!"

"Don't be foolish, Tribune. We would be too vulnerable at night in the desert."

Gaius' use of Sevilius' rank had the desired effect. He straightened his posture and wiped the fear from his mien. "What do you propose?" he asked, his voice more steady.

"Meet our enemy where he will not expect it, Hamad Rus."

Sevilius wiped his lips with the back of his hand and nodded. "Better to die fighting than running."

His remark, whether or not intended as an insult to Gaius, made sense.

"But not tonight," Gaius suggested. "First, we must prepare."

Sevilius nodded. "Yes, yes. Prepare."

Gaius looked into the faces of his men and saw newborn fear. If two centuriae could not face the enemy, how could their few numbers? He had no answer for them, but he knew that they must try.

Before retiring for the night, he sought out Rashid. He found the Berber sitting alone outside his tent. Gaius frowned when he did not see the assigned guard. Rashid looked up as Gaius approached.

"The Tribune is a fool," Rashid spat, "even for a Roman."

"Likely, he is. We go to Hamad Rus."

"You go to your death if you follow such an *akuzzi*."

"What is an *akuzzi*?"

"Gas that is passed from the anus in a noisy fashion."

Gaius smiled at Rashid's apt description of Sevilius. "This invisible foe is enemy to both our people. Will your people join us in the battle to defeat them?"

Rashid snickered. "Romans and Berbers fighting side-by-side? That would be a sight worth dying to witness." He shook his head. "But I cannot speak for my people. They fear the Inyosh. They fear Romans as well. We desert people are not as foolish as Roman Legionnaires. We do not seek out the Darks Ones."

"Better to stand together than to die alone."

"I can but ask. Perhaps in this way you will see that we are not to blame for the Roman deaths."

He abandoned his original plan of allowing two days of rest. The demise of Sevilius' troops was too disheartening to his tiny, beleaguered half-centuria. If they didn't march on Hamad Rus soon, he feared a mutiny. If captured, it would mean their deaths, but frightened men didn't think straight.

"Good. We leave in the morning for your village, and then on to Hamad Rus."

As he spoke the name, a chill wind blew across the desert, raising whispers from the sand. He wasn't certain, but it sounded as if they called his name.

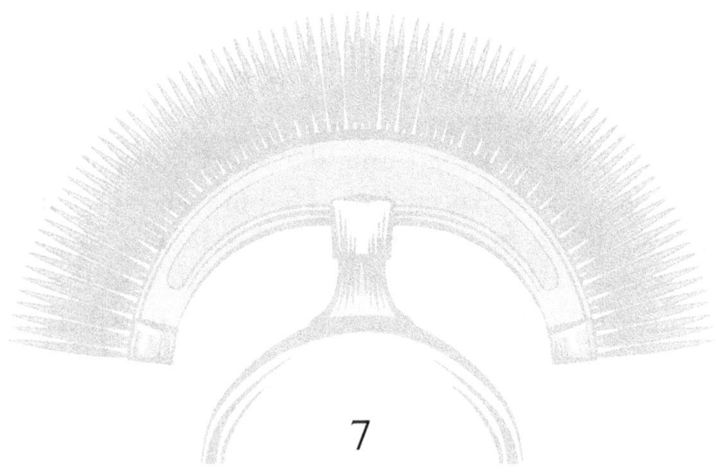

7

By sunrise, the encampment on the ridge had vanished as if it had never existed. As impermanent as any structure except solid stone in the wind-scoured desert, Castra-Augustus was gone, a mirage on the horizon, leaving only the scraggy date palms, the uncompleted rock wall, a jumble of footprints in the sand, and a litter midden to indicate that people had once lived there. The wind would soon scatter the garbage and erase the footprints, eliminating all signs of human occupation, as it had with previous civilizations.

Gaius wondered how many bones of earlier civilizations like Hamad Rus lay buried beneath the ceaseless sands. All civilizations fell. Rome had lingered longer than most. Would she, too, vanish unremembered, her grave marked only by stubs of broken marble columns jutting from the sand and half-remembered legends of her greatness.

He rode beside Tribune Sevilius, followed by his foot legionaries, his newly recruited natives, and two supply wagons. The other mounted cavalry patrolled the column's flanks to avoid ambush. The Tribune had made certain that everyone knew he commanded the column, bellowing orders at the top of his lungs, as they made ready to depart. Gaius remained out of his way. He did not wish to confront the Tribune unless necessary.

The day had dawned oppressively hot, almost as if anticipating and opposing the army's march. Little conversation accompanied the move. Most of the soldiers kept their eyes fixed on the horizon, which seemed to draw no closer as the day wore inexorably on.

Sevilius' men marched apart from the others with their eyes on the surrounding desert, as if expecting the sand to come alive and swallow them. Their story had spread throughout the encampment, eliciting a sense of hopelessness that Gaius feared would soon infect them all.

Flavius rode behind Gaius, equally absorbed by the scenery, or by its lack. League after league of featureless desert surrounded them, featureless save for the series of low dunes that served mainly to break up the rhythm of the journey. He dismissed them as too small to hide an army, *unless*, he reminded himself, *that army was invisible*. He quietly berated himself for harboring such sinister thoughts. Though unseen in the darkness, he was quite certain they would provide ready targets in full daylight and would therefore hide at the sight of armored legionnaires.

Gaius had not broached to the Tribune his plan to recruit Rashid's people in the fight with the *Inyosh*. He was certain the Tribune would reject it, but equally as convinced they would need as many men as possible. He would wait until the last possible minute to inform Sevilius of his plan.

The column meandered slowly across the desert, avoiding the areas of softer sand and the high dunes for the sake of the heavily laden wagons. They marched southeast toward Rashid's village; avoiding Hamad Rus. Sevilius questioned their direction.

"You informed me the city lay due south. Why do we bear so far east?"

"There is a small oasis and spring we can use. Approaching from the west allows us to use the dunes as cover. From the north, the ground is too open. We would be observed."

It was not all lie, and Sevilius did not argue.

Allowing only short rest breaks and an equally short cold lunch of hardtack biscuits with honey, they covered many leagues before camping for the night. With no wood or stone available, they could construct no protective barricade. They would have to rely on alert sentries.

"Flavius," Gaius said as he dismounted his horse, "set double sentries at all points with more men at the ready. Rotate them at three-hour intervals. I want no man closing his eyes on guard duty tonight." He paused. "Place the soldier who preached mutiny farthest out atop the dunes."

Flavius grinned. "Aye, dour Allectus has often espoused his disdain for authority. Perhaps a tiny domain to call his own will quench his desire." He rushed away to assign duties.

As his aide walked Apollo to the rope corral, Gaius chose a spot in the lee of a sand dune to make his bed. They would erect no tents on this trip. Men in tents made easier targets than did men sleeping around an open campfire, weapons at ready. His aide returned bearing a bowl of water. Gaius washed his face and hands to remove the dust of the journey and ordered him to give the remaining water to the horses.

Sevilius spread his blanket at a spot near Gaius but distant enough to show his contempt. He looked unused to sleeping on the ground, but he would not allow Gaius to see his discomfort. Quintus Cantos, his devoted aide, laid out silver dishes and a silver cup for his meal. *He's not roughing it too much,* Gaius mused. The disgruntled Tribune had spoken few words during the entire journey, but his frequent looks of hatred directed toward Gaius made up for the lack of communication. Gaius would sleep with his sword handy even if there were no other enemy to consider but the Tribune.

Soon, the aroma of spitted meat and pan-fried bread filled the air. With no breeze, the smoke and the cooking smell hung low, permeating the slight depression in which they had made camp. Most of the scrounged firewood gathered came from dead acacia and beech trees that had thrived in the Sahara savannah before the time of the Egyptians, buried by the encroaching sand but later uncovered by the ever-present winds, as they had uncovered dreaded Hamad Rus.

The odor of burning wood reminded him of more leisurely times between wars when he and his son camped out on the slopes of Mount Vesuvius, gazing at the stars. The slopes trembled and the summit glowed red from the fires within. He had explained that Vulcanus, weapon forger of the gods was hard at work at his forge and anvil. Those memorable times were rare. His certainty of more such times grew rarer with each passing day.

Gaius satisfied his appetite with a small piece of roasted mutton, bread, cheese, dried dates, and wine with just a smidgen of henbane, yarrow, and rhubarb to ease his stomach. After the meal, some of the normal routine returned to the weary soldiers, who joked and bragged of their exploits as soldiers do. However, Gaius noticed the new recruits, his native *aclis* bearers, remained ominously silent. They sat together as a group facing the desert with the fire at their backs. Their javelins lay across their laps, their curved blades stuck into the sand beside them. The fierce expressions on their faces disturbed him, as if they sensed danger nearby.

Flavius returned from his rounds munching on an apple. He tossed the core aside and plopped down in the sand across from Gaius, one arm resting on his knees. His sword arm, Gaius noticed, remained close to the hilt of his scabbard. "We will have a moon tonight," he said. "The men see this as a good omen."

"Do you?" Gaius asked.

Flavius shrugged. "I pay no attention to omens or signs. With a moon, perhaps we can see our mysterious enemy if he shows his face."

"So you are certain our enemy is human."

Flavius squinted to stare at Gaius to see if his commander joked with him. He detected no humor in Gaius' face. "You believe the Berber's wild tale?"

Gaius smiled. "I would not bet a copper *as* on his words," he said. "I believe our enemy is cunning and deadly, but as human as you or I." He spoke as assuredly as he could, despite his doubts. He could not betray his suspicions to his optio.

Flavius nodded at Gaius' reference to the lowest denomination coin in the Roman Empire. "As do I. Once our men draw first blood, this melancholy will vanish as quickly as the morning dew." He grabbed a handful of sand, letting it trickle through his fingers, as he stared at Sevilius. "I fear our young Tribune has lost his way. His eyes are empty.

His men see this and are frightened as well."

"What of our Berber friend?"

Flavius jerked his head toward the group of native recruits camped a short distance from the others. "He sits with his kind, although they do not trust him any more than do I. It is strange. They seem to defer to him, as if he is of a higher status than they are."

"Yes, he strikes me as more than a simple salt merchant. I wonder where he learned his Latin."

Flavius snorted derisively. "Probably from a captured Legionnaire just before he slit his throat."

Gaius winced at the thought and hoped Flavius was wrong. Something about their Berber captive disturbed him, but he didn't think him a murderer. He could have easily killed Gaius and the three remaining men during the sandstorm, taken their water, and escaped, but he had not. For some reason, he wished to remain with them. Gaius determined to find out why.

He noticed Flavius' furtive glances. "You have a question, Optio?"

"I can read maps. Why do we approach Hamad Rus in such a roundabout fashion?"

"Because we first go to Rashid's village to convince his people to fight with us."

Flavius did not explode, as Gaius had thought he might, but his face reddened. "Fight with Berbers? First Tebu, now Berbers. Dare we turn our backs?"

"We need the Berbers. They are aware of the danger of the shadow creatures. We share at least that bond with them."

"They might offer us as sacrifice to these Dark Ones. There is no love lost between our peoples."

"We must take that chance. We must win this battle at any cost."

"What of Sevilius? Does he know of your plan?"

"Not yet."

Flavius chuckled. "I thought not. He has not called for your death. If old enemies become friends, what does this foretell about the Empire?"

"Here in this deep desert waste, we have more in common with the

Berbers than we do with the Empire. I fear we face a determined enemy, evil and ancient. If we do not defeat him, he will spread. All the Empire could be in danger."

Flavius sighed. "I am an old war horse. Politics and Empires are beyond my addled brain. I follow you wherever you lead, Centurion."

"It is all I ask."

Flavius rose. "I will see to the men."

Night fell with the finality of a drawn curtain, but a shimmering display of fingers of fire streaking across the blood-red sky marked the sharp division between day and night.

"Falling stars," some of the men called out at their appearance, "a sign from the gods."

Gaius watched the celestial event with rapt attention, awed by the display of undulating color, until Flavius remarked, "An ill omen. They are all headed south toward Hamad Rus."

"I thought you took no notice of omens," Gaius replied.

"Not of the reading of entrails, the color of the moon, or the chattering of soothsayers, but perhaps this is the gods speaking to us."

Did Gaius read fear in Flavius' eyes? "The gods have forsaken this land."

Even as he said it, he wondered if there were gods older than the Roman ones he knew so well but in which he had so little faith. Rashid's story of *Nergal* and undead shades of the god's minions seemed like mad ravings in the light of day when the earth was alive and filled with the sounds of the living, but it took on new strength at night when darkness and silence conspired to blot out even the memory of life.

Flavius smiled. "If this is true, then we have nothing to fear. Still," he said as he got to his feet, "I will check the sentries again."

The moon rose a short time later, so large that Gaius felt he could reach out and touch it. Only somewhat comforted by its cold, ethereal light, he doused his small campfire, a small victory on his part. The added heat had made him uncomfortably warm, and yet he found himself clinging to it. Only the forlorn look of Sevilius broke the spell of the flames. With a sigh, he roused and went to the Tribune. His leg ached, but he refused to allow the tribune to see him limp.

"Tomorrow, we turn farther east," he said. "We will reach Rashid's village day after tomorrow."

Sevilius sat with his knees drawn up to his chest and his arms draped over them. A plate of uneaten food sat beside him. A small jerboa timidly hopped over and nuzzled the bread with its whiskered nose. The mouse's ears were almost as large as its body to keep it cool in the desert heat. Sevilius stared at the jerboa for a moment before asking Gaius, "What manner of enemy can defeat two centuriae without showing themselves?"

Gaius wondered if the Tribune had even heard him. "I don't know. Perhaps your men ran."

Sevilius glared at him with unbridled hatred at the reminder of his similar accusation flung at Gaius. "Evil follows you."

The Tribune's statement stung Gaius but also confused him. "What do you mean? How can you blame me for the loss of your men?"

"The gods abandoned us in Parthia after your disgrace. A plague swept through the legions, killing hundreds in Armenia and Syria. Before I left Marzuq, I received a dispatch from Leptis Magna. The eastern plague has now entered Rome. People are dying in the streets. Now, you come to Tripolitania, and death follows you here."

Plague, the worst thing that could befall a country, second only to war. Gaius worried for his wife and child. After his disgrace, he had sent them from Rome to stay with his uncle in Ischia to avoid the taint of his ignominy. The island should be safer than the mainland, but he had seen plague ravage entire cities. No place was truly safe against an enemy the sword could not touch. *Much like the dark, formless specters.*

"Why did you not tell me of this upon your arrival?" he demanded. "I have family in Ischia. My men have families in Rome and adjoining provinces."

Sevilius lowered his head to his knees as he spoke. "Their fates will be sealed long before any of you could reach them. I, too, have family in Rome." When he glanced back up at Gaius, the look of defeat and resignation in the Tribune's face dismayed him. "Our fates will be decided here in Tripolitania."

"Do not inform the men," Gaius warned. "They are frightened

enough. They might attempt to abandon their posts and return to their homes."

A strangled laugh escaped Sevilius' lips. He picked up a rock from beside him and hurled it at the hapless jerboa, now sitting on the edge of Sevilius' gold plate devouring his food. The stone caught the small rodent squarely in the head, killing it instantly. It lay with its lifeblood bleeding into the sand. The senseless act of violence against a hapless creature angered Gaius. He resisted the temptation to run his sword through the useless Tribune; then turned and stalked away, leaving Sevilius to bask in his personal misery.

The moon's pallid light swept the dunes with a ghostly glow, casting long shadows that danced with the moon's movement. As Gaius reclined on his blanket looking out over the encampment, he noticed shadows that danced apart from the other deeper shadows, drawing nearer. Alarmed, he leaped to his feet. At that moment, a man's blood-curdling scream in the distance ripped the night, Allectus, the flogged sentry, giving the alarm as he died.

"To arms!" Gaius shouted. He drew his sword and faced the movement. In the distance behind him, he heard Flavius' voice calling the men to arms.

He cast a glance at the Tribune. Sevilius stood and held his sword in his hand. Quintus Cantos stood beside him, his head swinging wildly from side to side searching the crests of the dunes for the cause of the alarm. Neither man took notice of the approaching shadows.

"The shadows!" Gaius warned. "Watch the shadows!"

The shadows circled the camp like a dark dust cloud, disappearing as they merged with other, moon-cast shadows. He had difficulty tracking them. A low, mournful moaning, the wretched sound of tortured men's souls crying out for vengeance, poured from the creatures, a sound Gaius could not decide if a call for battle or a dirge. Then, as if on command, they darted forward into the ranks of men. The screams of the dying mingled with the metallic clatter of swords and shields and the yells of frightened men:

"There! Behind the wagon."

"Look out!"

"Stand still, damn you!"

"Close ranks! Swords out!"

This last came from Flavius, urging his men toward the center of the camp and the protection of the fires. With a sickening feeling, Gaius realized how alone and exposed he had become at the edge of the encampment. As he raced to join his men, from the corner of his eye he saw a shadow sweeping across the sand toward him. He turned to face it with his short sword, doubting its worth against such an amorphous foe. Inside the dark, shapeless shadow, twin red orbs so intense they dazzled him, gazed at him with an unnatural hunger. A deeper blackness representing the creature's maw yawned, and a soft keening emerged, like voices whispering in a breeze. The eerie sound chilled Gaius' soul and raised goose bumps on his arms. Other shadows joined the first and began to encircle him. He spun slowly on his heels, his useless sword pointed toward his enemy, watching their movements.

Suddenly, Rashid stood beside him, holding his amulet in his hand, mumbling words that sound like no *Tamazight*, the language of the Berbers that he had ever heard. The words exploded awkwardly from Rashid's mouth, as if unsuitable for utterance by human lips. They sounded ancient, older than even the Berber tongue, perhaps from a time when the older gods walked the Earth. The jewel in the amulet glowed deep azure. Its light swept the sand around them. The sand fluoresced, reflecting the cerulean light. To Gaius' amazement, the shadows halted, as if obeying the strange words or taking heed of the strange light.

"Stay beside me or die," Rashid hissed in warning.

Believing the Berber, Gaius obeyed. The shadows didn't leave, but they drew no nearer. The night became strangely cold, and the familiar odor of death floated in the night air. The shadow creatures surrounding Gaius and Rashid did not attack, but the rest of the camp was not as lucky. Screams rent the night, wrenched in horror from dying men's throats. Gaius turned his head just far enough to see the thin ranks of his men flounder under a swarm of shadows. The banked fires faded, as if the marauding shadows were devouring their light. Swords flailed uselessly and hurled javelins pierced shadows but fell harmlessly to the sand beyond.

Sevilius and his aide stood apart from the others. As Gaius watched, a shadow moved swiftly across the sand directly toward the Tribune. His aide, Quintus Cantos, leapt in front of him with sword drawn. He disappeared as the shadow engulfed him. His dying scream pierced the black veil covering him, muffled as if coming from afar. The shadow withdrew, leaving only Quintus' sword behind. Gaius applauded the aide's noble sacrifice in his attempt to protect the Tribune. He had sorely misjudged the man based solely on his effeminate appearance and mannerisms without bothering to learn more of his character.

A second shadow now confronted Sevilius. The grisly death of his aide proved the last straw in breaking him. The color drained from his face, and his mouth opened, as if wishing to scream but unable to. Seeing the specter now focused on him, the Tribune threw his sword to the ground and ran toward the fires.

"We must save him," Gaius urged Rashid.

"If we move, we may die," Rashid replied.

"Stay then," Gaius yelled in reproach. "I must go. We need him in this quest."

Gaius detested the fact that the Tribune, the one person who could aid him in regaining his lost stature, was such a coward. He had the ear of the Emperor. His report on the Inyosh, in spite of his personal animosity toward Gaius, would allow the Emperor to set aside his earlier pronouncement without the appearance of having made an error in judgment.

Rashid shrugged. "Very well. Follow closely."

Gaius resisted the urge to run to the defense of his besieged men, begrudging the Berber's snail's-pace approach. Each new scream pierced Gaius' heart like a dagger thrust. The shadow pursuing Sevilius caught up with him, but to Gaius' amazement, it did not swallow him as it had the others. Instead, it reached out a shadowy protuberance, touched the Tribune's face like a lover's soft caress, and withdrew. Sevilius screamed and ran blindly away from the fires into the night.

Gaius veered away from the fires, intercepted the Tribune, and grabbed Sevilius' arm as he raced by, arresting his panicked flight by jerking him to a halt. The Tribune's eyes were wide open with fright, but he saw nothing. A whimper escaped his quivering lips. Spittle oozed from the corner of his mouth and dribbled down his chin. Gaius dragged the Tribune behind him toward the center of the camp.

Finally, as they drew within ten paces of the rapidly dwindling group of survivors, the shadows abruptly withdrew into the night, leaving bloody shreds of clothing, swords, helmets, and sandals littering the blood-splattered sand in their wake, but no bodies. With a quick count, Gaius gauged he had lost over a dozen men.

Flavius, his pale face streaked with blood, hovered on the edge of skewering Rashid with the aclis he held balanced in his right hand. Gaius held out his open palm to stop him.

"Hold, Flavius. We owe him our lives."

Flavius eyed the glowing amulet Rashid held out with obvious distrust. "What manner of witchery is this?" he said, jabbing the point of the javelin dangerously close to Rashid's neck to indicate the amulet.

"A talisman, a ward against evil," Rashid replied. "It has been in our tribe for centuries."

"I say kill him and take the charm." Flavius' angry eyes did not leave the Berber.

Gaius forced a smile at his optio's straightforward manner – Kill the enemy and seize his weapons. He glanced at Rashid. "I daresay it would be useless without the proper incantations. We need him."

Flavius seemed unconvinced, but lowered his javelin and jammed the point in the ground at his feet with a disgruntled growl. Around him, the men cowered nervously, their eyes straying from the Berber to the surrounding darkness, fearing attack from either quarter. Just over eighty men remained alive.

"Iron does not stop them," Flavius said. "I saw them, but they had no shape, just an amorphous black mist gliding across the sand. They descended on a man, and he was gone, leaving ... this." He kicked at a bloody piece of cloth with his sandaled foot. It landed atop Rashid's sandals. He stared hard at Rashid. "You know these creatures."

"I have never seen one. They are the *Inyosh*, the undead dark spawn of Lilith."

"How do we kill them?"

Rashid stared at Flavius as he answered, "How does one kill that which does not live?"

Gaius, seeing the sorry state his men were in, had more immediate concerns. "Will they attack again tonight?"

Rashid sighed, "I do not think so."

The Berber sounded uncertain, but the men were in no shape to face another such attack. They could do no more to prepare against it than they already had. "Flavius, see to the men. Give them a double ration of wine. Build the fires higher and keep the sentries within the perimeter of the camp." He handed him Sevilius' arm, like passing a package. The Tribune, lost in a world of his own creation, did not resist. "Take him to safety. In the morning, we move fast for the village. We do not camp until we reach it."

Gaius noticed that Flavius' eyes scanned the darkness nervously as he listened, but he nodded. "Aye, I'll stand watch myself." He glanced at Gaius. "I do not think I would welcome sleep this night."

Flavius took Sevilius and escorted him to the nearest fire. The Tribune sat so close to the flames that Gaius feared he would combust. Gaius didn't blame him. Fire seemed to be the only thing the creatures respected. Certainly, Roman iron did not daunt them.

After Flavius left, barking orders to the men, Gaius turned angrily to Rashid. "You are no salt merchant," he accused.

Rashid smiled. "Truly I am, but I am also a prince of my tribe. As such, I have access to all the lore of my tribe and the wisdom of the elders. Like this amulet, such knowledge has passed from father to son for many generations." The amulet no longer glowed. "You look at me as if I hide some great secret. I assure you, I know only what my father has told me. The power of the amulet is beyond me. The Dark Ones fear it or respect it; I do not know which, but it will not kill them, merely protect its bearer and those around him."

Gaius nodded. He could not argue with facts. He had witnessed the creatures' reluctance to approach the amulet. "It saved us tonight."

"Not all, I fear. Many died, yet you still insist on marching on Hamad Rus. What is it that makes you Romans so mad?"

"The need for glory," Gaius answered truthfully.

"I fear your glory will be short lived."

"Glory lives on long after the man dies," Gaius answered, believing his words.

Rashid chuckled, "Yes, chiseled in stone for all to see; yet you have seen Hamad Rus. It, too, once held carved likenesses of its heroes, now crumbled to dust. Rome is like that."

"Rome is eternal," Gaius replied, "Like the sky and the earth."

Rashid said nothing. He simply shook his head and stared into the darkness. Gaius' blood churned hot in his veins. He desired a foe upon which he could vent his frustration, not some formless shadow of the night. His grip on his sword tightened until his knuckles turned white before he thrust it into his scabbard.

"Why did you withhold the truth about yourself?" he demanded.

A quick smile played on Rashid's lips. "Romans have held princes for ransom. My people are poor and could pay no ransom."

Gaius nodded at the truth in the Berber's words. He had often held dignitaries of the enemy for ransom and sent severed heads or hands if they did not pay.

"If the amulet can protect those around it, why did your men die?"

Gaius knew he had struck a raw wound when a look of distress crossed Rashid's troubled face. In a voice much softer than earlier, he said, "I grew restless in the night. I walked away from our camp and sat watching the stars, as I often do. I heard screams. By the time I arrived, they were gone, as are your men. I wandered aimlessly searching for them half-mad with distress when I saw your fires."

"You think you abandoned them." Gaius guessed at the source of Rashid's guilt.

Rashid winced. "I am their prince. They were my responsibility."

Gaius nodded. "I have lost men, too many men. At first, I, too, felt responsible for each death, each maimed soldier. That faded over the years. Soldiers die. I cannot prevent all their deaths. I can only hope to use them wisely."

"My men were not soldiers. They were herders, wood carvers, and weavers who followed me to gather salt, not sack a city. They did not seek death nor expect death to come for them from the shadows."

"You can give meaning to their deaths by helping me defeat this common enemy."

"To me, their deaths have meaning. You Romans venture into the heart of the desert and disturb everything around you. Your presence awoke these monsters." He stared at Gaius. "You would sacrifice your men to regain your lost glory. Is that using them wisely? You cannot put sword to this enemy. You have witnessed their invulnerability. Why do you persist in this insanity?"

Gaius stiffened. "Because I am Roman."

Rashid shook his head slowly. "Go home. Save your men. The desert will swallow you as it does everything that opposes it. The desert has endured for thousands of years, some say since time itself. This evil grows restless. Now, it has tasted Roman blood. Do you think your civilization greater than those that once flourished here?" He sneered. "That is typical Roman vanity."

"Careful you do not evoke typical Roman wrath," Gaius advised.

Rashid spread his hands wide and bowed. "My apologies. We both bear the marks of our guilt. No scrubbing will wash that stain from us."

Speaking with Rashid always troubled him, as if the gods had sent the Berber prince to remind him of his inadequacies. Gaius wanted to dismiss him, but one question disturbed him. "Why did you save me?"

"If you died, do you think your optio, Flavius the Distrustful, would allow me to live long? I saved you to save myself."

Gaius tried hard not to smile at Rashid's apt nickname for Flavius. "A truthful enough answer," he replied. "Go, join your countrymen."

Rashid scowled. "They are not my countrymen. They are of the Tebu tribe from the Harouj Mountains far to the east. They are Roman lapdogs who have too long lived among your people and think they are civilized. They fear me because to them I am a wild Berber." Rashid stalked away, leaving Gaius angry with himself for allowing the Berber's words to provoke him.

Gaius knew something of the Tebu people. He had inquired about them before hiring them as bearers, as any good officer would. They were a strange, laconic people from deep in the desert south of Cyrenaica. Many of his fellow Romans considered them vacuous and lazy, but he found them to be proud, intelligent, and assiduously responsible if treated, if not as equals, at least as human beings. Traders who ventured to *Gebel Harouj* reported a land of dead basaltic volcanoes and hidden valleys, a place of stark landscapes but also great beauty. If the reports were not fantastical whims of the observers, trees did not grow in oases, but in deep pits that marred the *hamada*, the wind-swept rocky plain. Such a land of extremes created people of extremes. The Tebu were not Romans, but he trusted them, as much as he trusted any non-Roman.

Marcellus, skeptical of Rashid's estimate that the shadow creatures would not attack again, dogged the men relentlessly, urging them work faster, as they used most of the wood loaded on the wagon to build fires, and then uprooted dried shrubs to build them higher. He constantly twisted his head trying to keep his single good eye focused both on the men and on the surrounding darkness. Deeming the flames insufficient, he ordered oil poured oil on them to make them blaze higher still.

The sharp tang of the blood of the dead drifted on the wood smoke. The disheartened men huddled in the pools of light cast by the flames, as if death itself dwelled in the shadows, which it did. Flavius stalked the camp relentlessly, urging the sentries to remain vigilant at their posts. Marcellus followed close on the optio's heels, stopping beside each soldier to offer a few encouraging words and a friendly pat on the back. The imperturbable veteran's quiet manner in the face of danger pleased Gaius. The men respected Marcellus almost as much as they feared Flavius. Sometimes respect urged men to greater effort than fear.

The Tebu auxilia once again sat back to back, facing outward toward the darkness. They had lost two of their number during the attack and were undoubtedly reconsidering their decision to join the Legion.

Occasionally, one would glance in Rashid's direction and glare at him, but the Berber seemed oblivious of their disdain. He studied the amulet by the light of the fire as if trying to coax meaning from the undecipherable script around its edges. Gaius wished him luck. The amulet had proven the only protection they had against the Dark Ones.

Gaius had no stomach for magic, witches, or truthsayers. He considered them all charlatans and frauds. No reader of entrails had ever successfully predicted the outcome of a battle. The omens had been good before the battle at White Rock Pass, but he had lost a third of his men and his command. If magic resided in the amulet around Rashid's neck, he did not trust it any more than he trusted the Berber prince.

Marcellus's wary glances at Gaius revealed a reluctance to approach, as if the latest calamity had lowered his respect for his new commander. Finally, he summoned his courage and approached. He stood in front of Gaius with blood splatter on the patch over his eye and blood seeping through a crude bandage wrapped around a fresh wound on his left forearm. The wound bled profusely, but he paid it no attention.

"The men are frightened," he said.

"And you?"

Marcellus scuffed his sandal in the sand and stared at the mark he had made; then erased it before looking Gaius in the eyes. "I fear only failure."

"Then we must not fail."

"The men will not sleep this night."

Gaius studied Marcellus. *He fears only that his men will fail him, not the shadow creatures. He is a good man.*

"Then we will break camp late to allow them to sleep in safety after dawn arrives. Perhaps the sun will allay their fear."

Marcellus nodded. "As you wish." Still, he did not leave.

"There is something else, Tesserarius?" Gaius asked.

Marcellus lowered his voice. "It is the matter of the Tribune Sevilius. He has broken. His spirit is gone. His men see this, and they have lost all hope. If we do not do something soon, they will be useless as fighting men. I have heard grumbling of desertion."

"I will speak to them." He glanced at Marcellus' injured arm. "Perhaps you should have the *medicus* see to your wound."

Marcellus grinned. "This? It is nothing, a mere scratch from an overfriendly dark demon. The men see that I ignore it and become less concerned about their own wounds. Besides, the physician was one of the men lost this night. I will stitch it up later. My hands are steadier than were his."

As Marcellus walked away, Gaius realized he had chosen his third in command wisely. The old veteran knew more about the minds and habits of the common legionnaire than he ever could. Born patrician, Gaius hadn't mingled with the lower classes, while Marcellus had fought his way from slave, to gladiator, to soldier. Then, his duty to Rome done, he reenlisted. In his heart, Marcellus remained one of them.

Heeding Marcellus' request, Gaius approached the Tribune's men. In spite of their recent battle against a common foe, they still sat apart from the Castra-Augustus garrison, conversing little among themselves and not at all to the others. As Marcellus had remarked, they no longer resembled Roman soldiers. Discarded armor and unattended weapons lay scattered in a careless manner around their fire. The stink of fear rose from them stronger than the sour odor of sweat on their bodies. They stared at him with dour faces as he approached.

"Tonight you have met an enemy no Roman has ever faced, and you have driven them off." That part was not true, but he needed to bolster their spirits. "These creatures seem unstoppable, but we must endure against them. We no longer fight for Rome; we fight for our survival. If you resist one whit below your ability, you will never go home to your families. We may all die in this burned-over land of scorpions and shifting sand, but we must remember who we are. We are Roman Legionnaires."

He received no rousing cheer or salutes of honor, but a few looked at him as if ashamed of their forlorn hope and straightened their postures. Others remained undecided, shifting nervously as they sat, their eyes not meeting the gaze of any of their comrades. Fear of the night's battle still coursed fresh through their veins, fear and doubt. He would have to depend on their sense of self-preservation rather than their sense of duty.

"You now know or suspect, no Berber killed your comrades. These creatures did. We go now to seek the aid of the Berbers." This produced a few rumblings from the men. "We have a common enemy. Every extra sword increases our odds of survival."

One older soldier, his shoulders covered in scars both old and new, asked, "If we cannot kill these creatures, why do we seek them out?" Others mumbled their agreement.

"The desert at night is not safe. If we return to Marzuq, they would pick us off a few at a time during the night, as they did your comrades." His pointed remark struck home. The soldier nodded. Gaius continued, "We must bring the battle to them. We will find a way to defeat them."

The old soldier licked his lips and nodded again. "I will follow you, Centurion, but I do not believe we will go home. I do this for my family, for my comrades, not for the glory of Rome."

Gaius reached down and clasped the soldier's shoulder. "What is your name soldier?"

The soldier looked uncomfortable at the attention. "Antonius Pontius Cossus."

"Well, Antonius, that is all I ask of you. If you do not fail me, I will not fail you."

He hoped he could keep his promise to them. He had failed his men in Mesopotamia where the enemy was mere flesh and blood. How could he hope to defeat the undead? His only hope lay in the knowledge that they feared the Berber's amulet, and they feared fire; therefore, though already dead, they were not immune to destruction. They had weaknesses, if only he could discover a means to exploit them.

"Now, see to your weapons. Join my men. You will depend on one another in the coming battle. We must work as one unit, each man watching the other's back."

Gaius settled down comfortably on his bedroll but did not recline. With his back to the fire, his sword thrust into the sand between his legs, his eyes swept the darkness. Around him in the strangely silent camp, others did the same. However, his mind did not dwell upon the threat posed by the shadows of the night. He focused instead on his looming failure.

Only thirty days had passed since he had left the city of Leptis Magna, and already he had lost a third of his small force. Was he foolish to seek out his unseen enemy? Less bold leaders would have said so, but Gaius Marcus Linneus had never considered himself timid. Sitting behind a useless *vallum*, a half-completed stone palisade, waiting for death did not appeal to him. If he must die, let it be with a sword in his hand facing his enemy. His enemy waited in Hamad Rus.

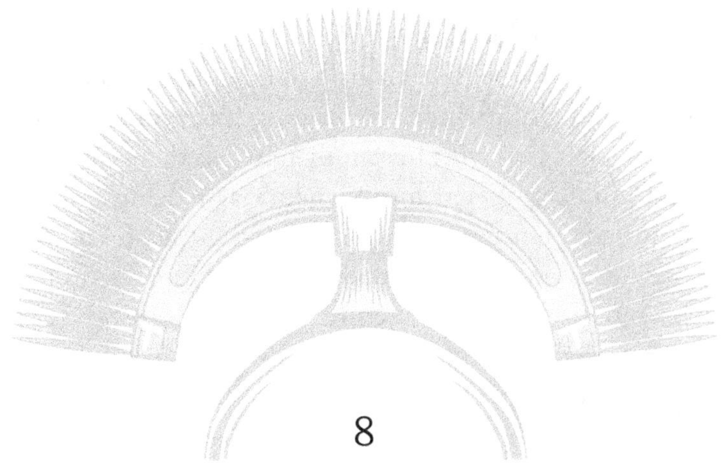

8

Gradually, as the first welcomed golden rays of the sun caressed the horizon, men succumbed to fatigue and slept, secure in the knowledge that daylight, even with its deadly heat, was now their ally. Gaius dozed in restless fits but did not sleep, and when the midmorning heat became unbearable, he roused the men and ordered them to break camp. They moaned and grumbled, but he took comfort in their complaints. Soldiers griped as naturally as women bore children. A silent soldier was a soldier afraid.

He worried about Sevilius. The Tribune had retreated into a world of his own creation. The bizarre events of the previous night and the horrific loss of his aide had been too much for his orderly, straightforward mind to accept. He allowed men to help him onto the back of his horse and remained upright in his saddle, but his cold blue eyes now gazed into places far beyond the sea of sand surrounding him. He rode beside Gaius, with the occasional whiny of Apollo correcting the Tribune's horse whenever it strayed from the path.

The Tribune of Marzuq was the least of Gaius' worries. He had been in command of his new desert legion for less than a week and had only a brief, terrifying glimpse of the enemy. He had already lost nearly a third of his force and had no prisoners or enemy corpses to show for it. If he did not succeed, the desert would save him the indignity of taking his own life.

Suicide was acceptable to most Romans as a means to escape long illnesses, infamy, or shame, but Gaius had a family to consider. He had refrained from killing himself before meeting Emperor Marcus Aurellius in exchange for a last visit with his family to see to their safety. When the Emperor had publicly offered him a chance at redemption, he eagerly accepted, even though it meant banishment to the wastes of Tripolitania where salvation was unlikely. He knew that if he remained in the desert for much longer, he would never return. The Sahara absorbed life. It did not give it. His Shadow Legion, or as Rashid put it, his Legion of the Damned, would be his last command.

As they marched, the heat soon became searing, silencing even the grumbling of the men. Gaius couldn't believe that something as mundane as sand could simultaneously cook one's body and drain it of the will to continue. He had always enjoyed the feel of damp sand on the bottom of his bare feet during his visits to the beaches of Fiuminico where the Tiber entered the Mare Nostrum. However, here the sand held no trace of moisture. Instead, it drank the moisture from everything it touched, as it sapped life from anything foolish enough to enter its domain.

They traveled southeast toward Rashid's village. They didn't approach close enough to Hamad Rus to see it, but Gaius felt its dark presence beyond the sea of dunes that separated them drawing him like a beckoning Siren. The dead city's cold, shadowy, malevolent tentacles reached out across the sand to grip his soul in an icy fear that the heat of the sun could not dissipate. He feared no man or no army, but he feared Hamad Rus. If his enemy were ensconced in the cavern-filled bluffs nearby, he would have to ride into the city to meet them in battle. His Roman pride and his last chance at redemption offered no other course of action.

The three survivors of his ill-fated excursion to Hamad Ras had spread the story of the dread, dead city until the entire company was aware of what they faced. Their gazes continually leapt to the horizon where the city lay, as if, like him, they could sense its presence. Each league distant from it increased their ease.

Gaius halted the march for only briefs periods of rest. The men ate their meager rations on the go. Though weary from the leagues of hard travel, stumbling up and often falling down treacherously steep dunes, the men seemed eager to complete their journey. At sunset, Gaius ordered torchbearers to flank the column. He didn't think it would prevent an attack, but the men took heart from their presence and continued marching through the night.

Marcellus rode up alongside Gaius. His single eye searched Gaius' face for a moment before speaking. "The darkness steals the men's courage. If we are attacked, I fear they will scatter."

"If they do, they will die. Make them realize this."

"I can try," Marcellus replied, "but standing against a shadowy enemy is not an easy thing to do." He spoke as if remembering his own experience.

Gaius hardened his face until it looked as if carved from stone, unyielding, eternal. "Kill the first man to break ranks. Tell them I ordered it."

Marcellus nodded, but his stance indicated he didn't like the command.

Gaius felt the need to explain his reasoning. "If they run, they will die. With one less pair of watchful eyes and one less sword, the man next to them will die as well. Only if a man knows his comrade is at his side watching his back will he fight, if not for himself, then for his comrades. Deep down they know this. They will understand."

Marcellus dropped back to pass along Gaius' orders. Flavius glanced in his direction, but said nothing.

"You don't approve?" Gaius asked.

"It was necessary."

"But do you approve?" Gaius insisted.

"Yes, I approve. I did not think you had the temerity to set such an example."

Gaius laughed at Flavius' undisguised gibe for allowing the Berber to live. "You do not know me well enough to judge me, Flavius. I did not protest the slaughter of my men in Parthia because I am unwilling to send men to their deaths, but because their deaths were unnecessary. Their lives were wasted. I will spend every man's life to destroy this enemy we seek, including mine. Not for glory or a way home; that path seems too far beyond reach at this moment, but because I fear for Rome's safety."

"I meant no disrespect to you, Gaius. I have never doubted your courage or your honor. Now, I do not doubt your motivation."

"It is good that old soldiers know each other well."

As the moon broke free of the surrounding dunes, it cast a soft golden light across the desert sand. Gaius rejoiced inside that it was not red. The desert at night was baleful enough without the added reminder of the blood it had taken. The stars beyond the dunes sparkled like a handful of freshly minted Roman coins flung into the sky. The *Via Lactea*, like a jug of milk spilled across the sky, appeared brighter and much closer than the familiar bright smear of light over his family's home in Tarquinii in Northern Italy. He felt as if he could almost reach out his hand, grab a handful of the multicolored specks, and hold their beauty in his fist to remind him of what he had left behind. Its splendor was incongruent to the stark landscape spread beneath its celestial majesty.

During one brief halt for rest, a commotion in the nearby dunes raised consternation among the men. Swords hissed as they slid from scabbards. The tips of javelins pointed outward like the thorns of a cactus. When a long-eared desert fox, a fennec, strode from behind a dune with the bloody corpse of a hare in its mouth, the men relaxed. Other than the jerboa, the fennec represented the first sign of animal life Gaius had seen since arriving in the desert. He took heart from the desert fox's manifestation, hoping it a good omen.

By sunrise, the men were unable to continue. The long, forced march had sapped their strength, and the rising sun had dispelled the fear that kept them moving through the darkness. Though he begrudged the time lost, Gaius informed Marcellus to order a halt. Some of his men helped Sevilius down from his horse. They were respectful of his rank, but refused to make eye contact with him. The Tribune, as silent as a mannequin used for target practice, sat motionless on the sand where they placed him, refusing any food and drinking only a little water fortified with honey for energy and only then when dribbled down his throat.

Though Gaius had no love for the Tribune, his condition evoked sympathy. If anything of the acerbic Tribune remained within the cold, silent shell, he would undoubtedly abhor the spectacle he made and detest the lack of dignity with which most patricians cloaked themselves. Gaius had seen men so shocked by the carnage of battle that they never recovered. Such an unseen injury left no visible scars but haunted the wounded as surely as a missing limb or eye. He wondered if Sevilius would prefer a quick thrust of a dagger to his heart, rather than a lifetime of drooling idiocy. Gaius knew he would prefer it for himself.

He quickly ordered the cooks to start fires to prepare a hot breakfast before the men, weary and footsore, fell into a stupor. Soon, the sizzling of meat searing on the hot griddles and the hearty aroma of wheat porridge boiling in large black pots wafted over the camp. Gaius' stomach rumbled in anticipation when his aide brought him a bowl of porridge filled with bits of seared pork bacon, leeks, and honey. He dug in with gusto, ignoring the slightly gritty texture of the pervasive sand that infiltrated everything. The men hardly spoke, silently wolfing down their porridge and chewing on leathery loaves of bread. Later, with filled bellies and the sun in their faces, they slept.

Weary as Gaius was, sleep would not come to him. His mind refused to remain quiescent long enough to allow Somnus', the god of sleep, welcomed visit. In truth, his resistance to sleep took root more in his deep dread of a visit from Morpheus, Somnus' sinister son, god of dreams and nightmares. Each time he slept, the image of the horrid monster became clearer and more defined. He feared to see it in its entirety lest it send his mind reeling as it had Sevilius'. He rested his body as best he could for a time; then kept busy moving through the camp examining the condition of his men, dismayed at what he saw.

Their exhaustion marred their faces. Many tended to suppurating blisters on their feet from the searing sand. Others rubbed olive oil onto their sun-broiled skin to ease the sunburn. If attacked now, they were in no condition to fight. Did he push them too hard? Did he push himself too hard? How could a man know his breaking point until he reached it? Once they reached Rashid's village and recruited help, they would rest before continuing to Hamad Rus.

Rashid had remained silent since the attack, remaining apart from the others all day and throughout the night, becoming more morose as the next day progressed. The Berber showed no eagerness to reach his village. Gaius wasn't certain if the Berber prince feared for his people's safety from the Romans or from the Inyosh. A dark cloud of retrospection at guilt over his lost men sat on Rashid's shoulders like a heavy mantle. Gaius knew because he had worn that same look many times after a battle, reliving every moment of each conflict, replaying every order he had given, following each thread as it wove itself into the tapestry of the event. He had learned that such scrutiny led only to self-doubt and guilt, neither of which was conducive to the next encounter.

Flavius lay with his focale thrown over his eyes to block out the sun, his head resting on his saddle, but Gaius doubted the optio's sleep a restful one. His sword hand jerked as if gripping and flailing at an enemy with his gladius, and his feet twitched in a frenzied dance of parried blows and rapid attacks. Whatever dream world foe he faced, it could be no worse than the one they faced in the real world.

Marcellus sat with his back against a rock speaking with Dracus Armis. Gaius regretted that the press of command had not allowed him the time to become better acquainted with his sesquiplecarus. The young lieutenant had thus far shown himself capable and was popular among the troops. Like many young legionnaires, Dracus had not been born in Rome, but in one of the outlying Iberian provinces near Cadiz. Gaius, who had campaigned with Iberian auxilia against Germanic tribes as a young Centurion, recognized the heavy Iberian accent with which the lieutenant pronounced many Latin words. The manner in which the young lieutenant deferred to the older and more experienced Marcellus spoke highly of the veteran's admiration among his subordinates.

After a brief discussion, Armis left Marcellus to post sentries atop nearby dunes, something Gaius should have remembered to do. Just because the creatures attack only at night didn't mean there weren't other, more human enemies eager to take advantage of the Romans' perceived weakness.

Gaius allowed the exhausted men to rest until mid-morning. Any longer, and their fatigued muscles would stiffen, making further travel impossible. The men staggered into roughly formed ranks and began the day's march with no fanfare or ceremony. They marched as if each step were a challenge, each dune they climbed a mountain. Their eyes remained focused on the man in front of them, never wavering, slowing when he slowed; stopping when he stopped. Even the horses snickered and started at every whisper of the wind, each rattle of armor.

The blazing sun bore down on them like a relentless torture device, licking every drop of moisture from their beleaguered bodies. Gaius ordered water bearers to travel up and down the ranks with water skins to relieve their thirst. This quickly reduced their water supply, but Rashid had earlier informed him that his village stood on the site of an ancient well along an even older caravan route. Gaius hoped to replenish their dwindling supply there.

By late afternoon, the dunes began to give way to a vast plain of bare stone and gravel. A row of low red hills rose in the distance, dancing on the heat waves rolling across the sun-baked ground. Rashid finally came out of his stupor.

"At the foot of the next valley lies Aduar Tereesh, my village," he said, pointing to a deep depression some three leagues distant. "We will reach it before dusk."

"Your people were Massylii, weren't they?" Gaius asked.

Rashid smiled. "You know your Amazigh history. Yes, I am of the Meshwesh tribe. We were part of the Massylii Kingdom of Numidia, allied with the Carthaginians many years ago during your Punic Wars. When you Romans defeated the Carthaginians, we moved deeper into the wastes of the Maghreb."

"The Masaesyli of western Numidia allied with the Romans. They remain in their ancient homeland."

"Yes, but they are now Roman lap dogs – Farmers and merchants dealing in grain, figs, olive oil, and beans for Roman kitchens. Their glory is ended."

Gaius noted the bitterness in Rashid's voice. "All things pass."

"Especially at the point of a Roman sword."

"Your hatred of all things Roman is obvious; and yet you claim you do not kill us."

"I hate the desert, but I do not try to kill it. It is too vast. It would not notice my feeble pinpricks."

Although hardly an admission of innocence, he believed Rashid. "I will send riders ahead to announce our arrival and to tell them that you accompany us."

"Very wise. They would not dare attack you with me as your hostage."

"You are not our hostage. You may ride ahead if you wish, but you must leave the amulet with me."

"Ah, I see. I am no longer your prisoner, but my amulet is. I will remain with it and with you."

As difficult as the crossing the *erg*, the vast sea of crescent-shaped sand dunes rolling for many leagues, had been, the uneven rocky terrain of the wind-swept *hamada* proved even more torturous. Apollo carefully picked his way among the stones and holes, but weary men stumbled often and fell, bruising shins and egos. Where the sand was hot and stealthily found its way into every bodily crevice, the bare rock seared naked flesh when touched. Gaius ignored the curses; glad the men were taking out their frustration and anger on the inanimate stones.

When the column neared the valley, the two riders returned.

"The village is deserted," one said.

Gaius glanced at Rashid. Rashid's face paled, but he didn't seem surprised by the report. "Abandoned or ...." Gaius stopped before completing his thought. If the Dark Ones have slain the villagers, he would know soon enough.

The scout cast a look of sympathy toward the Berber before focusing his attention on Gaius to complete his report. "Food is still on tables. The animals are in their pens. We searched several houses but found only bloody clothing."

Rashid nodded. "I expected as much when I saw no cook fire smoke or sentries on the surrounding hill."

The grave news disturbed Gaius as well. Any hope of strengthening his small force had vanished. He would have bypassed the deserted village if possible, but his physically drained men could go no farther without food and rest. They needed shelter from the blazing sun.

"We enter Tereesh," he said.

Rashid hung his head in dismay, as he rode beside Gaius, his last hope for his people vanished. Now, he traveled alone in the midst of strangers he did not trust and with whom he could not assimilate. Sevilius, if he understood the scout's report, gave no indication of it, but he became restless nevertheless, fidgeting, and gazing out over the plains behind them as if he expected to see something on the horizon.

Wind-sculpted columns of pink and buff-colored stone guarded the entrance to the valley like rows of grotesque frozen sentries. Some bore wide, flat tops resting atop spindles of stone so thin Gaius feared the drum of marching feet and the low rumble of the wagons' wheels would bring them crashing down. Slivers of red rock resembling fish gills stood so tightly packed that a man could not pass between them. Arches and half-arches of stone, many of them spanning the entire width of the valley, formed a vaulted roof lacking only trailing vines and marble statues to create a natural Roman portico. Carved by the relentless winds that scoured the *hamada,* the arches had once been a part of the massive outcropping of rock that bordered the valley. Their resemblance to enormous bleached bones gave the valley the appearance of a graveyard for some gigantic creature.

A pack of barking dogs met the column of strangers as they entered the village, but they remained at a safe distance, sensing these men were different. Chickens roosted in the lower branches of trees seeking shelter from the heat. Twenty unpainted, sun-baked brick structures lined a winding path that led from the highest point of the narrow valley down to a small oasis in its center. Tamarisks with their reddish-brown bark, thorny acacias, and the occasional oleander tree shaded the rear courtyards of the homes. Except for the dogs, the village laid deathly silent.

A small grove of olive trees and date palms surrounded the oasis. Beyond them lay irrigated fields of melons, squash, long beans, and millet. The horses caught scent of the water and began prancing nervously eager for a drink.

Gaius motioned Flavius to his side. "Set out sentries at each end of the village. Gather wood for large fires before dusk. The men must rest this night or they cannot continue."

Flavius' face betrayed no disappointment at finding the village empty. "Do you expect attack from the shadows or from the Berbers?"

"Watch for both, but perhaps the creatures' dark business with this dead village is done."

"Perhaps the dead seek dead places," Flavius countered.

"If that is so, then we can find no succor in this dead land."

"The Tebu recruits refuse to enter the village."

Gaius looked back at the remaining bearers he had pressed into service as auxilia. He didn't blame them. The village wore a mantle of death around the bones of its buildings. "Post them near the entrance to the valley. They will be too afraid of the dark to stray far, but post four legionnaires with them to keep an eye on them. Use Sevilius' men."

Flavius nodded at Gaius' decision. "They will be glad to be away from Sevilius."

"The Tribune became agitated as we neared the village. Perhaps he sensed something. I fear he might do something foolish. Keep a close watch on him."

Now, Flavius smiled. "It seems we will all be watching each other this night. Now, I fear for the wraiths."

Flavius walked away chuckling quietly to himself, leaving Gaius wishing he had half the optio's reserve of courage and hope. He searched for Rashid and saw him standing before the entrance to one of the homes. His distressed face bore the pain of his loss. He beat his clenched fist on his leg, but he did not enter. As Gaius approached him, he made coughing sounds in his throat so he wouldn't startle the Berber. At the sound, Rashid turned to look at Gaius. Tears ran down his cheeks, leaving tracks through the accumulated dust of their journey.

"It is my home," he said.

Gaius had guessed as much by the Berber's anguish. "Are you going inside?"

"I fear what I might find or not find."

"I will look for you," Gaius offered, as he stepped past Rashid.

"No, it is my place," Rashid sighed. "I will find nothing, and that is worse than finding their bodies."

"Your wife?" Gaius asked, surprised that he had not considered that the Berber might have a family.

"A wife and two small sons. I should not have gone to the salt plain."

"Then you would be dead as well," Gaius pointed out.

"That is how it should be."

"Dead, you would not be able to help us strike back at your enemy."

Rashid's eyes blazed with anger. "I do not need you to attack my enemies." He lifted the amulet. "This is my shield." He withdrew a dagger with a curved blade from his robes. "This is my weapon."

Gaius pulled his gladius from its scabbard and held it aloft. "I will place my weapon next to yours. Together, we shall extract revenge from our mutual foe."

Rashid nodded and walked into the building, while Gaius stood by the door peeking inside. Fruit and cooked meat sat on a low table surrounded by cushions. Nothing looked disturbed by a struggle. No blood stained the colorful woven rug covering the sand floor or rough stucco wall.

"Perhaps some of them escaped," Gaius said.

"No. They would have remained near the village and watched for our approach. They would have seen me." He turned to leave. "I cannot sleep in this house tonight. I will sleep on the ground beside the fire."

Gaius understood Rashid's reluctance to confront the ghosts of his family. Gaius had faced enough ghosts in his past to recognize the turmoil the Berber endured. Such moments of grief should be private matters, but he needed the Berber and his amulet nearby.

"Do not leave the village," he advised.

Rashid shot him a bitter look of rage, but it faded quickly. He touched the amulet beneath the robe to show that he understood Gaius' reasoning and nodded.

Though an air of tragedy hung over the village, the soldiers were glad to be in a defendable position. Flavius allowed them time to drink their fill of water and rest, but did not let them sleep. First, he chose three adjacent houses and had the men seal all the windows and doors except for the entrances with bricks, rocks – anything they could find. Then, they gathered dead wood for large fires laid before each doorway. Rashid suggested using the thin outer bark from a large shrub called a *torha*. The bark, he explained, made an excellent kindling for quickly starting fires without using oil.

He did not consult Rashid, but ordered several of the chickens and goats slaughtered for their meal. The blood he ordered collected in large earthenware urns sealed with fitted lids. They questioned his request with their eyes, but followed his bidding. Fresh meat would soothe their troubled bellies if not their minds. He had a purpose for the blood that he preferred not to reveal yet.

Gaius watched his optio moving among the men with a heavy hand here or a soft word there, delivering what each man needed to urge him on. He realized the optio's gruffness hid a sincere love and respect for the men under his command.

"Sleep now," Flavius told them. "We will get no rest this night."

Finally, satisfied that he had done all possible to secure a place to sleep, Flavius removed his armor, leaned against the shaded side of a building, and closed his eyes.

Before finding a place for his own nap, Gaius searched for Sevilius. He had lost sight of the Tribune after entering the village. He found him sitting on the floor of one of the houses. In his hand, he held a child's doll made of wood, cloth, with a dried gourd painted to resemble a child's face for a head. At first, Gaius thought Sevilius might be coming out of his inner exile, but, as he watched, the Tribune's somber face turned to one of rage. He pounded the doll with his fist, and then ripped off its head and tossed it aside. When Gaius' shadow touched the Tribune's body, he shrieked and cowered on the floor. Gaius didn't know what had instigated the Tribune's rage against the doll, but he would bear watching.

As Gaius walked away from the Tribune, he thought, *this cursed land works it spell on each of us.*

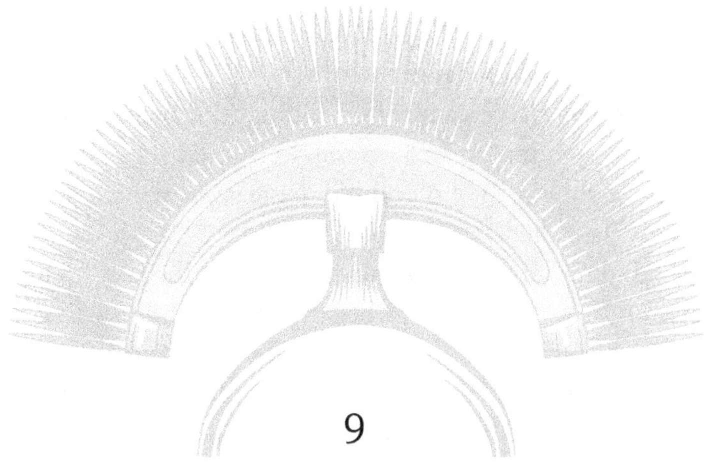

9

Gaius divided the men among the three houses he and Flavius had chosen, with Flavius, Marcellus, and himself in charge of one each. Each house offered a commendable view of the entrance to the valley and the other two houses. The Tebu auxilia and four of Sevilius' soldiers camped at the foot of the valley leading into the village. Their open position exposed them to the creatures, but Gaius suspected that the Dark Ones would seek out the greatest concentration of men, leaving them undisturbed. A large fire burned to dissuade any attack. After a short sleep, a hot meal, and mulled wine, the men's spirits improved dramatically. They now joked among themselves and played games of dice. They kept their weapons at ready and occasionally glanced reassuringly at the bonfire outside the door that cast its light over the building, but their fear remained in check.

Gaius kept Rashid near him but placed Sevilius under the care of Marcellus. After witnessing his recent attack on the doll, he didn't want to face the mad Tribune. The Tribune's odd behavior worked at his bowels like bad wine or the cancer eating him, nagging at him but unable to free himself of the irritation. Something cold and evil had taken up residence in the Tribune's mind, and it battled for what was left of his soul. What would happen if that something won? He trusted Marcellus to keep a close watch on Sevilius, but he had quietly given him permission to kill the Tribune if he proved a danger to others.

The first sign of attack came after midnight. It began with a growing chill invading the room. At first, Gaius welcomed the cooler air, but as the fire's orange glow turned blood red, he realized the danger.

"To arms!" he called.

Men around him instantly became alert, pointing javelins and swords at the doorway. The village's dogs began barking and howling, followed by yelps of pain. Then, the dogs became silent. A loud scuttling outside betrayed the enemy's presence, but it was not the enemy for which Gaius had been waiting. It was instead a more subtle danger.

"Scorpions!" one of the guards shouted. "Thousands of scorpions!"

Outside, spilling across the open ground between houses, the sand became black with the shiny carapaces of scorpions the size of a man's hand. Gaius's eyes went wide open and his throat closed until he could not draw a breath. The black mass of scurrying arthropods sent icy fingers of fear lancing into his chest. He wondered what manner of control the Dark Ones had over the scorpions, for under control they were. They zeroed in on the three inhabited houses as if they knew men waited inside.

He fought to break the fear controlling him. He had seen scorpions before, if never so many. If he did not act, his men would die. "Pour oil on the ground in front of the door!" he called out.

As quickly as the oil hit the ground, he put a torch to it. The roaring blaze singed his arms and face but slowed the advance of the scorpions. However, it did not stop them. They climbed up the outside walls and onto the roofs, trying to force their way inside through any crack and crevice large enough to admit them. Men slammed at the scorpions with the flat edge of swords and stomped them with their sandals. Gaius stabbed one through its grotesque ebon body with the point of his gladius and tossed its dead husk across the room.

"Use burning brands," he shouted to them.

Using the torches, they killed most of the venomous creatures pouring inside. The men were frantic, but the scorpions were natural creatures they could see and deal with, unlike the shadowy creatures. By the time the battle began to wane, several men had been stung. Two lay on the floor, writhing in pain. Gaius didn't have time to wonder how the other men were faring. By the time he noticed the scorpions in retreat, the shadow creatures were upon them.

The wraiths did not enter, but instead clawed frantically at the outside walls beyond the reach of the firelight, as if trying to dig their way inside through the sun-baked clay. He heard shouts from the other buildings, but no sounds of battle. The flames kept the creatures at bay, but he doubted the walls could withstand such a concentrated attack for long.

He spotted Rashid holding the amulet in his hands and realized that the amulet's azure glow filled the room with its brilliant radiance. Slowly, the blue glow expanded outside the building. The Berber's contorted face revealed the concentration needed to expand the amulet's reach to encompass three groups of men in three separate abodes. It seemed too much for him to bear. If Rashid's concentration lapsed, Gaius knew someone would die, maybe many.

One soldier, too curious for his own good, moved too close to the open doorway to peer outside. He thrust his javelin at one of the passing spectral shadows. A dark cloud enveloped the tip of the javelin and yanked the soldier outside. His screams created panic, but no one approached the door to attempt to rescue him, knowing it too late. When the stones used to block the windows began to rattle and shake, and then bulge inward under the pressure of the creatures, Gaius grabbed a shield and braced it against the window nearest him with his body. Others joined him. The attack ceased and the windows held.

The creatures were relentless, continuing their attack for over an hour, but the amulet's power stymied them. The men remained vigilant and cautious, emboldened by the loss of only a single life. Then, as suddenly as it began, the attack ended. The chill disappeared and the flames once again resumed their normal color. No one expressed their relief aloud, but the tension holding the room in its icy grip relaxed.

"Are you all right?" Gaius yelled to Marcellus next door.

"No one hurt here," he replied.

Flavius' loud voice yelled from the next building over from Marcellus, reporting only two injuries. Gaius searched the room for Rashid and found the Berber collapsed on the floor bathed in sweat, breathing heavily. His ashen face and twisted lips trembled from the exertion. He still gripped the amulet in both hands. Gaius helped him to a sitting position against the wall. Rashid's eyes fluttered and flew open.

"Have they gone?" he croaked.

"Yes, you kept them from the buildings."

He nodded. "I could feel the amulet's power flowing through me like cold flame, but it almost overwhelmed me." He stared up at Gaius. "I saved Romans, but I could not save my own people. What does that make of me? The creatures are now aware of the amulet's power. They will try to take it."

He tried to rise but was too weak. He hung his head and folded his hands in his lap.

"It will be dawn soon," Gaius assured him. "We'll be safe then."

"It is always night within the caverns of Hamad Rus. We will have no protection there except for the amulet. I do not know if I can wield it long enough for us to enter and return. I am a weak vessel for the power handed to me by my father."

"I have a few surprises for these damnable creatures."

"They must be great surprises indeed if you expect to survive this journey."

"I expect to survive and return to Rome in triumph." Gaius surprised himself with the confidence of his words. Even against a seemingly undefeatable enemy such as they faced, he held out hope for victory. He would accept no other outcome.

"If the gods will it."

He walked across the room, limping from the renewed pain in his leg. Rashid noticed and called him back.

"Your leg pains you, *Centurion.* There will be herbs in this house. It belonged to a healer." His face contorted at the memory. "A mixture of dried gentian and henbane will both ease the pain and help heal the wound. We use gentian to draw poison from the body from snakebites or scorpion stings. If you allow me, I will make a poultice for you and your stricken men."

"Why would you help me?"

"My fate is in your hands, Roman. Your death will mean mine. Any encumbrance of yours could cause your death. "

"Make your poultice, Berber. Remember well that your fate is indeed in these hands." Gaius held out his hands and showed them to Rashid; then, he turned to his men. "Sleep now. We march at dawn."

The predawn darkness clung to the valley as if draining the life from the already sterile soil. A hundred paces distant from the well, nothing grew except thorny weeds and stunted brambles. Small gardens of beans, melons, and millet, nourished by water from the well and protected by the shade of the oasis palms, barely produced enough food to supplement the villagers' diet of goat's milk and meat. The goats and camels scrounged the valley floor for enough food to survive. Rashid's people were not nomads, traveling from meager pasture to meager pasture. They had chosen to remain in the valley, and other than a dependable source of water, Gaius could see nothing to keep them there.

After the trials of the night, fingers of light gleamed like hope on the jagged hilltops surrounding the valley, but deep shadows burrowed into the narrow canyons and rocky crags, a warning of what awaited them. The men stumbled from the buildings, eagerly scanning the faces of their comrades to see if any had vanished during the night. The four soldiers and the new Tebu recruits returned unmolested from the valley mouth, having seen no signs of the creatures or the scorpions. Two men had died from wounds inflicted by the wraiths, and one of a scorpion sting. The poultice Rashid contrived for the remaining two scorpion-stung soldiers removed most of the venom, and it seemed they would live.

Gaius knew they had escaped greater numbers of dead only because of Rashid and his mysterious amulet. The creatures were determined and would have eventually broken through their defenses. He wanted to thank the Berber for his actions but did not wish to imply a sense of comradeship or a debt upon which the Berber could demand recompense. Gaius' distrust of the Berber prince waned, but he would still kill him if he proved dangerous.

The poultice Rashid applied to Gaius' thigh reduced the swelling and eased the dull throb, but it did nothing to ease his heavy burden. He had come to Rashid's village seeking help. Instead, he had found a dead village and had exposed his men to more danger. His enemy continued to vex him at every turn.

As the camp cooks prepared the morning meal, Gaius strolled to the well in the center of the oasis, the only sign of life in the sun burnt valley. The well, a wide, deep gash in the rock, looked more ancient than the village that had sprouted along its edges. A series of hand-hewn steps led to the bottom. He wondered at the tens of thousands of people who had trod those steps over the centuries. The wells were the lifeblood of the desert. If they went dry, the people either died or moved away. According to Rashid, the village had existed for ten generations, a long time for any culture.

A line of men passed jugs of water hand-over-hand and emptied them into large wooden kegs and empty water skins. Others carried them and loaded them onto the wagons. He waited until they had finished, and then, at the top of the well, he stripped off his uniform and walked down the steps naked. The stone felt cool on the bottom of his bare feet, but the warm water embraced his naked flesh. He floated on his back with his eyes closed, allowing the water to replenish the moisture in his desiccated skin. He could easily forget where he was, what he was about to do, and imagine himself back home in his scented bath. If he opened his eyes, his wife would be waiting for him with a towel to dry him off. The sounds of men preparing to march sounded dully through the water in his ears. He sighed and opened his eyes. Not his wife but Flavius stared down at him.

"We must talk," he said and walked away.

Flavius waited at the door of one of the buildings with a dour expression creasing his already craggy face. His eyes were on Sevilius, sitting inside the house on the floor. Crudely drawn images in charcoal covered one entire wall. The charred stick used to draw them lay at the base of the wall. The series of dizzying swirls and jagged lines that, at first, made no sense, as he stared at them became a roughly depicted humanoid torso and head. Beyond that, all resemblance to anything human ended.

Gaius' sharp intake of breath alarmed Flavius, as did the Centurion's suddenly pallid face. "Are you all right?" he asked.

Gaius said nothing. His gaze remained fixed on the grotesque drawing. His stomached knotted until it became a fist punching him in the gut and his heart pounded unmercifully in his chest. The Tribune had reached into his mind and sketched the image of the creature that had been haunting his dreams. The creature stared at him with two great, blood red eyes that stood out from the charcoal drawing. Gaius noticed the blood dripping from the palm of the Tribune's hand. He had cut himself and used his blood to color the eyes. Octopus-like tentacles surrounded the oversized mouth. The lower torso rested on a dozen large tentacles instead of legs. The roughly sketched lines created an air of motion to the creature. As Gaius stared at the creature, he could almost see tentacles writhing, reaching for him.

"After the Tribune drew this, he slashed himself to bloody the eyes," Flavius said. "When Marcellus tried to stop him, he struck him."

"Is Marcellus all right?"

"He is fine, but the men who witnessed the Tribune's actions are frightened. What shall we do about him?"

Gaius tried to focus his disjointed thoughts. Did he and the mad Tribune share the same nightmare? He suddenly grew afraid of the Tribune. He knew that Flavius would not hesitate to kill Sevilius if he ordered it, but his reluctance to murder a Roman officer, even one as deranged as Sevilius stayed his hand.

"We will watch him more carefully. Bind his wound. If he resists, a light tap to the head with the butt of your sword would not be out of line. We may need this Tribune before this war is over."

Flavius nodded, but clearly, he wanted to do more than tap the Tribune's head lightly. Given the Tribune's state of mind and his connection with the Dark Ones, Gaius almost gave the order to do so.

"The scorpions were an added entertainment," Flavius said. "Did you suspect the Inyosh could control living creatures?"

Gaius had found little time to consider the implications, though far-reaching they were. "It came as a shock. Perhaps the creatures and the scorpions both serve the same master."

"This Nergal the Berber speaks of?"

"It may be so."

"We live in interesting times when myths arise and the dead live."

Gaius grinned at his optio. "Indeed."

After a hearty breakfast of hot porridge, roasted goat, and bread with butter and honey, the men lined up for the march to Hamad Rus. The night's tribulations had given them a new sense of purpose. The men were not cowards. Most had faced enemies before. This new, unseen enemy was unlike any they had encountered, but they still had faith in their officers. As long as Gaius kept them alive, they would follow him and fight when ordered.

"Marcellus, take men and gather all the palm date oil in the village. Find wood for fires and rags for torches. Gather anything that will burn."

"There are rags plenty enough," Marcellus replied, "If you do not mind Berber blood." He chose half a dozen legionnaires and hurried away to gather oil.

Gaius cringed at Marcellus' grim comment about the dead villagers. He no longer harbored any ill will toward Rashid or his Berber kin. They were not the enemy. Indeed, they were victims of the Dark Ones just as were his troops. He imagined the horror and terror of unarmed, untrained villagers confronted with shadowy demons from hell. His trained Romans legionnaires had done little better. It seemed Roman iron was useless against the creatures. Only Rashid's mystical amulet wielded any power over the shadowy Inyosh.

As they had on the journey to the village, they would make no camp before reaching Hamad Rus. Gaius set a pace he knew the men could endure for hours. They stopped often to rest. The vast, open plain of sand and rock allowed them to see for leagues in any direction. They felt confident no enemy, not even shadow wraiths, could sneak up on them.

The day wore on hot and endless. The men moved in a silent, undulating line. Only the soft crunch of rocks beneath their sandals or the creak of the wagon wheels broke the eerie quiet.

Sevilius sat atop his horse as if at the head of a parade, his back straight, and his eyes staring straight ahead. He ignored those around him. Gaius noticed the Tribune's freshly bound wounded hand and wondered if Flavius had resorted to violence to accomplish it. The charcoal drawing had unsettled Flavius. Gaius had not allowed the optio to see how much it had disquieted him as well. The crude drawing resembled nothing he had ever seen. Gaius questioned if it sprung entirely from the troubled Tribune's fertile imagination, a part of his growing madness, or had the touch of the Dark Ones deposited it in his mind.

During one rest stop, Gaius pulled Rashid aside. With his foot, he drew in the sand a rough sketch of the Tribune's creation. Rashid's face immediately paled. He quickly kicked sand over the drawing, erasing it.

"Do not give life to such nightmares," he warned.

Rashid's reaction troubled Gaius. "What is it?"

"My grandfather once drew something similar when I was very young. I remember his hands shook as he drew it." He glanced down at the scuffed sand where the drawing had been. "I think it is *Nergal*, the god of the Inyosh."

"How could the Tribune know of it?"

Rashid glanced at Sevilius, studying the taciturn Tribune for a moment. "One of the Dark Ones touched him. Perhaps he saw into its mind. If so, I would not trust him."

Even coming from Rashid, whom he did not fully trust, it seemed sound like sage advice. Now, he had one more item to add to his long list of worries.

The wagons, heavily laden with jars of oil, wood, and extra food from Rashid's village, mired often in the soft sand. The men dug the sand from around the wheels to free them, only to repeat the procedure a few minutes later. Progress slowed to a crawl. The men grew restless, eager to move on even if it meant abandoning the wagons, but Gaius knew they could not. Six times during the morning, they freed the wagons before they reached harder packed sand.

By mid-day, Flavius allowed the men to place their heavy shields in the wagons to ease their burden, but they did not relinquish their swords or javelins. Several men suffering from severe heat exhaustion or fatigue and the two soldiers stung by the scorpions joined the armaments in the wagons. The extreme heat began to affect Gaius as well. His mind felt drained and his thoughts disjointed. He could not concentrate or develop any plan of action once they reached Hamad Rus. It was difficult enough simply forcing his body to continue. He relied on Apollo to guide him rather he guide the horse. When a wave of dizziness swept over him, he clamped his thighs against the four-pommel saddle to keep from falling off.

The day wore on interminably, hours passing with no let up from the heat or the endless desert. Once, he felt Apollo quiver beneath him, rousing him from his disorientation.

"Steady, boy," he said. He patted the horse's head; then, noticed the men standing instead of marching. Their faces bore looks of alarm. "What is it, Flavius?" he asked.

"Did you not feel it? The earth shuddered and groaned. A rippled passed along the ground, as if a large fish passing just beneath the surface of a pond."

Gaius, in his dazed state, had not felt the quake, but Apollo had. "I must have dozed." He glanced back at the column. "Are the men well?"

"Aye, frightened, but unharmed." In a quieter voice Flavius asked, "What if the earth moves while we are underground? What if we are trapped, buried alive?"

"Do not dwell on the worst that could happen," Gaius advised. "Consider scenarios we can remedy."

"Do you have a plan, Centurion?"

Flavius' question caught him off guard. He scowled. "Do you believe I am so reckless, optio? I have a plan of attack. Do you believe we need a plan to retreat as well?"

"No, Centurion. If we need to retreat, it will be too late."

Gaius started Apollo walking again. "That is my thought as well."

He had not lied to his optio, at least not entirely. His plan, though only half-formed in his mind, was simple enough. Much depended on what they encountered in the dark caverns. Flame and the Berber's amulet seemed their only effective defenses, so he would keep both close by. The creatures could not pass through stone, as proven by their inability to enter the houses. If they could seal the caverns with the wraiths inside, the problem would end. He just wasn't sure how to seal the cavern.

The day slowly dissolved into another night. Once again, men carrying torches flanked the column. They did not grumble when told they would not stop for the night. They were eager to reach any safety, even the stone walls of Hamad Rus. Wary and weary men cast furtive glances into the shadows, but they did not come under attack. Despite what little relief he might have felt, Gaius attributed the lull to the shadows waiting for them at Hamad Rus.

Morning brought relief from the darkness, but not from the heat. The sun scoured the land around them. After two days of forced march, fatigued men stumbled, tripped, and fell. Horses moved slowly with whinnies of distress. The column rested, drank water and wine, and ate sparingly at intervals, but their weariness grew too great for a short rest to offer much solace.

Gaius tried to remain alert, but the heat sapped his strength, bearing down on him as if Jove had singled him out for punishment. His mind wondered between dark images remembered from snippets of his nightmares and a vision of his wife. Would he ever see her again? Did she already number him among the dead? He realized his pride and ego had forced him to abandon her when she needed him most. Returning to her depended on defeating the enemy. For that reason, he was eager to reach Hamad Rus before nightfall. His men were slowly losing their effectiveness as a fighting force. Another day on the sand would finish them.

Several minutes passed before Gaius realized that Apollo had stopped moving. He opened his eyes and stared ahead. The dark openings of the cliffs loomed like hollow eyes warding the dead city of Hamad Rus below them, a warning to any intrepid visitor. The sun sank below the horizon, deepening the shadows already enveloping the city like an ebony cloak. He turned to see Flavius watching him intently.

"For what do we wait?" Flavius asked. The optio's dusty face bore the strain of his fatigue.

Gaius glanced at Sevilius. The Tribune sat on his horse as if willing himself to become part of it. His took no notice of the ancient city before him. He had not spoken all day. His days of leadership were over. He had become an empty shell filled with Gaius knew not what. Gaius tightened his grip on the reins and kicked Apollo in his flanks. The horse snorted, reared, and galloped down the slope toward the city. Gaius hung on, allowing the horse his head.

"We wait for nothing," he called back to Flavius.

He entered the city alone, daring his unseen enemy to strike him dead and end his misery. A soft murmur of voices rode the hot breeze, the ululant whispers of the dead. He ignored their taunts and rode directly to the ancient temple. As before, the temple seemed to drink in the darkness of the evening, growing more substantial as night encompassed it. The shadows surrounding it rippled, as if stirred by a breeze he did not feel. He contemplated the macabre frieze above the door, as his men marched up behind him breaking the silence. The carving depicted a thing of loathing, a creature whose eyes revealed an enmity for all things living. Men did not worship it out of love, but from fear. Only a people who had given up all hope would pray to such a god. In the end, it had done them no good.

As the dying sun slowly kissed the desert sands, long shadows crawled down the empty streets of the dead city like an advancing black tide. The darkness pooled in the yawning cave entrances on the bluff billowed out of the mouths of the caverns and spilled down the rock, streaming to join the growing pool of gloom engulfing the city. Gaius felt the uneasiness of the men. Darkness brought the enemy. This time he was prepared. He pointed to the same building in which they had earlier made camp.

"Set up camp there. Place braziers of oil at each opening."

He smiled. This time death would not catch them unawares. He didn't enter the temple to see if the blood of his men still stained the altar. He pointed to the doorway.

"Have men bring stones and seal this door. Large stones. Let's see if these creatures can make sacrifices to their dark god now."

While Marcellus oversaw the men and the camp, Gaius, Rashid, Flavius, Sevilius, and two others rode toward the bluffs. He wanted a closer look at the strange tombs. A narrow path, carved from the rock, wound back and forth across the lower face of the bluff until it reached a man-made plateau hewn halfway up its flanks. Something about the caves disturbed him. Then he realized what it was.

"Where is the rubble?"

Flavius turned to him. "What?"

"The city was carved from native stone as were these caverns. Where is the rubble from their construction?"

"Carted away for another purpose," Flavius posed; then dismissed the question for a more practical one. "Do you think our unseen enemy resides within?"

"For what purpose?" Gaius asked, ignoring Flavius' question.

"What does it matter where the rubble went," Flavius growled, "unless our invisible enemy uses it as ammunition for invisible catapults?"

"I think it matters," Gaius replied, though he could not say how. He did not like mysteries or unanswered questions.

Sevilius stared grimly at the cavern entrance. He pulled his cloak tighter around his body. After a while, he broke his long silence. "Only the dead dwell here."

"The dead is who we seek," Gaius replied.

After speaking his few words, Sevilius returned to the world in his head, ignoring all further attempts to draw him out.

A chill, dank breeze smelling of long dead things issued from the nearest opening with a ghostly sigh. The caverns gaped uninviting and threatening. The thick darkness within could, as Flavius suspected, hold an army of enemies ready to pour forth and overwhelm his small band of men. He felt exposed. A shudder passed through him.

"Come," he said. "We must prepare for tonight."

It was a difficult thing to turn his back on the openings and ride back to the dead city of Hamad Rus, but he had questions for Rashid he must ask in private.

That preparations proceeded as he had ordered pleased him. The men's exhaustion did not impede their sense of duty. They had sealed the single door to the temple with a double mound of large stones. No more sacrifices would occur there. Oil-filled brass braziers burned at each window and in front of the solitary door of the building in which they camped. If the enemy feared fire and light, they should be safe. He posted no guards outside the building but doubled the guard inside. Large fires burned inside on both levels. Satisfied he could do nothing more, he settled down to dine with his men.

Men who should have been famished by the forced march picked nervously at their food, eating little. Gaius gnawed on a roasted pork cutlet, but the meat left a sour taste in his mouth and in his stomach. He dipped bread in honey and chewed it instead. He ordered wine distributed to the men to dull their apprehension. As he stared into his goblet, the dark red color of the wine reminded him of blood. He forced himself to take a sip, surprised that it tasted only of fermented grapes.

Sevilius alone sat huddled in a corner, his cloak pulled about him like a security blanket. After his dire warning at the caverns, he had once again retreated into stony silence. His men avoided him with their gaze. Sevilius did not notice their rejection of him. He seemed unaware of anything, lost in his growing insanity. Gaius feared he would become a hindrance inside the cavern, but he could spare no men to watch him and did not wish to bind him and leave him behind to almost certain death.

After the meal, as Gaius peeled an apple with his dagger, Flavius broached the subject he had so far avoided. "Why are we here?"

Gaius let the long peel drop to the floor. "Because the enemy is here."

Flavius held his arms spread wide. "He seems to be everywhere. Why are we here?" He pointed to the floor, tapping it with his finger. "What is your plan?"

Gaius took a bite of the apple but found it tasteless. He frowned, wondering if any food would ever satisfy him again. He tossed the apple onto the fire and watched the flames devour it. "It is my intention to enter one of the openings in the cliff and seek out the enemy."

Flavius' jaw dropped. "Are you mad?" he bellowed.

Gaius frowned. "You dare call me mad?" he shot at Flavius.

Flavius squared his chin and confronted his superior. "I dare when the darkness is our enemy."

"If the enemy ventures from his home at night, then night is when we should investigate his home."

"That is like poking a stick into a bee's nest just to lick the honey from the tip. I fear we shall stir up the nest and reap small reward for our troubles."

Gaius was adamant. He knew Flavius dared not disobey an order, but he needed his optio to understand his reasoning. "We brought sufficient oil and torches. I will leave men under Marcellus' command outside the entrance to keep a large fire burning to prevent the creatures from returning. If our enemy still dwells inside the caves, we must drive them out into the open, into the daylight where we might see their faces."

"There are many caverns. Perhaps our enemy outnumbers us."

Gaius could see Flavius mulling over the idea in his head. His objections became more specific – logistics rather than dissention over the idea of his plan.

"Protected by fire and with our backs to a stone wall, no one can defeat us. We will burn their homes, destroy their supplies, and kill their women." He revealed the reason he felt comfortable confronting the enemy in his caverns. "We have the Berber and his amulet."

Flavius' sneer told him all he needed to know.

"You witnessed the amulet at work."

"I witnessed a blue light and witnessed the creatures depart. Perhaps it was on the Berber's orders. I do not trust him any more than I trust his magic."

Gaius nodded. "Forthright and honest. Very well. Your job will be to kill the Berber at the first sign of betrayal. I think it is a task to which you would apply yourself with zeal."

"Aye," Flavius growled. "His death would please me, but I will abide by your wishes. He dies only if he deceives us."

"We will leave Marcellus with sesquiplecarus Dracus and four seasoned men, as well as the native auxilia, outside the entrance. The Tebu would not enter the caverns even if we flogged them. If we fail, Marcellus' task will be to report our deaths to Leptis Manga. We leave six hours before dawn."

"What do think we will find there?"

"Redemption or death." Gaius shook his head slowly. Sevilius' strange behavior had driven his thoughts to darker levels. "I fear our Berber friend is right. We face no normal foe. Something evil resides within those deep caverns, something that has been waiting a very long time. Egypt, a once great nation fell mysteriously many centuries ago. Civilizations far to the east have disappeared just as quickly – Sumeria, Ur, Babylon, Hittite, Persia, and Akkad. Hamad Rus was once the beating heart of the Saharan desert. Now, like the others, it is a faded memory. I believe our enemy is a destroyer of nations. It has now tasted good Roman blood. I think it will leave its dark places and seek out Rome."

Flavius stared at Gaius in shock. "You test these creatures, offering our lives so that Marcellus might determine the enemy's true strength and purpose."

Gaius admired the quickness Flavius displayed in divining his purpose. "If we cannot defeat them, we will not return. Our deaths will be the Emperor's proof of the danger."

Flavius glanced at the men, all sublimely unaware of what was to come. As a veteran military man, he could smell defeat. "I will sharpen my blade." With that, he nodded curtly and turned to walk away.

Gaius stopped him. "I have one other trick that may work."

Flavius lifted an eyebrow.

"The goats' blood. The creatures do not attack animals. If we douse our bodies with the blood of the goats, perhaps it will mask our scent for a time."

Flavius wrinkled his nose. "Cover ourselves in animal's blood? That seems unwholesome."

"Perhaps, but if it gives us any edge, however slight, it will be worth the discomfort. Inform the men of my plan."

Flavius nodded. "I will tell them."

As Flavius walked away, Rashid said, "He is right. We will not return."

Gaius started at Rashid's words; then scowled at him. He had not heard the Berber approach. "You walk like a cat."

Rashid smiled. "Even cats fear too many rats. If we enter the *aguram*, the Tombs of the Dead, my amulet might not protect us. I do not know the limits of its power. I could not use it in time to save my people. It is said the caverns run to the center of the earth, to hell."

"Then we will meet Charon the boatman of the River Styx and pay him his copper coins to ferry us to Hades."

Rashid stared at him, uncomprehending his reference to Roman lore. "If we encounter a river in this dry land, it will be a river of blood, Roman blood."

"And yours, Berber," Gaius reminded him, "yours as well."

"I would hate to deprive your Flavius of his pleasure, but the Dark Ones might have other plans for me."

"If you fail me, he might turn his blade on me."

Rashid arched one eyebrow in mock surprise. "A Roman killing a Roman? That would be … barbaric."

Gaius pointed a finger at Rashid. "Your tongue might be your death, Berber."

"A man must speak what he perceives as the truth, or he is no man."

"Then you believe there are versions of the truth?"

Rashid shrugged. "There is, of course, Roman truth, and then there is the Truth."

"You speak like a politician. You would make a good Senator."

"Were my skin not dark and my manners not so rough? Were I a Roman?"

This brought a smile to Gaius' lips. "As I said a true politician. Are all Berber princes politicians?"

"All Berbers are politic. That is how we survive in a hostile land."

"Will my plan with the goats' blood work?" Gaius had doubts, but could think of no other subterfuge that might gain them entrance into the caverns.

Rashid paused. "I do not know. It seems logical to make the attempt. We might fool the creatures' nostrils, but we will not fool their eyes."

"A few minutes might be all we need."

"We are entering their domain, the *tabyni*, the deep darkness. I know not your entire plan, but I fear it will prove inadequate for what we encounter. The dark wraiths that were once Inyosh waged war against the Kashites for many years. The Kashites are no more. These shadow creatures are not mindless beasts. They will work together to defend their domain." Rashid uttered a soft hiss of disproval. "Do you think to surround them and subdue them with fire and sword? Do you think I alone with my amulet can defeat them?"

Gaius stared at Rashid. "I suggest you sleep. It might be your last."

He watched Rashid cross the room and make a pallet with his blanket in the corner away from the others. The Berber intrigued him. If fate and birth had not made them enemies, Gaius thought he might have made a good friend. If he feared death, he did not show it. Gaius had dwelt upon death many times, during many battles, and most of all after his banishment from Rome when he had contemplated death by his own hands. Such an end would have pleased the Emperor but would have brought further disgrace to his family; therefore, he had meekly accepted his punishment. If death did not find him in this hostile, barren land, he would once again return to Rome and confront the Emperor, this time with a Legion at his back.

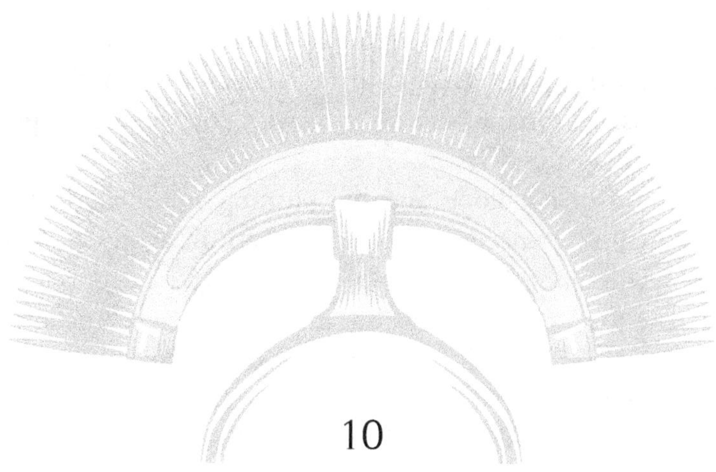

10

Gaius thought he had faced darkness before, both darkness within the mind and the darkness of the deepest night, but staring into the entrance of the ominous cavern was like gazing into a bottomless black pit. He felt it drawing him ever-downward in a dizzying spiral. He leaned farther over the edge … and felt a hand touch his shoulder.

"Why this particular one?" Flavius asked, leaning on Gaius' shoulder to look past him into the depths of the cavern as nonchalantly as one might inspect a closet.

The goat's blood splotching the optio's face and arms and staining his tunic made him appear battle bloodied. The stench of days-old goat's blood was far worse than most battlegrounds Gaius remembered, but if it tricked the creatures, it would be worth the discomfort.

Gaius shook his head to clear it. He pointed to the carving above the entrance. "It is the same as that of the temple in the city."

Flavius motioned to the men surrounding them. They each lit a torch, beating back the darkness and revealing their own coating of goat's blood. Each one also carried two more unlit torches thrust through their belts. Several men bore urns filled with oil. They had dipped each torch in oil mixed with sulfur and lime to waterproof it. The torches produced a unique stench of their own. Such precautions puzzled Flavius; fearing water in the desert seemed incongruous, but Gaius had explored caves in Gaul, damp, dripping, stalagmite and stalactite filled chambers that easily extinguished torches. He did not wish to risk such a possibility when faced with deadly wraiths.

The odor of goat's blood and the burning sulfur worked together to gnaw at Gaius' stomach, exacerbating the dull agony caused by the cancer. He wanted nothing more than to lie down in a cool place with a flagon of wine to allow it to settle, but matters were reaching a head. In a few hours, he would have all the time he needed or his discomfort would no longer matter. The dead feel no pain.

Marcellus and the men he had chosen had constructed an enormous pyre in front of the main entrance with wood carted from Rashid's village and what little wood they could scrounge from the countryside. Gaius noticed Antonius Cossus, the old veteran, among them. He nodded to him, glad to see Marcellus had an experienced man he could depend on. Antonius nodded back.

Gaius' orders to Marcellus had been simple. If he did not return, Marcellus would march back to camp, and then send riders to warn the garrison at Marzuq. To prepare, they had soaked the wood with oil. At each of the smaller entrances, they placed burning braziers. The Tebu natives helped, but stayed as far from the dark entrance as possible. They had balked at marking their bodies with goat's blood. Only physical force would have convinced them, and Gaius needed them too badly to risk driving them away. Their allegiance to their new Roman masters went only so far.

Flavius stared at the carving on the lintel. "It looks as if it was once a man."

That thought had crossed Gaius' mind as well. The eyes bore a strikingly human quality, although they possessed no touch of pity or mercy. They were the eyes of a natural killer. He hoped the carving merely symbolic, some artist's whimsy, but he suspected it once was the face of their enemy transformed upon their cursed deaths to shadowy form.

The flat ledge upon which they stood stretched from one end of the crimson bluff to the other, a distance of about 1,600 Roman *pedes*

– almost half a league. Six entrances dotted the ledge, some too small for a man to enter on hands and knees. Peering inside each, Gaius saw that they sloped downward into the depths of the earth. Only the main entrance was wide enough to admit men. Strange carvings adorned the lintels and fluted columns set in front of them – nightmarish creatures, disfigured figures that might have been men, and runes that held the eye captive, revealing more malevolent detail the longer one stared. The relentless march of the eons had sand-etched their heavily pitted carved surfaces beyond recognition, but just their rough, blurred outlines troubled Gaius. They resembled nothing he had seen in Rome, in Greece, in Egypt, or in any building or temple in the Middle East. He wondered what manner of people once lived in these lands.

The men still thought of the caverns as tombs, but Gaius doubted they would find anyone buried within. However, that didn't mean that men had not died there.

"All is ready," Marcellus announced, wiping his hands on his tunic. "We have scrounged all the wood this desert has to offer."

"Strip the wagons if necessary," Gaius ordered, "but keep the fires burning until after dawn."

He eyed Gaius for a moment. "I still think I should accompany you. You might need my sword. Dracus Armis can mind these native recruits and Sevilius' men."

Gaius smiled, touched by the veteran's sense of duty. It was true that he wanted the veteran legionnaire's sword by his side, but Dracus was young. If he arrived in Leptis Magna with a tale of deadly living shadows, dead cities, and a defeated legion, they would dismiss him as a coward, or worse, a deserter.

"You have your orders if we fail."

Marcellus snapped to attention and saluted. "You will not fail, *Legate*."

"*Centurion*," Gaius reminded him.

"In my mind, you will always be a commander."

He spun and returned to his men. Gaius spotted Rashid sitting with his back against the cliff studying the amulet and went to him. Unlike the reluctant Tebu, the Berber had not hesitated dousing himself with goat's blood. His eyes peered out from a blood-red mask.

"It is time," Gaius said.

Rashid rose slowly, tucking the amulet carefully inside his robe. The blood had dried quickly in the desiccated desert air, making the robe stiff. He looked at the sky, and then at the desert around them as if fixing the image in his mind, *or as if he expects never to see them again,* Gaius realized grimly.

"I do not believe they have exited their lair as you hoped. I think they are waiting within for us."

"Why do you believe this?"

Rashid shrugged. "Because they have not yet attacked us."

Gaius could not refute Rashid's logic. "Are they men or beasts?"

Rashid's hand went to his breast as if to assure him the amulet still rested there. "Perhaps a bit of both originally many centuries ago, but now they are shadows of what they once were. They are evil itself serving a thing even more evil."

Gaius chuckled. "I thought Romans were evil itself."

The outer edges of Rashid's lips turned up. "You are but a little evil. Your empire will crumble as others have, as Hamad Rus fell. The Dark Ones are eternal. Their evil god existed before time itself."

In spite of himself, Gaius cast a quick glance over the ruins of Hamad Rus and shuddered. The ruined city was barely visible in the darkness but just as foreboding. Would Rome join it in its ignoble death? *Not while I breathe,* he swore. He grabbed a torch from one of the soldiers and marched into the darkness with resolute steps. "Let's go."

Flavius cautioned Gaius back, insisting that four men bearing torches lead the way. Gaius understood Flavius' prudence, but the men moved too cautiously. He crowded them to urge them to move faster. They had to reach their destination, wherever that might be, before dawn. Rashid, vigilant but subdued, walked alongside Gaius. Flavius followed Rashid. "Where I can watch him," he explained. Sevilius trudged along beside Flavius oblivious to his surroundings. His only expression was an occasional tic in his jaw. Gaius kept a close watch on the mad Tribune, hoping to use him as a bellwether to determine if the wraiths were near.

The short entrance opened into a large square chamber with roughly carved, unadorned walls. The torches barely illuminated its voluminous interior. Along one wall, toppled and broken statues half-covered by drifting sand and dusty cobwebs stood behind a stone altar. They were representations of the original gods of the people of Hamad Rus, long forgotten during their war with the Dark Ones.

The altar was not of the same slick black stone as the temple in the city. Cruder, carved from the same soft, red rock as the cavern, it projected none of the sense of malevolence the black altar possessed. It was dust-filled from centuries of disuse. Any gods it represented either existed no longer or had fled the area long ago.

Gaius scanned the ceiling but saw no bats overhead. No animal tracks marked the floor. In fact, the deep sand bore no prints of any kind, but Gaius did not doubt that the cavern was occupied.

Watching him, Rashid said, "Nothing living enters these caverns if you fear another attack by scorpions. Perhaps the creatures of the desert have more sense than men."

Directly ahead, a wide opening plunged deeper into the mountain, sloping steeply downward. Gaius pointed to it and said, "There is no reason to linger here."

Four men could walk abreast in the wide tunnel, and the torch Gaius held above his head could not touch the ceiling. Gaius noted the tunnel looked as if clawed from the solid rock rather than chiseled by the hands of men. The ceiling bore no traces of soot or black smoke marks, as if whoever or whatever used the tunnel had no need for light. The men noticed this also and became even more pensive.

After walking for an uneventful half an hour, they encountered the first side tunnel, smaller than the main tunnel and sloping upward. A faint breeze blew down the tunnel from the outside, bringing the scent of the desert. Gaius believed it connected to one of the smaller entrances on the surface. Fearing the mountain a honeycomb of such tunnels, Gaius dismissed Flavius' suggestion of exploring it.

"We cannot split our force. Leave a brazier with burning oil in the entrance. It might dissuade our enemy from emerging at our backs." Gaius worried that if they encountered many such tunnels, they would soon run out of oil.

The weight of the mountain above pressed down upon Gaius' senses. The claustrophobic confines of the tunnel played on his nerves, making him eager to finish the job he had started and return to the surface. By his reckoning, they had travelled ten *milliarium* from the entrance, the equivalent of the length of thirty Coliseums. His left leg grew numb above the knee and threatened to give out whenever the uneven tunnel made a sharp incline or decline. Several times, he stumbled, covering it up with a quick lunge to the wall to lean against it on the pretext of examining some new feature. He clenched his teeth against the pain. He fooled everyone but Flavius.

"Perhaps we should rest," he suggested.

Gaius shook his head. "Rest would not ease the ache of my old war wound. We can ill afford a delay."

"We can ill afford to carry you."

Gaius scowled and straightened up. "I will make it, Optio."

The caverns were more extensive than he had guessed. They had already descended to a depth well below the level of the city. Was Rashid right? Did the caverns lead to Hades? The air was warm and heavy, difficult to pull into his lungs, and tasted old and bitter, like wine gone sour. They had passed no structures, no carvings, and no rooms. He had seen no places for sconces or any type of lighting. The creatures that used the maze of tunnels beneath the earth needed no light with which to see.

The confined space magnified each sound, echoing down the tunnel ahead of them. Even his labored breathing pounded in his ears multiplied by the breathing of three score men. With the shuffling of sandaled feet on stone and the occasional rattle of armor or scabbard, he suspected they would not catch their enemy unawares.

They passed four more tunnels, leaving burning oil at each. Flavius considered each one a potential risk, but they had neither the manpower to post guards nor stone to block the pitch-black openings. Above them, the sun would be rising, bathing the desert in morning light. Marcellus, at least, would be safe. The Stygian depths they now prowled had never seen sunlight, had never tasted a fresh breeze.

Twice, they rested. Gaius was glad for the respite. He sat with his back to the stone wall to ease the pain in his thigh. The men ate mechanically from cold food in their kits, while their nervous eyes scanned the walls and the tunnel before and behind them. Roman soldiers fought in a phalanx, shields locked tight for protection. If they fought in the tunnel, it would be as individuals. The untested tirones began to doubt their skill, and doubt could kill.

The heavy stench of goat's blood did not staunch their appetites. *Hircina*, meat of the goats from the village roasted and dried, *caseus*, the cheese from goat milk, dried apples and dates, hardtack biscuits, *acetum*, or sour wine, and *sel*. Salt not only flavored the food, it replaced salt lost from perspiration. In the desert, *sel* was more precious than gold, the commodity for which Rashid's people had risked their lives.

As if to remind him of his mortality, Gaius' stomach awoke and began clawing at his insides like a burrowing creature. He did not know if its cause was the stench, the cancer eating at his stomach, or the tension. He poured a mound of the powdered henbane into the palm of his hand and ate it dry. The taste almost succeeded in making him vomit, but he took a sip of sour wine to get the vile concoction down his throat. Flavius eyed him questioningly, but said nothing. The medicine soon began to fight back the agony in his stomach, but it would not go away.

By Gaius' reckoning, it was mid-afternoon when they reached a circular chamber large enough to hold the Coliseum and the Forum combined; far later than he had planned. By its shape, it was a natural cavern; volcanic in origin, but the convergence of the many tunnels lining the walls was not. They dotted the cavern walls like rodent holes, but Gaius suspected things more dire than rats used them. The walls glowed softly, offering the equivalent of late twilight to the light-starved men. Gaius reached out his hand and rubbed it across the stone nearest him. It came away shiny, sticky, and glowing.

"Phosphorescent algae," he said with awe, wiping the tacky goo on his armor. "I've heard of such in deep caves in Gaul."

"Those caverns held no such sight as that, I'll wager," Flavius said.

Following Flavius' gaze, Gaius quickly discovered what had become of the rubble from the city above and from the tunnels. The roof of the chamber soared over their heads, fading into blackness with distance. A tower in its center, conceived by no human mind and built by no human hand, reached into the blackness of the roof of the enormous cavern. It was a dizzying construct, a truncated cone with many seemingly randomly placed flat protuberances and protrusions, and deep, narrow crevices and recesses. Gaius estimated it fell just short of the 12-story Coliseum, 187-Roman feet tall.

Rather than mortared with cement like sturdy Roman buildings, the various-sized stones appeared held in place by tufts of the phosphorescent algae. Zigzagging iridescent lines traced the entire length of the tower, as if cold fire inside were trying to erupt through cracks in the masonry. If not for its location deep in the bowels of the earth and its dark implication, it would have been a beautiful sight, a wonder more marvelous than the fabled Colossus of Rhodes or the Egyptian Pyramids. In Gaius, it evoked only revulsion. It was an evil construct built for dark purposes.

More ominous than the tower, a gigantic statue stood before it like a silent sentinel. The head and face resembled that of the frieze above the temple door in Hamad Rus, but the body passed all resemblance to human origin. Rather than a trunk with arms and legs, the creature's body consisted of a mass of writhing tentacles tipped with razor-sharp claws, each almost as large as a man. It looked so lifelike that Gaius half-expected it to open its eyes and step down from its stone pedestal to confront them. Its resemblance to the frenzied charcoal sketch by Sevilius disturbed him. He turned to face Rashid.

"*Nergal,*" Rashid whispered in answer to his unspoken question.

They moved closer. What the light of their torches revealed next horrified Gaius. He had witnessed the carnage of many battlefields; had seen the rotting carcasses and weathered bones of friend and foe alike scattered over vast plains, stony hillsides, and deep mountain passes, but the grisly scene before him chilled him to the marrow.

"I believe we now know where the bodies of our slain men went," Flavius said.

A carpet of skeletons and broken bones covered the entire floor of the cavern. Some skeletons, ghostly white in their freshness, retained tatters of flesh and pieces of Roman armor or Berber clothing. Others had yellowed with age. They lay in undignified heaps around the base of the statue, as if offerings. Smashed skulls stared empty-eyed at the assemblage of soldiers from atop boulders. In the center of the cavern, a deep pit pierced the cavern floor, as perfectly round and as smooth edged as a javelin thrust through flesh. More bones surrounded the lip of the chasm. An atrocious odor, stronger than that of the fetid rotting flesh around the statue, rose from the depths on a cold, damp, dank air. Scratching sounds, like millions of rats, spilled from the opening in the earth. The men began whispering among themselves. Witnessing the fate of their fallen comrades was an ill omen. A few covered their faces and whimpered.

Sevilius, too, stared at the macabre collection of bones. He recognized the armored corpse of Quintus Cantos, his aide, by the crest on the baldric he wore over his shoulder. A wail escaped his lips, the first sound he had uttered in hours. He broke and ran toward the nearest opening in the wall rather than the passage through which they had entered.

"Stop him!" Flavius cried to the stunned soldiers, his voice echoing in the chamber.

"No, let him go," Gaius said. His eyes remained fixed on the bone yard. He had no time to worry after a demented Tribune.

Flavius dismissed the Tribune's exit as quickly as he would a dead enemy. He focused on the tower. "I believe the tower is our enemy's fortress," he said. "We would need siege engines to take it."

Rashid stepped forward, stopping beyond the edge of the reach of the flickering torches, his sandaled feet almost treading on the bones. "I do not think taking the fortress is an option," he said. "Observe." He pointed toward the top of the tower.

At first, Gaius could not see to what Rashid pointed. Then, he noticed movement, dark shapes pouring from the openings and clambering down the side of the tower in an ever-increasing black tide. They were too distant to discern distinctly; then, an icy fear gripped his heart, and his hands turned cold and clammy.

"The Dark Ones," Rashid whispered.

The ebon creatures moved with a purpose, and that purpose was to offer the intruders to their dark god. Gaius judged they had only minutes before the first of the swarming creatures reached them.

"Bring oil," he called out. "Hurry!"

The rocks would not burn, but he hoped the algae used as mortar dry enough to kindle. If nothing else, they would have light in which to fight their undead opponents. Men rushed toward the tower with torches and urns of oil, giving the pit a wide berth, and began splashing oil along the base of the tower. Gaius feared they took too long.

"Smash the urns on the side of the tower," Gaius told them. "Save one urn for later."

On his signal, a lighted torch sailed through the air and landed at the base of the dark tower. Ignited, the oil-soaked algae flamed as Gaius hoped it would. Tongues of fire raced up the side of the tower, following the lines of dried algae, but his men did not have time to surround the entire tower with oil. Many of the creatures swarmed down the backside and spread out among the shadows, killing anyone who approached. He witnessed one creature explode into flame when it moved too close to the burning tower. The sight spawned an idea.

"Form ranks," Gaius ordered. "Pour oil on your swords and spears, and then light them."

Gaius doused his gladius in oil and touched it to a torch, turning into the Flaming Sword the Jewish texts said God had placed at the east gate of Eden after he expelled man from the garden. Its small flame did little to illuminate the enormous cavern, but as dozens more swords, lances, and arrow points sparked into life, their combined light illuminated the band of soldiers standing unyielding against their supernatural foe. Gaius felt pride for his men. Though obviously frightened by the swarm of shadows descending upon them, they did not panic. Though unlike any enemy they had ever faced, they now faced an enemy they could see, and training took over. Their formed ranks behind the wall of shields did not waver. They waited. The sagittarii fired first. Their flaming arrows arced through the air like bolts of lightning from the gods, landing among the attacking mob of monsters. Any creature struck by the flames exploded, leaving only a fine black powder that drifted to the earth

In almost every battle, one soldier, buoyed by the rush of battle-born adrenaline, inevitably broke ranks and Legion discipline, and attacked the enemy, urging his fellow soldiers onward. Gaius lauded his courage but damned his stupidity. He died quickly beneath a horde of wraiths. Another man tossed a flaming javelin at one of the wraiths. The javelin passed through the creature's body, but the wraith burst into flames and exploded. Emboldened by his success, more men dropped their heavy shields, broke ranks, and attacked with flaming swords and javelins. Arcs of flame scattered the shadowy mass, but the men became separated in the heat of the mêlée.

"Reform ranks," Flavius yelled, but the bloodlust of battle was upon them. Days and months of constant fear sent them into a killing frenzy.

If their numbers had not been so few, Gaius felt certain his men could have held their ground, but for each creature that fell in flames, dozens more took its place from the surrounding openings in the cavern walls. The scene of battle became clearer as raging flames completely engulfed the tower. Burning wraiths cascaded from openings like drops of ebony rain, their ashes scattering on the breeze. The growing light forced many of the creatures back into the openings along the side of the chamber. Curiously, they avoided the rim of the pit, as did his men. Fearing the creatures would fall upon his beleaguered men from behind; Gaius ordered the cornicen to signal them to regroup. The bugler's brass horn echoed from the walls of the cavernous space, becoming a full *symphonia* of blaring *buccina*, *cornu*, and *tuba*. The reverberations became the pounding rhythm of beaten *tympanum*. Even the creatures paused in their attack at the sound.

"Back into the tunnel," he yelled.

He waited as the men filed past. However, Flavius didn't respond to the order to retreat. He stood surrounded by a half score of creatures who had ignored the growing light of the fires. The optio's flaming sword swept scythe-like through the air, but the flames were slowly dying, and they had no more oil. Gaius charged forward. He fell among the wraiths swinging wildly and clearing a path to Flavius' side. Flavius bled from a dozen wounds inflicted by the razor-sharp claws of the creatures. His tired breath came in ragged gasps, and his blows grew weaker, took longer to execute, leaving his side exposed.

Together, he and Flavius held back the black horde, but as Gaius watched in horror, one shadow wraith slipped beneath Flavius' reach and seemed to merge with him. Flavius' eyes went wide in agony. He dropped his sword and fell to his knees, screaming. The creatures fell on him, covering him in shadow. Gaius attacked the group, but when he dispelled them, Flavius was no longer there. Only his sword and bloodstained leather vest remained. Gaius stared at the spot where his friend had died until a hand grasped his shoulder.

"We must leave," Rashid urged.

A sea of creatures encircled them, but they drew no nearer. The amulet in the Berber's hand glowed with bright azure light. Any creature the light fell upon vanished in a puff of ash. Gaius glanced one last time to where Flavius had fallen and nodded. He could nothing for the optio.

"Lead us from this place."

Now, the black tower, fully ablaze, pulled fresh air from the outside to feed the flames. A rush of air swept through the cavern, raising a cloud of dust and black ash from vanquished demon creatures. Rocks and boulders the size of men broke free from the disintegrating tower and tumbled down its sides, bouncing across the floor of the cavern. Realizing the tower could collapse at any moment, Rashid hurried, leading Gaius away from the battle, madly dodging the barrage of deadly boulders. He approached the circle of waiting creatures. They fell back before the amulet's potent radiance and made an opening through which he led Gaius.

Two soldiers with torches flickering in the stiff breeze waited at the entrance of the tunnel.

"How many made it out?" Gaius asked them.

"Twelve counting us," one of the soldiers replied.

Gaius cursed. He had lost three-quarters of his men, and they still had to traverse the long tunnel back to the surface.

"Is Optio Flavius following?" the soldier asked, staring over Gaius' shoulder.

Gaius shook his head. "The optio has fallen."

The soldier nodded and entered the tunnel. Before they could follow, the entire chamber groaned and shuddered. Rocks, loosened by the raging inferno, dropped from the ceiling. The entrance to the tunnel collapsed on top of the soldier, sealing the exit behind tons of rock. Boulders bounced down the slope toward them. The remaining soldier dove one direction, as he and Rashid rolled in the opposite direction. Their luck proved more fortuitous than did the soldier's. A boulder caught him midstride, carrying him down the slope, leaving a bloody trail in its path.

Gaius glanced back at the burning tower. The top half swayed drunkenly for a moment before crashing to the ground. A cloud of dust swept from the base of the tower and enveloped them. Gaius coughed to expel the disgusting dust from his lungs, groping blindly to the cavern wall to orient himself. He found the wall and leaned against it, wiping his eyes to clear them. Through a gap in the dust cloud, he saw the grotesque statue shudder, as a large boulder struck its lower tentacles. He waited for the statue to topple from its pedestal, wishing to glean some small measure of satisfaction as it shattered. Instead, it moved.

At first, he thought his eyes had deceived him. Then, several of the tentacles shifted slightly. *No*, he realized with a sickening feeling, *the tentacles came from the pit*. Round tentacles, each as large around as a wagon wheel, swept from the pit. They gripped the statue and pulled it down, shattering it into a dozen pieces. Then, with a ghastly howl that shook the entire chamber, the creature within the pit rose, brushing aside stones and bones. The remaining creatures cowered from it. Any minion touched by the massive tentacles gibbered in fear before bursting into flames. Finally, the head of the creature appeared over the edge of the pit. As in Sevilius' drawing, the head held two large, blood red eyes and a lipless mouth surrounded by a nest of writing smaller tentacles. Gaius trembled as the dead red eyes swept over him; then, dismissed him as insignificant.

"Come," Rashid urged, frantically grabbing at his hand.

Gaius turned to face him. The Berber had not seen the creature through the dust and remained unaware of their peril. The presence of the wraiths drove his fear. The truth was overwhelming. Gaius' mind, trained by Greek and Roman philosophers, had no place in its well-ordered world for creatures such as this. The Inyosh worshipped a terrible god that held even its minions in appalling contempt.

"It's alive," he said.

Rashid stared at him as if he were mad, as perhaps he was. He had seen an impossible creature arise from the depths of Hades. Surely, that was as mad as one could become. Would he now follow Tribune Sevilius' path into madness? He looked back at the pit to reassure himself that he had been mistaken, but smoke and dust now filled the cavern, shielding it from his view. Terror coursed through him like a fire. A consuming desire to flee the cavern and the dark tunnels engulfed him, submerging him in darkness as deep as that from which the creature had risen. In all his battles, facing death with any lucky enemy thrust of the sword or by a well-aimed arrow, he had not known fear. Now, fear was all he felt. It washed away all other sensations – courage, curiosity, steadfastness. Like a coward, he ran.

Gaius expected an attack by the creatures from each opening they passed, but none came. The appearance of their god had driven them deeper into their burrows. Choosing an opening at random, he raced up the steep slope. He barely noticed the pain in his leg or the presence of Rashid behind him, and then realized the azure glow of the amulet the Berber wore on his chest illuminated the way. He ran until his legs cramped and his chest begged for more air. Finally, exhausted and recovering a small portion of his senses, he collapsed on the floor of the tunnel. He listened, but heard nothing – No pursuit, no footsteps, no clanking of armor, no sounds of battle. He heard only the rumble of falling stone and the rasping sound of his and Rashid's breathing.

"Why are you running so blindly?" Rashid asked between deeply drawn breaths.

"Did you not see it?" Gaius demanded.

"See what?"

The words burst from him, "The creature, *Nergal.* It emerged from its lair."

Rashid stared at him for a moment and shook his head slowly. "Surely, it was a trick of the light."

"No, it skewered me with its evil gaze, and then began moving, its tentacles writhing in the air like a squid."

"You saw the statue tremble. Stone does not move."

"And shadows do not eat people," Gaius shot at him. "Why is one nightmare so easy to believe and not the other?"

Rashid did not respond to the question. Instead, he said, "I think we are lost within this mountain."

"We cannot go back. I will not go back," Gaius insisted.

"Then we continue forward." Rashid sniffed the air. "The air is fresh. It must lead outside."

Gaius marveled at the Berber's sense of smell. His nostrils detected nothing but the stench of death.

As they continued walking, Gaius spotted a glow ahead of them. "A light," he said.

A small fire still flickered in an overturned brazier, one of the braziers they had left on the way in.

"This is the main tunnel," Gaius pointed out with a sigh of relief. He stopped to listen but heard nothing. "Where are my men?"

He doubted that he and Rashid could have fallen so far behind the main group. His unease increased when they began to encounter more overturned braziers, their flames dead, along with scraps of bloody clothing and discarded weapons. The soft whispers of ghosts filled the tunnel both behind and ahead of them.

"It appears you were right," he told Rashid, as a sense of despair descended over him over the loss of his men. "It looks as though we will not return alive from Hamad Rus."

"If my god is willing, perhaps we shall."

"The gods are capricious," Gaius mused, and then laughed aloud.

"What petty gods men worship! To think that such gods as I have witnessed this day walk this earth."

He would pit himself against any adversary – animal or human – but these dark killers were neither human nor beast. They were creatures born in the pits of hell, serving a master who was ancient before the beginning of time. The minions were deadly enough. Now, the master had awakened. Why did he not prostate himself upon the ground in fear?

He realized the henbane coursing through his body sedated his senses. Had the henbane been the source of his glimpse into Hades? Had his drug-befuddled mind created an enemy greater than the one that had defeated him and killed his men? No, his imagination was not that vivid. He had witnessed something rising from the pit. He was sure of it.

The pair finally emerged from the confines of the tunnel into an ash-gray light. Dust clouds covered the western sky, the precursor to another savage dust storm descending on them. The sun rode low on the murky horizon, a smudge of light through a veil of sand. Gaius fell to the ground breathing in great lungfuls of clean, cool air to flush the stench of the burrows from his nostrils, but the smell of death remained. Of Marcellus and the men he had posted to guard the entrance, he saw no sign. The pyre still burned, though it now burned low, casting eerie shadows on the cliff face. The daylight didn't erase the memory of the darkness haunting his soul.

"We are too pitiful to oppose such a creature," he said from his knees, shaking his head. "We are but mortal men. Even the gods could not defeat such a creature."

"They are wraiths, but they die. You saw them."

Gaius sobbed. "Not the *Inyosh*, their master, *Nergal.*"

Rashid stared at him. "It is but an idol of stone."

The ground shuddered beneath them. A wail like the screams of a thousand dying men trumpeted from the cave entrance behind them, echoing from the smaller tunnels as well. Gaius covered his ears and rolled into a ball on the ground.

"Hear?" he yelled over the terrifying sound. "He wants us."

"It is escaping air from the cavern collapsing. Nothing more."

Gaius laughed. Rashid rose from the ground slowly, grabbed Gaius' arm, and urged him to stand. "Come. We must find shelter before dark."

Gaius saw no reason to stand. He resisted. "There is no hiding from the gods."

Rashid persisted, tugging on Gaius' arm. "We hide from the Dark Ones. It is almost night. Come, Roman. I need you to clear my people of your men's deaths, but I will leave you here to die if I must."

Gaius stared at Rashid. "You have no idea of what we have awakened. Your people will all die, as will mine. Pitiful mankind will be swept from the face of the earth."

As he spoke, he allowed Rashid to draw him to his feet. Numbness now replaced fear. He looked out over the ruins of dead Hamad Rus below them. Had they tried to come to some arrangement with *Nergal* and his minions, exchanging their worship for safety? If so, it had done them no good. Such a creature from the abyss of time, alien to anything human, had no regard for worshippers. Their deaths had meant no more to the loathsome creature than the deaths of its Inyosh minions inside the warren. Could Rome, with its panoply of gods borrowed from the Greeks, accommodate another god? He did not believe so. Nergal would not tolerate Rome's lack of conviction toward the beings she worshipped.

Already, the early evening shadows were gathering like blown sand against the shaded eastern side of the buildings, awaiting the fall of full darkness to spring forth like hungry animals to devour him and his companion. Free of the dark confines of the cavern and with the effects of the henbane wearing off, the panic that had consumed him slowly faded. Summoning the dignity of the Roman officer he was, he straightened himself and dusted off his tunic. If he must die, he would face death like a man, like a Roman soldier.

Spotting a full urn of oil, he picked it up and smashed it inside the entrance to the cavern. He then took a burning piece of wood from the pyre and tossed it inside. The flames erupted in a fireball, chasing back the shadows within. He knew it would not stop *Nergal* or burn away the centuries of corruption and death committed within the walls, but it might give the creatures pause.

He drew his sword. "Come. Let us face death as equals."

"All corpses are equal," Rashid replied.

Gaius held out his hand. "You saved my life. Let us then face death as friends."

Rashid eyed the proffered hand with some amusement, but grasped it tightly. "Friends with a Roman. What will my people think of me?"

The mountain shuddered so violently, the pair stumbled around like drunkards to keep from falling. Slabs of rock broke away from the cliff face and slid down the slope. Rocks pelted them. The fluted columns in front of the cave entrances cracked, and then crumbled and gave way, submitting to the trembling earth after centuries of long sentry duty. Gaius danced out of the way as a splinter of rock twice his height broke away and skewered the ground where he had been standing.

"*Nergal* comes," Gaius cried, staring into the opening.

Rashid followed Gaius' gaze. "*Something* comes," he said. The tone of his voice indicated he longer felt as certain that Gaius had imagined *Nergal* climbing from the pit.

They exchanged worried glances, and then, as one, fled the rocky ledge. The ground beneath them churned and quaked as they ran down the zigzagging road to the desert floor, dodging boulders that chased after them rolling down the slope. They raced for the city of Hamad Rus. The ground shook at regular intervals, like the strides of a gigantic creature but originating deep in the earth. Gaius had given no thought to their destination. Though he knew the soft stone walls of the buildings of Hamad Ras would not keep out the creature, the city offered the only cover on the otherwise flat, empty plain. As a cockroach caught in the sudden brightness of a lit lamp, he didn't want to present a visible target to *Nergal*.

The monster wasn't their only problem. Encouraged by their master's presence, the creatures would enter the city like a vengeful horde bent on their deaths.

As the pair entered the city, Gaius raced directly for the temple. Around him, buildings that had stood for a thousand years collapsed, spilling their walls into the narrow streets. At the temple, the tremors had scattered the rocks his men had used to seal the entrance. He stood at the door and peered inside. The black basin overflowed with fresh blood. It ran down the sides of the altar and spilled onto the floor, an offering by the creatures to their bloodthirsty god. The thick, dark liquid, once the essence of men's lives, rippled with each tremor.

His stomach tightened at the ghastly sight. He cringed at the thought of Flavius' blood being there in the basin. A rage overtook him. He drew his sword intent on destroying the altar, saving his men from at least the ignoble fate of becoming a blood offering to an ancient evil.

Rashid's amulet burst into life, illuminating the room in bright, azure light. Gaius paused, his rage dissolving with the knowledge of Nergal's presence. Each increasingly powerful tremor sent fresh spasms of fear coursing through his body. He tried to pray to Jove, but knew Jove's power could not match Nergal's ages-old strength. Compared to Nergal, Roman and Greek gods were but children. The light of the amulet kept the creatures at bay. He heard their wails and yammers outside the temple above Rashid's incantation in words as old as time itself.

The azure light fell upon movement in the corner of the room. Gaius gripped his sword tighter and positioned himself for a better swing of his blade. The shadow moved again. It was no wraith, but a man.

"Show yourself," he yelled at the figure above the din of the earth shaking.

Sevilius stood, his filthy uniform tattered and bloody, his armor and mantle missing. In his hand, he held a bloody dagger. His blank, expressionless face was as white as milk. He stared at Gaius without comprehension.

"He is lost to us," Rashid warned. "That is not Inyosh blood on his dagger."

Gaius saw the self-inflicted slashes up and down the mad Tribune's arms, as if he tried to cut away the darkness inside.

A deathly silence fell over the city, but a dark presence remained. Suddenly, a look of abject terror twisted Sevilius' face. His scream seemed inhuman, incapable of issuing from a human throat. Gaius dropped his sword and covered his ears with his hands to drown out the piercing shriek. Sevilius' body began to spasm. He danced around the room like a marionette with tangled strings, jabbering strange words. The floor cracked and erupted at the Tribune's feet. Tentacles as big around as a man's body thrust through the earth and stone, showering all three men with fist-sized chunks of stone flooring and dirt. A foul odor, the stench of death and corruption, issued from the crack in the floor.

A tentacle whipped in Rashid's direction, but he held the amulet steady in both hands. Azure light shot from the amulet and struck the writhing appendage. It withdrew amid a tremendous roar from within the crack and a renewed shuddering of the building. The second tentacle sought Gaius. He pulled his dagger and stabbed at it, but the creature's flesh was as tough as stone. He ducked its wild gyrations and rolled across the floor beyond its reach. Before Rashid could react, Sevilius snatched the amulet from his hands. The tentacle lashed out and struck the Berber in the chest, lifting him and smashing him high into the wall. He slid down the wall and collapsed in a heap at its base. The mad Tribune held the amulet above his head, grinning.

"I am its master," he yelled. "I am safe."

Gaius rushed to Rashid's side. The blow stunned the Berber. His face was drained of color. He breathed slowly and shallowly, but his pulse remained steady. Gaius dragged him away from the groping tentacles.

Sevilius, his face now dark as soot, his eyes filled with hate, glared at Gaius. He pointed his finger. "I will order this creature to kill you. You are the cause of all this evil, you and your cowardly men."

Gaius had had enough of the Tribune's accusations and demented raving. The amulet was useless in his hands, but if he could rouse Rashid, they might yet survive. He flung his dagger underhanded at the Tribune. It struck Sevilius in the throat. The look of surprise on Sevilius' face as his life's blood ran down his tunic brought Gaius no pleasure. There was no glory in killing mad men. He sought only to retrieve the amulet. He almost failed in that task as well. The amulet dropped from Sevilius' dying hand and bounced across the floor of the temple toward the yawning chasm beside the altar. As Gaius lunged for the amulet, he ducked a tentacle that swept over his head and encircled the Tribune's body. The claw at its tip ripped into Sevilius' stomach, gutting him like a fish. Blood and intestines spilled from the gaping wound and mingled with the dirt and rubble. As the tentacle withdrew, it dragged Sevilius' lifeless corpse into the ground with it.

Gaius caught the amulet by its chain as it slid over the precipice of the chasm. As his hand grasped the amulet, it flared to life for a moment, sending a surge of cold heat through his arm and into his chest. The brief flash of azure illuminated the depths of the chasm. What he saw below made him realize he had not been hallucinating in the wraith cavern. Writhing tentacles blurred the creature's form, but two massive, crimson eyes stared up at him from the darkness. It took all his willpower to break the hypnotic pull of the malevolent orbs and crawl from the brink of the chasm.

Holding the glowing amulet before him like a torch, Gaius picked up the unconscious Rashid, slung him over his shoulder, and dashed out the door. Behind him, the temple exploded, as a dozen tentacles thrust into the air through the roof. The shattered roof rained debris around them as he ran. The walls crashed outward, missing Gaius' heels by a hand's width. The Inyosh ignored him, caught up in their worship of their ancient god of death.

At the edge of the cursed city of Hamad Rus, a ghost galloped at him from the darkness – Apollo, his Andalusian warhorse. He threw Rashid across Apollo's neck and leaped on behind him. He kicked the horse in the flanks and held on as the horse raced through the dead streets. Apollo was as eager to leave the stench of death city as he was. The horse sped away into the *Sea of Lost Souls*, leaving the deafening roar of the ancient god behind him.

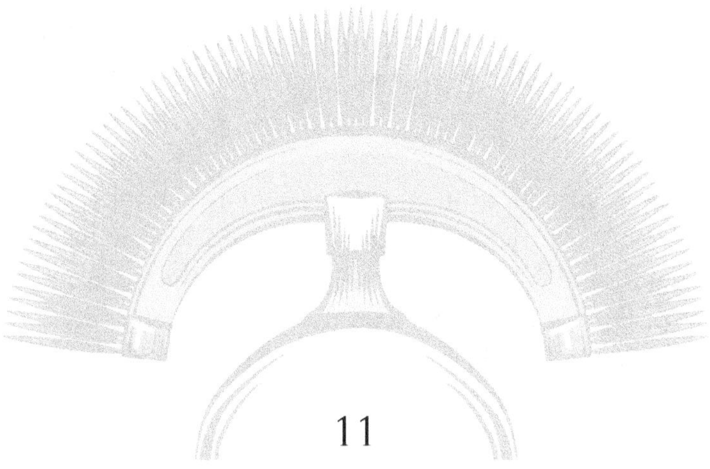

11

Morning found them many leagues from dreaded Hamad Rus. Exhausted by his underground ordeal; Gaius had difficulty remaining upright on Apollo's back. His head reeled from the horrors he had witnessed, and his mind languished between the realm of sleep and the fear of the nightmares he was certain sleep would bring. Rashid lay doubled over on the horse's broad neck, oblivious to his surroundings. His chest did not move. Gaius did not know if the Berber still lived.

They had missed the full wrath of the sandstorm, but its outer fringes hammered them with sheets of windblown sand so thick Gaius didn't know if they were traveling in a straight line or going in a circle. He had half expected to see the city of Hamad Rus appear before him out of the sand like some ghostly apparition. He placed his trust in Apollo's sure-footed sense of direction and closed his eyes against the storm.

Finally, even the mighty Apollo could go no farther. Carrying two men taxed the valiant Andalusian warhorse's great strength. Through a break in the veil of sand, Gaius spotted a small copse of palm trees over a small rise and urged Apollo toward it.

The leeward side of a tall crescent sand dune blocked most of the wind and sand. To Gaius' disappointment, he found no pool of water or spring. Any water remained deep in the ground near the trees' roots.

He dismounted, slid Rashid from Apollo's back, and laid him on the ground. The injured Berber roused for a moment and gazed at Gaius with unfocused eyes.

"Where …?"

Guessing at his question, Gaius pressed the amulet into Rashid's hands. "Here it is my friend. We are safe for now. Are you badly injured?"

He lifted Rashid's upper body from the sand. Rashid grunted in pain, "*Ad uri tggrt!* Do not touch me. I think a have broken ribs."

Gaius nodded. "I will bind them," he said, but Rashid had already slipped back into unconsciousness.

Ripping a strip of cloth from the bottom of his tunic, Gaius wrapped Rashid's chest, pulling the binding tight to force the cracked ribs back into place. The Berber moaned from the pain but did not awaken. A water skin tied to Apollo's saddle held just enough water for a few sips each. He poured some of the precious liquid into his palm for Apollo. Without him, they would surely die in the desert. The horse licked the moisture from his palm gratefully, and then whinnied for more.

"Sorry, old warrior. There is no more save a sip for Rashid and myself. I would give you his share, but I might need him still." He brushed his parched dusty lips with a few drops of water.

Gaius wasn't sure where they were, but the sun lay to his right. They were heading north. He hoped the horse could carry them both to Castra-Augustus, though what they would do when they reached the abandoned fort he wasn't certain. He had left a small cache of water and food for any of Sevilius' men who might have survived and wandered in after their departure for Hamad Rus, but Marzuq was three day's hard ride from the fort and at least another twenty to Leptis Magna. Bearing news of Tribune Sevilius' death would not stand him in good stead with the garrison at Marzuq, but he couldn't bypass the city. It sat at the edge of the Great Sand Sea and only a well-organized caravan could reach the coast. He had arrived in Marzuq in just such a caravan and well understood the dangers the journey presented.

What could he tell them when he arrived? Could he tell them the Emperor's chosen had gone mad and tried to kill him? In the full light of day, the last moments inside the horrid warren seemed like a nightmare. Had he really seen a grotesque monster arise from the pit of Hades? It had to be so. There could be no other explanation for what occurred in the temple. He had seen the groping tentacles thrusting upwards from the floor, had seen the half-mad Sevilius ripped apart by them. He had stared into the primordial blood-red eyes of Nergal and felt his enmity to humans, perhaps all life.

If Sevilius were half-mad, then surely he was completely mad. How could he ever again watch a sunset and not dread what might lurk beyond the reach of the light? The thought sent chills coursing through his body in spite of the heat. He shuddered. Night would come all too soon, and with it the blood-hungry Inyosh. The amulet was no good without Rashid to control it, and Rashid hovered near death.

The ride through the storm had exhausted him. He removed Apollo's saddle and laid it on the sand. Then, his strength depleted, he sagged to the ground and slept.

He awoke with the sun stabbing his eyes. The sandstorm had passed. He shaded his eyes with his hand and noticed a bunch of dates hanging from one of the palms. He hadn't eaten for over a day, but he was more interested in their moisture to quench his thirst. He climbed up on Apollo's back and hacked off the limb off with his sword. Shoving one of the dates in his mouth, he bit down on it, realizing too late that the dates were not quite ripe. His gnawing hunger demanded some offering, some small token to appease it. He chewed on the unripe fruit and swallowed the bitter date seeds and all. The stringent sour juice puckered his swollen lips but eased the burn in his parched throat.

Rashid's eyes fluttered for a moment, and then opened. He looked around in confusion. Then his eyes settled on the bunch of dates Gaius had laid on the ground beside him. Rashid picked one up, sucked the moisture and flavor from the unripe date, and spat out the bitter pulp. Gaius poured the last of the water into his mouth.

"What is your plan, Roman?" he asked. His voice was weak but steady.

"We ride to Leptis Magna and warn the governor of the danger."

"You may go to Leptis Magna, but I may not. The creature will follow the amulet. It is aware of it now. I will not lead it into the midst of an unwary population of my people."

Gaius noticed the Berber made no mention of the Romans living in the city. "What do you propose?"

"That we march deep into the desert away from people. We lead *Nergal* and his dark army away from civilization. In this manner we do not increase the numbers of the creatures."

Gaius was disappointed. He had hoped the Rashid had a real plan. "That's it? March into the desert and die." He waved his arms around. "Why not die here in the comfort of this beautiful oasis?"

Rashid remained silent for a moment. "Perhaps we can lead Nergal and his minions back to the warren beneath the mountain at Hamad Rus."

Gaius choked on a bitter date seed. "Are you truly mad?" he shouted. "We barely escaped that foul place with our lives. Now, you propose we return."

"Hear me out, Roman. There are words my grandfather taught me when I was young but warned me against using. He did not explain, but I believe they summon a greater power from the amulet. If so, it might mean my death, but it may be sufficient to seal the creature inside the mountain. I would trade my life for my people." He stared at Gaius. "I am too weak to make the journey alone." He paused before adding, "It would probably mean your death as well, Centurion."

Gaius suspected as much. If what the Berber said were true, sacrificing their lives to stop the creatures would be the proper thing to do, but he had seen the sinister living shadows, had seen *Nergal.* He had sacrificed his entire Shadow Legion to obtain the information he now had. He had led them to their deaths with the promise that what they were acting for the honor of Rome. Rashid was a fool. Two men alone, especially a half-mad Centurion and a half-dead Berber prince, could not defeat the creature. What he proposed bordered on suicide, a futile gesture.

"No," he answered.

Rashid glared at him. "You refuse?"

"Yes, I refuse," Gaius snapped. He didn't like Rashid's accusatory tone. Let the Berber think him a coward if he wished. "Some mystical words your grandfather taught you that might increase the amulet's power; might, mind you, not will … I will not throw away my life on some tale from your childhood. Your amulet can kill the shadow creatures, but I harbor no such hope against *Nergal*.

"Look at you. Your pitiful appearance puts doubt to your claim of powerful savior. You can barely sit, much less ride. You might not live out the day." He fought back a sob, remembering the screams of his slaughtered men. "I have watched my men die all around me, and yet I survive. If the gods have saved me for anything, it is to bring warning to Leptis Magna so that more Legions can be brought to bear on this new enemy."

"You do not trust me," Rashid said.

"No, I do not trust you," Gaius shouted. The Berber had struck at the heart of the matter. "You care nothing for Romans, and your people are dead; therefore, why would you throw away your life? To save more Roman lives?"

He shook his head and began pacing in the sand. His nervous anger bothered Apollo, who raised and dipped his head while snorting. Gaius stopped and rested his hand on the horse's neck, but sensing his master's agitation, he remained wary.

Rashid grimaced as he moved his body slightly to see Gaius' face hidden behind Apollo's neck. "Can your legions with all their shining brass armor, sharp weapons, their trumpets sounding, and their banners held high stop *Nergal*? Send a thousand men, and the dark army would increase by that thousand. Neither Roman siege engines nor frontal attack by armored cavalry will defeat the *Inyosh* god. He is arcane power manifest and only such power can affect him. You are a fool to think your army can do what armies through the centuries have been unable to achieve."

Exhausted by his speech, he fell back gasping for breath.

Gaius eyed the Berber with suspicion. "What do you mean the creatures would increase? We killed hundreds in the caverns. Surely there is a limit to their number."

A deep rumble that might have been laughter rose in Rashid's throat. "Do you not see it yet, Roman?" he barked. "The creatures replenish their numbers from our living ranks. The spirits of the dead they kill become the undead. Their useless flesh, blood, and bones become an offering to their god." He began coughing, sending a spasm of pain wracking his body. When the coughs subsided, he continued, "Why do you think I am so tortured, Centurion Gaius Marcus Linneus? Each creature I see I must wonder if it is the shade of my beloved wife or children."

Speaking brought a renewed spasm of pain to him. He doubled over and held his ribs, coughing into his hand. The Berber's words stunned Gaius. He had not considered what fate had befallen his men beyond their deaths. Would he now face the shade of Flavius or the ghost of demented Sevilius in the form of a deadly shadow? How could they defeat an enemy that increased its ranks by assimilating the shades of the dead?

"Why did you not tell me this sooner?" Gaius demanded.

"What would you have done, Centurion? Would you have ended your mad quest to defeat another enemy and return to Rome as conquering hero?"

As he spoke, Rashid dabbed at spots of blood dotting his lips. More blood stained the hand he had used to cover his cough. He sucked in air like a furnace bellows heating iron for sword making. Gaius had seen such symptoms before. One of Rashid's fractured ribs had punctured a lung. Such wounds more often than not meant a slow death as blood filled the lungs.

"Very well," he said, "raise your Berber army. Feed them to the creatures if you must. You cannot survive without me, and I ride to Marzuq, and then on to Leptis Magna. We will depart as soon as you are able."

Rashid attempted to rise to his feet. The color drained from his face and he fell back onto the sand, clenching his teeth against the pain and gasping for breath at the effort. Gaius looked at the Berber and shook his head, marveling at his determination.

"You might not live to leave this oasis."

"I will make it. By the shades of my dead wife and child, I will make it, and I will return with my people to end this monster's reign."

"First, we must reach Marzuq," Gaius reminded him. He stepped to the Berber's side, wondering why he bothered keeping him alive. "I must rearrange your bandage or you will die. You might die anyway. I have rendered aid on the battlefield, but I am no physician."

Rashid didn't protest as he loosened the bandage and moved it higher up Rashid's chest, but when he began knotting it beneath Rashid's first rib, he howled in pain.

"Perhaps you should pray to your god, if praying to a Roman god distresses you."

"You Romans stole your gods from the Greeks, as you do everything you desire."

In reply, Gaius jerked the bandage tight and finished the knot, extracting another yelp of pain from Rashid. "That might help," he said.

Rashid didn't answer. The pain had been too much. He had lapsed into unconsciousness. Gaius hoped the additional pressure would pull the rib away from the lung. He could do nothing for the wound itself. It would seal in due course, or Rashid would die. It was in the gods' hands. *As is my fate.*

With nothing better to do, Gaius lay down in the shade of a date palm and slept.

When he awoke, the sun had traversed over half the sky. His shade had migrated away from his place of rest, and the sun's rays beat down on him with a fury only a dedicated enemy should possess, not a disinterested celestial orb. His sleep had been fitful, but he had no dreams of Nergal or his dark minions. A demon thirst possessed his body. He would have killed for a single sip of water or a taste of wine. He looked at Rashid to check his condition. The Berber still lived, and his breathing had improved. Gaius had mixed emotions about that. The Berber prince was a thorn in his side, a conscience he didn't need, but fate had thrown them together for a purpose, and he felt more lay in store for them.

He shook Rashid awake. "Come. We must go, Berber."

Rashid's eyes flickered open. At first, he stared at the face above him without recognition; then, as his mind cleared, he frowned. "It is you, Roman. I thought you might have left me for the *tamdda* to devour."

Gaius glanced up at the vultures that had been circling the oasis since the storm passed. "It was a thought. Can you ride?"

"We shall see," Rashid replied and pushed up from the sand with his arms.

With Gaius' aid, he rose to stand, leaning against the tree. Gaius brought Apollo to him, laced his fingers to support Rashid's foot, and boosted him up on Apollo's back. He grabbed the saddle, and leaped onto the horse's back. Once astraddle the horse, Rashid's strength failed him. He swooned, falling back unconscious into Gaius' arms. Gaius patted Apollo's neck affectionately. It would be a difficult journey for the horse, double-burdened as he was.

"One more trip, old friend, and I will release you from my service. You have been faithful and loyal."

The horse snickered and stamped his front hooves in the sand. Gaius thought once more of his family and his home in Italy, doubting he would ever see either again, and then dismissed them to concentrate on reaching Marzuq.

They rode north throughout the remainder of the day without stopping for rest. Gaius kept Apollo's pace to a slow walk, detesting the pace that would add hours to their journey, but necessary to conserve the horse's strength. Reeling with heat exhaustion, his mind wandered to far places – His home, Rome, Parthia, dreaded Hamad Rus. Only when an image so grotesque, so real popped into his mind that it frightened him, did he jerk awake. He opened his eyes expecting to see *Nergal* standing before him, ready to devour him. Instead, Apollo stood on the crest of a dune stamping his right hoof in the sand trying to get his attention.

Gaius starred down into a small basin below the crest of the dune upon a sight than warmed his heart – a Roman eagle flying atop a standard. The golden eagle did not travel before a legion; only nine men on horses rode beneath it, but that didn't matter to Gaius. One of the men was Tesserarius Marcellus Quintus. Another was Sesquiplecarus Dracus Armis. Four of Sevilius' men accompanied them, as well as the surviving Tebu auxilia leading two packhorses. Marcellus recognized Apollo and waved his sword in the air. Gaius urged Apollo down the dune's steep slope. The shifting sands made the horse's footing treacherous. Gaius clasped Rashid to him to prevent him toppling from Apollo's back.

Marcellus rode forward to meet them.

"Ho, Centurion Gaius Linneus," he called out. "I thought you dead with the others." He eyed the unconscious Berber with undisguised suspicion.

"Marcellus, help Rashid from my horse. Be careful of his broken ribs."

Marcellus dropped from his horse and directed the three Tebu to help Rashid down, while Dracus held Apollo steady.

"How did you escape Hamad Rus?" Gaius asked.

"We waited for your return, but when the earth began to tremble, most of the Tebu scattered in terror. Only these three remained. Shortly afterwards, a lone legionnaire, badly injured, emerged from the cavern with a tale of death and destruction before dying in my arms. I wanted to enter and find you, but I remembered your order and set out for Marzuq to warn them of what we had discovered." He stood at attention and saluted with his clenched fist across his chest. "Your orders, Centurion."

Gaius smiled at Marcellus' stoicism. He suspected the grizzled veteran had dozens of questions he wished to ask, but had set them aside as information unnecessary for the completion of his duty. Gaius was glad. He couldn't yet bring himself to describe what he had witnessed in the bowels of the earth. The horrors too fresh, he feared the recounting of events still unclear in his own mind would make him sound insane to his tesserarius who had not seen them. He faced Sesquiplecarus Dracus.

"Dracus Armis. I want you, two of the legionnaires, and the three

Tebu to ride ahead to Marzuq and report to the commander, Sunio Atticus, the destruction of our garrison at Castra-Augustus and the death of Tribune Sevilius and his centuriae. Warn them that Rome now faces a new enemy, more steadfast and deadly than the Garamnates or the Numidians. We now face a shadow army immune to any weapon save fire. They will not believe you, but report it anyway. I will write a letter and affix my seal. That should save you from reprisal from the disbelief of Praetor Augustus."

"Sir," Dracus said with a pained expression, "I would ride with you." He waved his hand at Antonius Cossus. "Let this man deliver your message."

"Antonius is a good legionnaire, but he is a mere foot soldier without rank. No one would believe these barbarians bearing such a tale. Only a Roman officer can deliver this report. A single sword, regardless of how skillfully you wield it, will not help us in our endeavor to reach Marzuq. I will keep Antonius and one other with me. If we fail, Rome must have warning."

Dracus nodded. "I will report as ordered." He backed away to converse with the three auxilia.

"Marcellus, my veteran friend, we enter the lion's den with this journey." He stared Marcellus directly in his eyes. "It will likely mean our deaths."

Marcellus grinned as he stroked his eye patch. "I have given much for the Empire. I would give all if needed."

Gaius threw his leg over Apollo's back and leaped down, stretching his back to ease his tight muscles from his long, cramped journey. It took him a long moment to realize his leg had not protested his dismount. He moved it experimentally a few times and felt only a dull ache. He had no time to marvel at its rapid healing.

"If nothing else, we will draw the enemy to us to ease young Dracus' journey to Marzuq. First things first. Do you have food, Marcellus?"

"Some native swill, such as it is, but it fills an empty belly. We have wine." He smiled. "I would not leave it to the shadow creatures."

"Good. We will eat and drink our fill; then, we ride north slowly. We do not wish to outpace our enemy."

As the others feasted on fruit, warm porridge, and wine, Gaius took parchment and penned two letters, one to Sunio Atticus in Marzuq; the second to the governor of Leptis Magna. Finding the right words was difficult. Though Romans openly declared their faith in the gods, in reality few believed in gods or demons. How could they believe in creatures such as *Nergal* or shadowy wraiths? He didn't include the descent into madness of Tribune Sevilius. Trampling upon his memory would serve no purpose.

He stated that the Berbers were not responsible for the Roman deaths, not that he believed the Praetor would heed his words, but he had promised Rashid. When he finished, he called Dracus to him and handed him the letter. He removed his family crest signet ring and caressed it with his fingers before dropping it into Dracus' hand.

"If I do not arrive in Marzuq, send this ring to my uncle in Ischia. Tell my family I died honorably. Divide the supplies and take one of the packhorses. I will need the other for our Berber friend. Ride fast, Sesquiplecarus."

Dracus took the ring and placed it inside his tunic. "I will not fail."

Mounting their horses, Dracus Armis, two of Sevilius' legionnaires, and the three Tebu auxilia rode away over the dunes. When they had vanished from sight, Gaius turned to Marcellus.

"They should have a safe journey. The creatures will turn their attention toward us."

"That is a comforting thought."

"Now, my friend. I would have food and wine. When night falls, I fear we shall be too busy for dining."

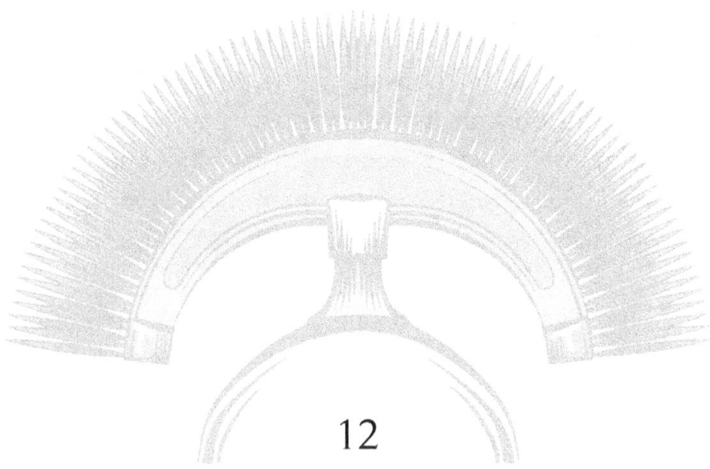

12

Gaius allowed Rashid to sleep as long as possible to recuperate from his injury, but a few hours after the sun had vanished and the darkness had thickened into a viscous curtain of shadows the air changed, becoming chilled and unnaturally still. The hairs on his arm rose to attention as if a summer thunderstorm were approaching, an unlikely event in the deep desert. Marcellus noticed him scanning the crests of the dunes, frowned, and slid his sword from his scabbard. He kicked Antonius Cossus in the rump to wake him and the other soldier sleeping beside him.

"It is time to earn your pay, legionnaire," he said.

Before Gaius could rouse Rashid, his eyes opened. "They have come," he said.

Gaius nodded. "I think so."

"Help me to sit upright."

He levered the Berber into a sitting position and shoved one of the saddles behind his back to prop him up. Gaius looked into the Berber's eyes and saw pain. "Are you well enough to use your amulet?"

"If I am not, we shall learn soon enough," he replied.

He pulled the amulet from his robes. The stone glowed softly like the moon's shadow on still water. As he recited a few arcane phrases in the ancient tongue of its creators, it sparked to life, casting a faint blue aura of light across the narrow basin. The weaker brightness of the amulet dismayed Gaius. In the warren, the light had blazed like a fire. The amulet was not only their sole weapon; it also provided their only light. They had no fire. They carried but two torches and no oil or wood to make more. Gaius wished to hold them in reserve in case Rashid's condition worsened. From the looks of the Berber, tonight might be that time.

"They are but a few," Rashid said. "They are scouts rather than an army." His voice fell to an almost whisper. "One or a hundred, it does not matter. I have little strength left."

Gaius had an idea. "In the warren you touched my sword with the amulet, and it glowed with the same blue light as the stone. Can you do it again?"

Rashid looked thoughtful for a moment. "I can but try."

"Better make it quick," Marcellus called out.

The crests of the surrounding dunes were dotted with black shapes visible against the dark background only by the faint starlight behind them. Gaius counted ten; more than enough to finish the job they had started beneath the mountain at Hamad Rus. Brief flashes of red pierced the darkness as the creatures' eyes focused on their quarry. The wind carried a soft keening that increased in volume as the creatures slid noiselessly down the slope and circled the camp just outside the reach of the blue light.

The creatures drew closer. Marcellus retreated to stand beside Gaius and Rashid. Antonius Cossus and his companion stood a short distance away, as if fearing the Berber as much as the Inyosh. The pair exchanged nervous glances and appeared ready to run, but to their credit as legionnaires, they remained steadfast, moving in to stand on either side of Marcellus. Marcellus' extended sword arm tracked the creatures' movements, but Gaius knew it posed no threat to the amorphous shadow creatures.

He glanced over his shoulder at Rashid. "If you are going to do something, Berber, do it now or we die."

Rashid spoke a few more words. Their utterance brought contortions of agony to his face. Their echoes lingered in the air like exhaled breath on a frigid day, multiplying, growing louder until they reached a crescendo. The amulet burst into azure flames that danced on the warped tip of each of its five points. Gaius touched the tip of his blade to one of the five points, and it, too, exploded into flames. From such a cerulean conflagration, he expected to feel heat in the sword, but it remained cool to the touch.

He experienced a strange connection to the stone within the amulet, a prickling sensation that extended up his arm, through his shoulder, and into his chest, the center of his being. The air around him seemed to brighten, as if more wood had added to the nonexistent fire. He realized that the power of the amulet allowed him to pierce the shadowy veil surrounding the creatures and to see them more clearly. He knew that if he concentrated hard enough, he would discern their true being. He wasn't sure he wanted too that badly.

"You next," he told Marcellus.

The old warrior stared at the flames in awe and in fear but recognized that the azure fire was the enemy of the creatures. With a quick thrust, he touched his sword to the flames of the amulet. Antonius Cossus added his sword more reluctantly, almost dropping it when the azure fire danced on his blade. His companion followed suit. Now, they had four weapons ablaze. Rashid gasped a heavy sigh and collapsed onto the sand. His part in the coming battle had ended. The light of the amulet extinguished, but the swords blazed brightly.

The Inyosh shades, seeing the amulet grow cold, attacked. Standing back to back over Rashid's unconscious body, Gaius, Marcellus, and the two legionnaires fought back. One of the creatures shot at Gaius from the darkness. With its shroud of darkness gone, he aimed for the center of its body, where he hoped its black heart resided and thrust. To his delight, he impaled it up to the hilt of his sword. A ragged blue line, like a crack in a vase, appeared where sword met shadow. The creature's mouth opened wider as it wailed in surprise and pain, so wide Gaius thought the creature would turn inside out. It burst into azure flame and exploded, showering both men with black ash. Working together, the four of them quickly dispatched three more of the creatures.

Then, the wraiths changed tactics and went for the horses. Two of them leaped onto the back of the packhorse like a pair of hyenas. The horsed reared and pawed at the air trying to throw them off, its eyes wide with panic. It did no good. Within seconds, black tendrils had penetrated the horse's flesh, drawing from it its life essence. The packhorse fell to the ground thrashing the sand with its flailing legs, and then lay still.

"We must save the horses," Gaius said. Afoot, they would never reach Castra-Augustus, let alone Marzuq.

Marcellus nodded and tapped Antonius Cossus on the shoulder. Together, they raced to the horses' defense. They fought off shadows attacking singly and in pairs, while Gaius and the other soldier kept watch over Rashid. The creatures retained the cunning of their human origins, feinting here and attacking there. Gaius slew another of the creatures, but he knew at some point one would get through their defenses. Out of the corner of his eye, he saw one preparing to attack Marcellus' back.

"Behind you, Marcellus," he yelled.

Marcellus swung around, but Antonius Cossus acted more quickly. He delivered a two-handed blow to the creature's head, cleaving it in half before it reached Marcellus. The wraith exploded into powder.

"Thank you for my life," Marcellus said.

"I may have given you only a brief respite. The creatures are determined to end it."

They stood back to back defending the horses.

Gaius' companion watched the exchange and allowed his attention to lapse for a split second, just long enough for one of the creatures to rush past his defenses and envelop him within its ebony folds. Through the shadowy veil, Gaius witnessed the creature's maw open wide, exposing hundreds of tiny, jagged teeth. The mouth closed over the legionnaire's head, severing it from his body. Blood spilled down the creature's featureless form before being absorbed into its mass. It rushed away, still embracing the dead man in its shadowy grasp.

The horrific sight sickened Gaius. If the men of his Shadow Legion had witnessed the gruesome manner of their companions' deaths and not just their sudden disappearance, they would have fled the desert long ago. He grimaced at the thought of more blood filling the black altar stone at Hamad Rus.

Now, three of the creatures came at him. He killed one and fended off the other two, but they maneuvered him away from Rashid's side. One flanked him and rushed at the unconscious Berber. As Gaius raced to intercept the creature, he felt certain Rashid would die in the next moment, dooming them all. To his amazement, as the shadowy creature touched the Berber, his body burst into a brilliant azure glow. Waves of power danced along his body like the flames of a taper, undulating slowly, growing larger and brighter. Then, like ripples from a stone cast into a pond, waves of brilliant azure radiance poured from his body, swept across the small basin, and washed over the dunes. The creature attacking him wailed and began vibrating rapidly, its shadowy outline blurring. Then, it vanished, leaving no fire, smoke, or black ash. It was simply gone.

As the waves of arcane power passed through Gaius' body, they left a slightly unpleasant tingle that resonated with the fluttering of power within his chest, but no heat. His *gladius* blazed brighter for a moment; then faded. So did the prickling in his chest. He felt empty inside, as if someone had reached inside and yanked out his heart.

The remaining Inyosh did not fare as well. Their blood-red eyes focused on the Berber's glowing body. Gaius thought he could detect fear in them. The first ripple of power passed through them, immobilizing them, as if skewered by an invisible blade. The ensuing ripples produced the same results as with the first creature. The small depression filled with high keening wails that passed beyond the range of human hearing. Then, like a flame blown by pursed lips, they went out, disappeared as if they had never existed.

Gaius staggered backwards and used his sword jabbed into the sand to steady him while he fought for breath. He stared down at the Berber's body. As the last ripple passed beyond the rim of the dunes, the glow enveloping him retreated, drawn back into the amulet as a sponge absorbs water. The light of the amulet smoldered for a moment, then extinguished. The amulet had protected its unconscious bearer's body with a different kind of energy than that displayed when wielded consciously by Rashid. Gaius wondered of what else it might be capable.

Marcellus sat on the ground, his sword stuck into the sand between his legs. He stared at the Berber's prostate body as if waiting for another miracle. "Are they gone?" he asked Gaius.

Gaius nodded. "I think they are vanquished."

Marcellus leaned back and rested on his elbows. His chest heaved from his exertions. "I have never seen such in my lifetime. This dealing with Berber magic, shadowy wraiths, and ancient gods is too much for an old legionnaire. Perhaps when this is all over, I will retire to a small house surrounded by trees and lakes in Tuscany with two nubile servant wenches to tend to my needs and a dog by my side."

Gaius sensed Marcellus needed to talk, to relieve his mind of the enormity of what he had witnessed. "You are not from Tuscany," Gaius commented.

"No, I was born in Gaul and brought to Rome to train as a gladiator, but as a legionnaire I passed through Tuscany once on the way to put an end to pesky Germanic raids in Noricum across the Adriatic Sea. Tuscany is a beautiful countryside. The wine is excellent, the maidens plump and large bosomed, and there is no sand within eyesight." He reached down, scooped up a handful of sand, let it sift through his fingers, and scowled. "This accursed sand covers much but uncovers things best left hidden from view, things I wish I could somehow unsee."

Gaius agreed with Marcellus' assessment. Two weeks ago, his only concern had been regaining his honor. Now, he struggled for not only his life, but for the life of the Roman Empire. That the fate of the Empire rested in the hands of two tired old veterans, a mystical Berber prince near death, and a dishonored legionnaire Legatii struck him as ironic. He caught the attention of Antonius Cossus, who still stood sword in hand staring at the dunes, as if he was unsure the battle was over.

"Antonius, when you have rested, see to the horses. I will tend to the Berber." He glanced around him. He no longer felt danger, but his sense of unease did not go away. To Marcellus, he said, "We should leave this place before more of these monsters find us."

Marcellus rose to his feet and brushed off the sand. "I can rest astride my horse." He went to the horses and helped Antonius saddle them, whispering to them and stroking their backs to calm their nervousness.

Gaius poured a little water into the palm of his hand and wiped it across Rashid's forehead. Rather than fevered as he expected to find it, his flesh was cool. Rashid opened his eyes.

"You are no *imalayka*," he said. He rose up and reached for the water skin in Gaius' hand. "No, an angel you are not, but your gift of water is a blessing." He took a long swig of water and sighed. "They are gone?"

Gaius nodded. "You don't remember?"

Rashid looked puzzled. "I remember using all my remaining strength to summon flame to your swords, and then …" He shook his head. "I recall nothing more."

"The amulet awakened and saved you, saved us."

Rashid glanced down at the amulet and frowned. "I think it spoke to me in my sleep. I do not understand the words, but the voice felt," He groped for a word, "reassuring."

"The power of the amulet swept out from here across the dunes. The others might have sensed it. We must ride before more come."

He reached to help Rashid to his feet. To Gaius' surprise, the Berber stood with no assistance. At his startled expression, Rashid looked down at his body. His fingers probed his injured side, and then he smiled.

"It seems I am healed," he exclaimed. "I feel no pain at all."

"More Berber magic," Marcellus mumbled from near the horses, clearly not approving.

"Your amulet healed you," Gaius said, "just as it protected you from the Inyosh." He stared at Rashid. "What else did your grandfather tell you about the amulet?"

Rashid's forehead wrinkled in thought. "He called it a sigil against evil." He stared into the amulet as if trying to extract meaning from the stone in its center. Gaius touched his shoulder to bring him back to the present. Rashid looked up and said, "He said it is a living thing."

"Living?"

"He said no more than that. I believe he was frightened of it, but knew he must pass down the lore of it." He frowned. "I think the stone forced him to."

Marcellus came over with the horses. "I gave them what water I could spare and some of that foul tasting Tebu mush. They wrinkled their noses in disgust but ate it." He handed Gaius and Rashid strips of dried goat meat and a piece of bread. "It is damnable chewy but provides nourishment." He eyed Rashid's condition. "I thought we would be tying you across your horse, Berber. You look haler than do I."

"His amulet," Gaius said.

Marcellus bit off a piece of jerked goat, raised the eyebrow above his missing eye, and said, "Aye, the amulet." He turned to walk away as if that were explanation enough.

Gaius marveled at Rashid's improved condition. He exhibited no outward signs of his injury. He moved nimbly, and his breathing sounded regular. By all appearances, he was as fit and healthy as any man could ever hope to be. The Berber took the small miracle of his rejuvenation in stride, but Gaius couldn't help but feel daunted by his unnatural recovery. Until now, Gaius had considered the amulet only as a potent weapon against Nergal and his wraith minions. Now, he had to wonder if the amulet's power might be a threat to Rome as well. A Berber army or any army capable of quickly healing their wounds would be a formidable foe.

The four men mounted their horses and rode north. Their mounts were eager to be free of the stink of the area, and Gaius felt as they did. Though the night was dark and the wraiths could find them anywhere, he felt better riding across the flat sand sea than among the dunes.

The remainder of the night passed without incident. They rode straight through until dawn before resting. During his southward journey from Leptis Magna to Castra-Augustus, Gaius had little bothered to observe his surroundings. His mind had been seething with disgust and resentment at his recent demotion and exile to Tripolitania. Then, it had been an endless, featureless expanse of sand, each league an identical twin to the previous leagues. Now, he awoke to the beauty of the region.

True, it was arid; broiling hot by day and chilling at night, and inhospitable to traveler and local inhabitants alike, but it possessed an indefinable quality that no other place had. Even in the deserts of Mesopotamia, though vast and uninviting, he had never felt such loneliness. Thriving cities, the ruins of ancient cities, small villages, and caravan roads scattered throughout the region like handfuls of stones cast onto a courtyard. They were remote and far between, but never had he spent more than two nights camped in the desert before encountering some inn, village, or oasis with bed, food, and water – A land that did not welcome travelers, but tolerated them.

The vast sand sea sweeping from Marzuq south into the heart of the Sahara was antagonistic toward life. Since the days centuries ago when the area had been wet and welcoming, the relentless climate and encroaching sand slowly swallowed everything it touched, grinding it into more sand and dust to further extend its reaches. The Roman Empire's claim to Tripolitania and Cyrenaica consisted of cities along the coast, a few towns situated along trade routes, and scattered castras like Castra-Augustus comprising the *Lime Tripolitanus.*

In truth, the Sahara itself was a vast, self-sustaining *lime*, a natural fortress of sand, scorpions, and sun more secure than any Roman-built wall of stone and sod, or wooden palisade. Vast sand-sea *ergs*, rocky *hamadas*, gravel-strewn *serirs*, salt-choked *chotts*, dry *wadis*, and impassable high *promontoria* – All acted as barriers to invading armies and intrepid explorers alike.

Perhaps by surviving the desert one began to understand it and appreciate its stark beauty. Each dune differed from its neighbor as two pebbles on the beach, each oasis a distinctive Eden, offering a diverse harbor for wandering men and beasts. Sandstorms, heat mirages, scuttling clouds all became daubs of paint on a sand-covered canvas. Each quartz crystal granule of sand sparkled like jewels in the Emperor's crown.

When Gaius caught sight of abandoned Castra-Augustus, now just an exposed rocky rib of the earth protruding through the soil, a jumble of mixed emotions passed through his mind. It had been his home for only days, but it saddened him to see it barren and empty with its unfinished stone wall, latrine, and its rubbish heap attracting vultures and rodents the only reminders that humans had once lived there.

Marcellus brought his horse alongside Gaius. "I hope young Dracus Armis didn't drink all the wine we left buried." He wiped his mouth with the back of his hand. "This tepid, sour desert water leaves my thirst unquenched."

Gaius patted Apollo's neck. "I am more concerned that they left oats for the horses. It is still a long ride to Marzuq."

As they entered the compound, Gaius felt the ghosts of the dead staring at him, as if silently asking why he had allowed them to die. He had no ready answer. Men died in battles. Only the outcome would determine if their deaths had been gloriously spent or foolishly sacrificed.

"We remain only long enough to eat and rest the horses," he said. "Then, we ride on."

The well was dry. It had finally given up its last precious drops of water and died. The tiny oasis could easily replenish itself after occasional use, but couldn't withstand the abuse of a permanent Roman encampment. Gaius knew it would never come back. Now, thirsty travelers and local wildlife would have no place to drink. One more death Rashid could blame on the Romans.

Two full water skins, salted meat, dried fruit, and stale bread, as well as oats and honey for the horses, remained in the buried cache of supplies. They unsaddled the horses, groomed, and fed them before tending to their own needs. The horses were more important to their survival than food or water. They rested through the heat of the day until just before sunset. As he lay there, Gaius felt slight, rhythmic tremors through the rock. Before an hour had passed, the vibrations became more noticeable. He knew their source and quailed.

"How can Nergal move so quickly?" he asked Rashid. "Surely such a ponderous creature must move slowly."

"It is said the earth is hollow with many deep tunnels leading throughout its width and breadth. Nergal travels through these. His domain is the deep earth. He draws strength and nourishment from the stone, as we draw it from the food we eat. He needs no rest or sleep. His pursuit is relentless. If we tarry, he will overtake us."

"Then we sleep in the saddle until we reach Marzuq." Gaius stood and buckled on his balteus and sword.

Antonius Cossus took a swig from the wine skin he and Marcellus shared. "Must we ride so soon? I am a foot soldier unused to horses. My backside burns like a desert fever."

"If you knew what followed us, Antonius, you would be on your horse by now."

Antonius Cossus stared at Gaius for a moment; and then, rose and saddled his horse.

"Come," Gaius said. "We will find no rest until we reach the walls of Marzuq."

In his heart, he doubted even the solid walls of Marzuq would be enough to deter Nergal's wrath.

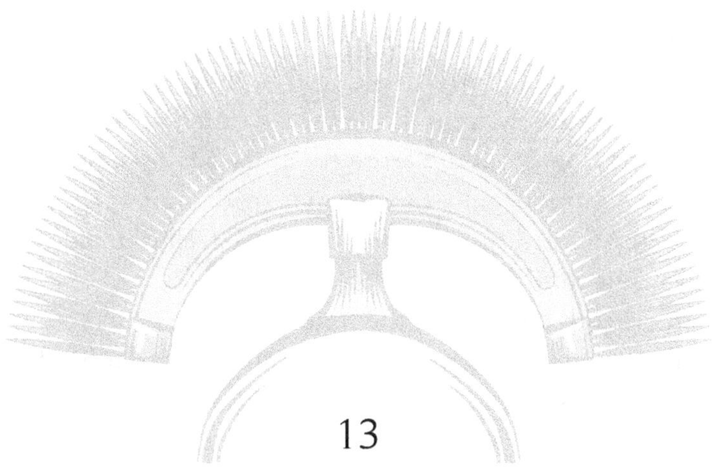

13

For two days and nights they rode, stopping only long enough to feed, water, and rest the horses. They dozed in the saddle, ate, and drank in the saddle. Conversation required too much energy, so they rode in silence. The heat savaged them by day, and the cold sucked out their life force by night. They were more automatons than men when they approached the walls of Marzuq on the morning of the third day.

The gentle swaying of the date palm trees in the breeze hypnotized Gaius as he sat astride Apollo and stared at the buff stone walls of the garrison. Around it, like young chicks at the feet of the mother hen, buildings of bleached, sun-baked brick, blocks of pink or buff stone, and tents of all shapes and sizes fought for proximity to the garrison's walls, creating a warren of narrow alleyways teeming with people, camels, horses, and carts. Tables of food, spices, jewelry, cloth, and weapons ate up what little space remained. The sight of so much life seemed alien to Gaius after his weeks in the deep desert.

As he watched, a squad of legionnaires rode out from the gates of the garrison to meet them. His unshaven face, filthy body, and tattered clothing wouldn't make a good impression, but he could do nothing about it. He straightened himself in his saddle and waited. The young officer, a *Principale* of undetermined rank, perhaps *optio centuriae* by his bearing, dressed in full armor except for helmet, stopped in front of him, withdrew a scroll from his tunic, and read from it.

"Centurion Gaius Marcus Linneus, by order of Praefectus Titilus Pontius Calidus, you are under arrest for crime against the Republic."

The officer motioned to the six men with him. They drew their swords and surrounded Gaius' small band. Marcellus' hand went to his sword, but Gaius stopped him.

"No, my friend. Now is not the time to die."

Marcellus scowled, reversed his sword, and handed it hilt first to one of the guards. Gaius and Antonius Cossus did the same.

To the young officer, Gaius said, "Did not Sesquiplecarus Dracus Armis arrive with my missive to the garrison commander, Sunio Atticus?"

The officer's face soured. "Praefectus castrorum Sunio Atticus is not here. He left for Leptis Magna a week ago. His wife is ill with the plague."

Gaius was aghast. "With Tribune Sevilius absent, he left the garrison without a commander? Who is in charge?"

"Praefectus Titilus Pontius Calidus."

"But he is the civil authority. Who commands the legion?"

"Myself and two other optio."

"By the gods," he snapped. "Did Dracus deliver my letter to the Praefectus?"

The young *optio* frowned. "He did, and with it a tale so unbelievable it bordered on jest. Even after twenty lashes from the flagellum ordered by the Praefectus, he refused to change his story."

Gaius fumed. "Tribune Sevilius Antonius Livinius is dead, as is his entire double-centuria, wiped out by these creatures of which my letter spoke. They march on Marzuq. We must prepare to meet them."

"We all know of your *gradus dejectio*, Gaius Linneus. Tribune Sevilius was much loved and respected in this garrison. The demise of two centuriae has left the garrison undermanned. We will not tolerate your perfidy with this Berber dog."

The officer made as if to strike Rashid with his sword.

Gaius held out his hand. "Stop! Strike him and you will die, *optio*."

"Do not threaten me, prisoner," he replied gruffly.

"Your prisoner I may be, and your men may kill me, but if you strike this man, I assure you, you will die."

The officer reconsidered, sheathed his sword, and motioned to the guards. They herded Gaius and his party before them through the narrow, winding streets to the gates of the garrison. Men stared down at them from the walls, their faces displaying their loathing. They, too, had heard of his letter, and like the Praefectus, refused to believe. Gaius noticed the sentries were spaced twenty paces apart, leaving large gaps in the defenses. Their escorts delivered them to the stables, a long, brick structure against the rear wall of the garrison. The stench of horse manure ripening in the sweltering heat assaulted Gaius' nostrils. The reek of urine from the latrine standing next to it added to the acrid pall. The open buckets for collecting urine for the laundry buzzed with flies, for which the alkaline urine was as delectable as vinegary wine to the soldiers.

At one end of the building, a heavy wooden door opened into a small room once used as a tact room for saddles, bridals, and reins. Now, it held only a small desk, a chair, and a wall with wooden pegs from which an assortment of flagellum and iron manacles hung. Gaius didn't envy the post of *optio carceris*, the jailer, in the unhealthy environment. He was certain only a low-ranking *milite* would draw such a disagreeable duty with extra pay and an outlet for sadistic tendencies the only benefits. A second doorway led into a narrow L-shaped corridor. They were pushed and shoved down the corridor until it ended at a large empty room save for two holes in the floor, each barely wide enough for a man to pass through. Gaius stared into the hole and backed away as the stench overwhelmed his senses.

"I demand to see the Praefectus," he yelled.

"The Praefectus will not see you, *fustuarium*."

Gaius shuddered. *Fustuarium* were crushed to death with heavy stones or beaten to death with cudgels. "We are sentenced to death with no hearing, no trial? Has the Republic fallen so low so quickly?"

The optio spat at him. "If I had been allowed, I would have run you through with my sword when I first met you. There is no room for cowards and traitors in the Legion. Your treachery threatens us all. Now, into the hole, or I will have the guards drop you in head first."

Gaius stared at the officer but knew he could not reach him. His superiors had deemed Gaius a traitor, and he had no reason to question them. Their Tribune was dead and they had no other enemy to blame but him. "Very well," he said and stepped off into space.

The floor of the prison was eight feet below the hole. He hit the rough stone heavily and fell against the wall. His face and hand came away wet and sticky, coated with moss, algae, and other substances too foul to guess at their origin. He moved aside just in time to avoid being struck by Marcellus and Rashid as they followed him into their prison.

"What of Antonius Cossus?" he yelled up through the hole. "He is one of Sevilius' men."

"He will join your sesquiplecarus in the next cell."

"What of the Tebu auxilia who accompanied Dracus?"

"Auxilia?" The officer laughed. "Surely you jest. The barbarian scum were killed as soon as they entered the city bearing Roman weapons. Soon, you will join them, as will the Berber."

Gaius sat down and leaned against the wall. He quickly regretted his decision. Decades of filth coated the slimy wall. The murder of the innocent Tebu infuriated him. They had joined the legion, served honorably, and deserved a better end. "It seems our warning was not heeded."

"Aye," Marcellus said. "We should have ridden straight to the coast and across the sea."

"This is my land, Roman," Rashid reminded him. "I have no other place to go. If *Nergal* comes, which he will, he will suck this country dry of life before moving on. I should have returned to my people to fight with them. We will die in this place."

"Titilus Calidus will speak with me soon," Gaius said with more conviction than he felt. "He'll have to. Once the Praefectus understands ..."

Rashid's sharp grunt of derision interrupted him. "He will never understand, Centurion. His mind is closed, as yours was. It took the deaths of your men to open yours. It will take the destruction of this town to open his. Then, it will be too late."

"I'll find a way out of this prison."

"What would you do to escape, Centurion?" Rashid posed, staring at Gaius across the expanse of the room. His face looked chiseled from cold marble, but his eyes glowed hot and angry. "Would you kill fellow Romans to reach the Praefectus' side?"

"Do not answer him," Marcellus advised. "He is a crafty one. He will have you do his bidding."

"My bidding is the saving of my country from the ravages of *Nergal* and his army of wraith minions. I cannot do it from here." He turned to face Gaius once more.

Marcellus's warning had given Gaius time to consider his answer carefully. He knew what the Berber wanted him to say, and he knew of no way around it. "The lives of a few legionnaires or principales mean nothing to the safety of Rome. If you know of a way out of here, Berber, tell me."

Rashid walked to the far side of the room, picked the cleanest spot he could find on the filthy floor, and lay down. "Sleep now, Centurion. Soon, our time will come."

For two days, they lingered in their dark, stinking prison cell, eating the foul food dropped through the hole once a day, drinking water delivered in the same buckets horses drank from, and relieving themselves in the corner of the room. The stench of their own bodily wastes added to their miserable existence. Lice gnawed at their flesh by day, and rats and cockroaches scurried over their bodies by night. The wraith scratch on Marcellus' arm became inflamed. Pus oozed from beneath the scab, and the flesh around the wound turned a sickly yellow. Marcellus shrugged off the wound with his usual insouciance.

"One good eye and one good arm is all I need to serve you, Centurion. I can still caress a woman's breast while she feeds me or pours wine into my mouth. Two arms are overrated."

Each day, Gaius demanded to speak with the Praefectus. Each day, they refused him. He grew weary of his incarceration and wondered about Rashid's plan, but the Berber revealed nothing. He sat with his eyes closed most of the day either praying or sleeping, Gaius couldn't tell which.

Antonius Cossus, Sesquiplecarus Dracus Armis, and the remaining soldier resided in the cell across the large room. The conditions of their captivity were even worse than that suffered by Gaius and his companions. The guards treated Sevilius' men as if they were cowards instead of survivors. The wounds on Dracus' back from his scourging became severely infected. A fever wracked his body, and Gaius' appeals for a medicus to treat his wounds were ignored.

Gaius wondered why they were still alive, why Praefectus Titilus had not executed them immediately. At the very least, fustuariae were usually banished to wander the countryside with the sentence of death hanging over their heads. In the desert, that meant a slow death. If the Praefectus feared to kill him for fear of incurring the wrath of Marcus Aurelius, then he would send a message to the Emperor asking for instructions. That could take months. Gaius feared they would be dead before then. Nergal was fast approaching the city.

The absence of pain became the only redeeming quality of his incarceration. His stomach voiced its revulsion at the food served them, but no more gut-wrenching stabbing pains wracked his body. Even his thigh barely troubled him. He wondered if the azure magic of the amulet had affected him as it had Rashid.

At least I will die healthy and free of ailments.

On the morning of their third day of captivity, the young optio who had arrested them appeared in the opening above their heads. He peered down at them with disgust, wrinkling his nose at the stench. A few minutes later, the guards lowered a ladder into the room.

"You, Gaius Linneus," he called. "The Praefectus wishes to speak with you. The Berber is to come as well."

"Unless I have been stripped of my rank during my incarceration, you will address me as Centurion Gaius Linneus. I still outrank you. You may inform the Praefectus I will not come unless first, I bathe, and then you provide a clean uniform. I will not appear before him in these stinking rags. The Berber prince as well," he added.

The optio scowled at him. "You will come as ordered or my men will drag you out of your hole."

"Any of your men that enter this hole will not emerge alive," Gaius threatened.

The officer licked his lips as he considered his options for a moment or two, finally deciding not to test Gaius' threat. "Very well. The two of you may bath first, under guard, but be warned; the Praefectus is not pleased with you."

"The Praefectus has bigger issues to worry over, as *I* have warned *him*."

As he walked to the foot of the ladder, he spoke briefly to Marcellus sitting on the floor holding his infected arm in his lap. "I will insist on treatment for your wound."

"I would prefer wine," he replied.

Rashid pushed up close behind him and whispered, "The time has come, Centurion. Nergal is near. I can feel his presence."

The Berber shoved a metal object into his hand. He glanced down to see Rashid's dagger. He stared at Rashid. "How?"

"They did not ask, and I did not tell," he said. "I am not a Roman Legionnaire to relinquish my weapons on demand."

Gaius tucked the dagger into his tunic. "I will determine if and when to use it."

Rashid spread his hands wide. "Of course."

The bright sunlight outside the building hurt Gaius' eyes. He covered them with his grubby hand, noticing the accumulated dirt and gods only knew what else beneath his fingernails. An officer of the Legion couldn't always be fastidious in his hygiene, but the indignity of parading across the open ground of the fort wearing filthy rags and was more demeaning than his incarceration. Away from the stable and the latrine, the air smelled of oleander blossoms and tamarisk. Gaius inhaled deeply to flush the stench of the jail from his lungs. The broiling sun he had learned to hate baked his bare head, but warmed his spirits.

Nearer the barracks, the pungent aroma of turmeric and the fragrance of sweet *silphium* drifting from the open kitchen door flavored the air. *Silphium* had become the major export from Cyrenaica to Rome's households. He had tried its curative effects for his constant stomach ailments, but it had failed.

Outside the barracks, steam rose from a simple communal bath constructed of native stone. There were no boilers or furnaces for a *caldarium*, a hot bath. Young native boys stoked the fires beneath the raised *thermae* with kindling and dried camel dung to heat the *tepidarium*, the warm bath. The bath, primitive by Roman standards, perhaps even crude, lay open to the sky. It boasted no statuary or mosaics. It contained no atrium where friends could meet and converse or changing rooms. No musicians provided soothing music while bathers relaxed. No slaves provided food or wine. Soldiers had no need of such luxuries.

As small as the bath was, the waste of so much water in a desert must have dismayed the natives at what they considered a Roman affectation. Its water drew Gaius' gaze like the gyrations of a half-naked female dancer to a sex-starved legionnaire. He didn't resist when the guard shoved him in the back to keep him moving toward the bath.

"Stand here," one of them ordered, pointing to a spot just before the steps.

Two young boys brought buckets of cold water and set them at Gaius and Rashid's feet.

"Strip and wash off the stink before you enter the bath," the guard said.

Gaius and Rashid discarded their clothing, poured the water over their heads, and rubbed down their bodies with their hands as best they could, flaking away the last of the crusted goat's blood that had fouled his body for almost a week.

Tone guard scanned the numerous scars covering Gaius' body. "Now you may bathe," he said, but his voice no longer held as much disdain.

Gaius reached down to pick up his clothing.

"Leave that pile of filth," the other guard yelled. "We will burn them."

Gaius did not intend to re-don his foul uniform. He used the opportunity to secret the dagger in the palm of his palm. As he descended the steps into the warm waters of the bath, he laid it on the bottom step beneath the waterline. His skin felt as it would drain the bath, absorbing the life-giving water into his desiccated flesh. He used a pumice stone and a wooden *strigil* he found on the edge of the bath to scrape away the layers of accumulated filth, vigorously scrubbing his flesh until it became raw. He sat on the steps chest deep in the warm water, allowing it to ease his aching muscles, while regretting that he had no capsarii to massage them.

Rashid seemed uncomfortable in so much water. He scrubbed his body clean, but glared at the water around him as if it might come alive and drown him. After only five minutes of luxuriating, the guards ordered them out of the bath. Gaius stepped to the edge of the small *frigidarium* and leaped in feet first. The waters of the cold plunging pool were barely cooler than the waters of the warm bath, but he emerged feeling more refreshed and invigorated than he had in many weeks.

Clothes had been laid out for them; a simple native robe and sandals for Rashid, but for Gaius a white toga with red piping, underclothing, sandals, and a gold pin to hold the toga over his shoulder was provided. The patrician clothing surprised him. He had expected at most a soldier's plain tunic and sandals.

"The Praefectus must have more in mind than informing us of the time of our executions," he said to Rashid.

"Perhaps that is the reason." Rashid pointed south to a dark cloud covering the southern horizon.

"A sandstorm?" Gaius asked, although he knew it was not. His chest ached from the connection between him and the dark cloud. His mind detected the ponderous writhing of Nergal's tentacles as they sped him toward the city, though his ears heard nothing.

Rashid shook his head. "No, it is a black shroud, a shadow in which Nergal conceals his hideous visage. It is wraiths, Roman, thousands of wraiths."

"Come now," the guard ordered. His gaze kept drifting back to the dark, turbulent haze. Fear clouded his face. "Centurion, did Tribune Sevilius truly die at the hands of demons?"

Gaius couldn't reveal that he had killed mad, demented Sevilius. He lied. "Yes, he fought bravely against the shadow creatures, but they overwhelmed him."

The guard nodded as if satisfied. "Our officers are frightened. Rumors abound from natives fleeing the villages to the south. They say a walking mountain comes."

Close enough, thought Gaius. "It is Nergal, the creatures' god. It is of him that I tried to warn the Praefectus."

"I heard it said that the Emperor judged you wrongly; that you fought well in Parthia and saved most of your men. Is this true?"

He knew he must speak the whole truth. As a legionnaire, he deserved the truth. "I listened to the Imperator and blindly sent my men into an ambush. Three hundred died. Their deaths weary my spirit, but the remainder I saved, yes."

Gaius expected the next words. "Can you save us, Centurion?"

"We will see," he answered as truthfully as he dared. He would make no more promises he could not keep.

Praefectus Titilus Pontius Calidus, a short, pudgy man with pallid skin, possessed the restless, darting eyes of a viper. His reddish-brown hair was the color of tamarisk bark, and his white and purple toga ill fit him like a blanket draped over a horse. The toga barely covered open lesions on his arms and legs. Gaius had seen such lesions before – *Morbus gallicus,* the wasting disease caused by unhealthy sexual dalliances, a common occurrence common among soldiers but never so openly displayed among patricians. The disease ate away bones and made men mad. He wondered how far down the path of insanity the disease had taken the Praefectus.

Titilus reclined on a cushioned marble bench in a room open on three sides. A bored young boy waved a palm leaf fan above his head. A bowl of grapes and dates sat on a table by his side. Purple juice from the grapes dribbled down his chin. A golden goblet held wine. Gaius glanced at the wine and licked his lips. He resisted the impulse to snatch it up and drain the cup. A small bowl held the mashed pulp of the poppy plant, morphine to ease the pain of his disease. Titilus jabbed his finger in the bowl, brought the paste to his mouth, and licked his finger. Then he waved his arm at Gaius and pointed to a shorter wooden bench bare of cushions.

"Sit, Centurion."

He didn't offer the same courtesy to Rashid. Titilus' civility confused him. "I will stand, Praefectus. I have wasted three days sitting in your stinking fusturium while Nergal and his minions draw closer." He pointed south. "You see their cloak now. Tomorrow, you will see their faces and know I spoke the truth."

"It is a difficult story to believe, Centurion – Terrible gods and vicious creatures who steal soldiers away in the dark for their blood. Surely, you see my dilemma. Tribune Sevilius was a …"

"Sevilius was a pompous fool," Gaius said. He had nothing to lose now by speaking the truth. "He held his position through family ties, not merit. He lost two centuriae to these creatures, though I cannot fault him for that. I lost my entire command, but he refused to learn from his mistake. The touch of the creatures drove him mad. Will you follow his example?"

Titilus' face reddened. He rose from his bench and sat upright. "I have heard disturbing reports from the few scouts that have returned and from villagers seeking refuge. They speak of shadows devouring people and of great rumblings beneath the earth."

"Send out no more patrols. Tonight, build fires, huge ones. Fire is one of the few things that ward against these creatures."

Titilus' eyes narrowed. "What is the other?"

"Now we come to the Berber prince." He indicated Rashid.

"I can speak for myself," Rashid said. He faced Titilus. "I am the bearer of a sigil that has power over the creatures." He held out the amulet. "As prince of my people, I alone possess the knowledge of its use. In Roman hands, it is worthless."

Titilus looked at Gaius, who nodded. "Only he knows the words that awaken the power within the stone."

"Will you take command of the troops, Centurion, under my ultimate command of course?" he added quickly.

"Yes, but first you must free all who came with me and send the *medicus* to tend to their injuries."

Titilus slapped his knee with the palm of his hand. "Done." He turned to one of the guards standing near the edge of the room. Gaius had not missed the fact that one of the guards held his aclis ready to hurl at Gaius' first threatening movement. "Do as the Centurion commands." To Gaius, he asked, "Can we defeat this creature, this Great Old One?"

In answer, he chose one of Rashid's aphorisms, "We can but try. I must take leave of you to make preparations for the battle to come."

He placed his clench fist over his chest and bowed slightly, just enough to show obeisance to the pompous Praefectus. As he turned to leave, he made a public display of returning Rashid's dagger. "I will not need it after all," he said. The startled look on Titilus' face was almost worth the days of captivity, almost.

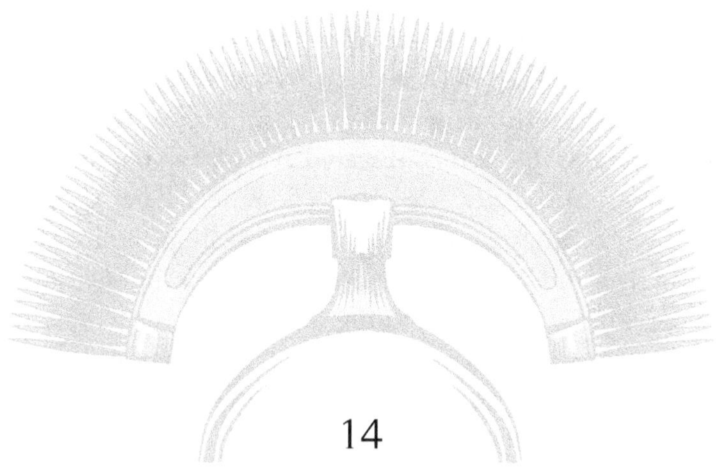

14

Gaius had men lift the garrison's three *Ballistae* to the roofs of buildings that rose above the wall to allow them to fire their bolts over the walls. The task was formidable, made possible only by use of hoists, blocks and tackles, and muscle power. Each three-foot-long shaft ended with a broad triangular iron tip as large as a spear tip, effective against flesh and blood enemies but useless against shadows. He ordered oil-soaked rags wrapped around the shafts near the spear point and secured with leather thongs. Fired with enough force, a heavy *ballista* bolt could penetrate a dozen human bodies before stopping. He hoped it could skewer and ignite that many wraiths as well. He wished they had twenty of the weapons instead of only three.

Three ballista and four medium-sized *onagers,* stone-throwing catapults, provided a moderate defense against a human army, but to Gaius' trained military eye, they were pitifully inadequate for repelling an unnatural horde of undead demons and a rampaging monster. They might as well toss pebbles at a charging war elephant. Pebbles and stones he had in plenty. Heavy rocks the size of a man's head wrapped in layers of cloth and soaked in oil would serve as ammunition for the onagers, as would clay pots filled with white-hot embers, which upon impact would shatter, scattering embers everywhere.

Blazing fires at multiple points along the walls and in front of each gate and door would keep out the creatures for as long as the fuel lasted. He left gaps in the South-facing wall to direct the creatures into the range of the siege weapons. He had confiscated every scrap of wood, jug of oil, and bolt of cloth in the city. Men had felled every date palm and shrub to add to the growing pile of kindling. Stockpiling food would not be necessary. If they did not defeat Nergal and his minions quickly, they would all die. There would be no long siege.

Once the wooden pyres were set ablaze, no citizen of the town could enter or leave the fort. Those who chose to remain outside would survive or die by their own defenses. Many were already evacuating the city. The burning pyres also meant that the defenders inside the fort could not escape. It was a nightmare scenario, the equivalent of chaining one foot to a stake in the ground amid a sea of attacking enemies.

He spotted Titilus Calidus hurrying across the courtyard toward him. He had no wish to speak with the Praefectus. Too many things took priority over listening to the frightened ramblings of a career politician. Gaius ignored him in hopes that he would go away. Instead, he climbed to where Gaius directed the crew positioning the last ballista. As he approached, his plump cheeks glowed rosy from the exertion of climbing the steps to the top of the wall.

Seeing that the siege engines were all pointed south, Titilus asked, "What if they surround us? Should not they be divided to cover all the walls?"

"We cannot cover all the walls from attack," Gaius explained. "We do not have enough men. With Sevilius' two centuriae massacred, the Third Cohort has less than four hundred men remaining. That includes cooks, grooms, wood workers, engineers, paymasters, supply clerks, standard-bearers, and musicians. Twenty men are tironii, here from Leptis Magna less than a month. They haven't completed their basic training. I have two hundred munifex culled from the thousands in the city capable of wielding sword, spear, or the bow. Still, it is not enough. We will build fires along the bottoms and on the tops of all the other walls and force the dark army to attack the south wall. I will position the onagers below the south wall as well."

Titilus waved his right hand in the air. "It seems a foolish move, but I have given you command of the garrison and will not interfere. What of the creatures' master?"

Gaius noted that the Praefectus shied from mentioning Nergal's name. Everyone in the fort could feel creature's movements as a dull rumbling in the earth. "Fire or walls will not stop him. If Rashid cannot summon sufficient power from the amulet …." He shrugged. "This is not a battle against any enemy we have faced. Our weapons are useless against Nergal. If we fail, he will seek out Rome and destroy it as well."

Titilus' face grew even more pallid than normal. "Rome fall?" He reached up his hand and pressed it against his chest, as if his breath had failed him. He shook his head slowly side to side, making his jowls flap. "It cannot be, Centurion. We cannot allow such a thing to happen."

Gaius' face grew stark as he said, "Men will die, Praefectus. We may all die, but the Berber must live. Impress that upon your officers. Rashid must live. Without him, all is lost."

Titilus nodded. "I will issue an order immediately. What else can I do?"

"You can pray to your family gods, Praefectus Calidus. If they have any power, we will need their intervention."

Gaius watched a dark line of men, women, and children, laden with all the possessions they could carry or load onto the backs of camels and even goats, streaming steadily from the city headed north, the first refugees of Nergal's onslaught. They had no carts. He had ordered all wagons, carts, and chariots broken up for the wood. The citizens of Marzuq had ignored his attempts to dissuade them from leaving. He knew they would never reach safety. The creatures, sensing easy prey, would hunt them down and devour them before attacking the fort, providing the raw material for more wraiths in Nergal's ever-growing army of the dead, or instead, as had happened is Rashid's village, control hordes of deadly desert creatures to attack them.

Praefectus Calidus too eyed the line of refugees snaking across the desert as if he longed to be among them. "If you succeed in this, Centurion Linneus, I will send a letter to the Emperor to extol your contribution to our defense. I will make no mention of the death of Tribune Sevilius. I am sure his death was beyond your ability to prevent. The Emperor may rescind his judgment and return your honor."

The Praefectus had no faith in Gaius' ability or in his plan. Titilus' only goal was to see that all responsibility fell on Gaius' shoulders; therefore, any blame for failure became his as well. Gaius turned on Titilus. He had heard enough of the spouting of hot-winded patricians to know how mercurial their praises could be. "No one can take my honor, Titilus Calidus. All that the Emperor took from me was a burden. Now, I have nothing to lose."

Titilus stared at Gaius, reached into his robe, and withdrew a leather bag. It clinked when he held it out to Gaius. "There are one hundred gold *denarii* here, Centurion, enough to buy an estate outside Rome, slaves, perhaps even your good name. It is yours if you assign twenty men to accompany me to Leptis Magna. I will send more reinforcements."

The Praefectus' voice pleaded. Perspiration dotted the flash above his lip. The stink of his fear and his disease poured from his body fouling the air. Gaius felt a momentary desire to run his sword through the fat, pompous patrician's belly. Instead, he let his anger find voice.

"You are an abomination, Praefectus. The Emperor's judgment upon me has freed me to speak my mind. Return to your apartments and pray to see the dawn. If you dare to bribe me or any of my men again, I will set you in front of the gates to await judgment by Nergal and his minions."

Too shocked to speak, Titilus backed away, almost stumbling over the edge of the wall. He recovered, trotted down the steps, and disappeared.

Speaking of the Berber raised the issue of Rashid's absence. The Berber prince, now wearing new robes more befitting his rank, had kept to himself since their release. Rashid had begged him to order all the population brought into the fort, but he had refused. He didn't have the manpower to spare rounding up recalcitrant Berbers, Tebu, and Maxyans were in the town trading in the marketplaces or passing through in caravans. He had compromised by allowing the families of any of the munifex assigned to defend the fort to join them inside the walls. Rashid's anger had been monumental but had made no dent in Gaius' armor.

He spotted Rashid in his customary position at the corner of the south wall, standing solitary vigil and staring out across the desert. The black cloud of the day before was now recognizable as an enormous, whirling dust devil. Gaius walked the length of the wall and stood beside the Berber. The black cloud looked even more frightening than the sandstorm for which they had first mistaken it.

"It is not sand," Rashid said, as if reading his thoughts. "It is the shattered bodies of the creatures. Nergal has sacrificed them to cloak his approach."

"I thought you said he traveled using underground tunnels."

"He does, but his movements disturb the soil above. The devil *tamzawit* covers his approach and fills onlookers with dread and awe, does it not?"

He gazed at Gaius. His once blue on blue eyes were now a dull, bluish gray – *lividis*, the color of contused flesh. They were sunken deep within his sockets, surrounded by black circles from lack of sleep. His lips were thin and pale, his cheeks gaunt. His brow furrowed by the concentration required to remain in contact with the entity within the azure stone, which now glowed continuously, even in bright daylight. His right cheek had developed a slight tic that danced when he spoke. He turned away from the image of the approaching dust devil when Gaius approached. He wore the mien of a condemned prisoner, as if watching it hour after hour wrenched away chunks of his soul. The amulet never left the Berber's hand. As he spoke, his fingers caressed its smooth surface.

"Yes, Centurion, I see your eyes observe my pitiful countenance. I told you the sigil is a living thing. All living things require nourishment. The stone draws sustenance from my flesh and my vigor. It is a small price to pay, for in exchange, it now speaks to me, tells me things of its history." He shook his head. "We cannot win this battle here, Centurion. I cannot stop Nergal. No power on Earth, not even the iharz I hold in my hand, can vanquish him."

At Rashid's confession, the enormity of it all descended on Gaius like a sudden downpour. His legs became rubbery and failed to support him. He grasped the wall beside him to prevent falling to his knees. He had gambled everything on Rashid's ability to stop Nergal and protect Rome. Was he lying to allow Romans to die? He searched Rashid's face; read his eyes and his expression, and saw that the Berber spoke the truth. The amulet had told him so, and the truth ate at his soul.

"But … but I felt its power in the temple," he said, remembering the sensation of the amulet in his hand, the tingling in his chest while clutching the blazing sword when attacked on the journey to Marzuq. "It healed your wounds. It healed my leg. Nergal recoiled from it. I witnessed it."

"The sigil wounds him, even frightens him, if such a creature can feel fear, but it cannot kill him. However, it can bind Nergal to his underground lair where men wiser and more powerful than me imprisoned him eons ago when the world was young. For millennia, he remained asleep, confined in his subterranean cell by runes and signs set in stone by his jailers. Then, first the Greeks, then the Carthaginians, and now you Romans come to my country with thoughts of conquest. Your blood lust has awakened him. He feels in you a kindred spirit, a despoiler of civilizations."

Rashid's tirade taxed his energy. He collapsed and sat on the edge of the wall, gasping for breath. Gaius moved toward him to aid him. Rashid stopped him with a sharp wave of his hand.

"I do not need your help, Centurion. See to your defenses. They will fail, but you must try. It is your way." His tone softened. "I do not hold you responsible for what has befallen my people, Gaius Linneus. I see now that refuge within these walls was an illusion. For a Roman, you treated me well. You are no longer the typical pompous Roman ass you once were. You know the truth of Nergal and his dark minions, but you still consider the Inyosh an enemy to defeat. Each death here in this city, in this fort, will create more wraiths. They will spread across the land like a plague of locusts. It is a battle you cannot win."

Gaius abhorred admitting defeat before fighting the battle, but he knew Rashid was right. Despite his frantic preparations, they could not win. Every military leader relied on his gut instinct to foresee the outcome of battles. Gaius' gut spoke of defeat. "What then do you suggest?"

Rashid looked up. His eyes now held a glimmer of hope. "You seek my counsel? It is as I first suggested when we fled Hamad Rus. We must lure the creature back to its pit and bind it there with the sigil." He squeezed the amulet in his hand with renewed vigor.

"I cannot abandon these people."

"You abandoned mine readily enough," Rashid wailed; then, shook his head. "It is useless, Centurion. The creatures will sense blood and be eager to overrun the fort and the city. Appoint someone to command your troops, someone to see to the defenses." His voice took on a pleading tone. "You must accompany me to Hamad Rus. You have shared a small portion of the amulet's power. If anything happens to me, perhaps it will suffice to allow you to complete the task."

Gaius considered Rashid's suggestion. Abandoning his post went against everything he believed in, everything drilled into him by years of training and battle, but had he not done it once before when he took his entire Shadow Legion to Hamad Rus? Then, it was on a chance to regain his lost honor, a way out of Tripolitania. Could he not do as much to save Rome?

Quickly his sense of duty took over. "No. Marcellus is still weak. The other officers are young and inexperienced, unfamiliar with the tactics I propose to employ. If I leave, the fort will fall and the garrison will be lost."

Rashid sighed and seemed to collapse into himself, as if the possibility of Gaius accompanying him to Hamad Rus had been his last hope. "Perhaps you have not lost all of your Roman pomposity after all," he sighed. "Your warrior's ego betrays you. You fear to loosen your grip on a power you know, however futile, to grasp a power that can save all. You plan a foolish gesture. Dying gallantly among your troops will earn you a Roman epithet, but by doing so you throw away Rome's only chance of survival, as well as my country's only chance. One day you Romans will leave this land, conquered by another, as you have conquered so many. Some fledging empire will take your place, but the Tamazight will continue to live in this desert as we always have. It is our home."

The truth of Rashid's words stung him. Was his ego betraying him, just another ineffectual gesture on his part, another White Rock Pass, but this time with him saving no one? He was a legionnaire, a soldier. It was a soldier's nature to fight. The situation called not for bravery and the sword, but for abandoning his nature, his calling, to follow Rashid on a madman's quest. The conflict raging within him made his mind a churning cauldron. He could not think straight. Then, he focused on the one thing that had always been true to him, the image of his wife and child in Ischia. Could he protect them there by throwing away his life within the fort's walls? In the end, did it really matter where he died?

His decision surprised him. A deep sigh, sounding as if wrenched from his soul, escaped his lips. He felt as if he were betraying everything he held dear. "You win, Berber. I will accompany you to Hamad Rus, but I must direct the first attack. Their first encounter with the wraith army will break their spirits. They must see me on the wall, unafraid, or they will not rally for a second attack."

"Are you, Roman? Are you truly unafraid?"

Gaius considered Rashid's question. Did he feel fear or dread, as with any other battle? He had never gone into battle fearing for his life. His skill as a tactician determined the outcome, barring the capriciousness of the gods. He feared for the safety of his wife and child. He feared for Rome. He did not fear for himself.

"No, Prince Abdullah," he answered using Rashid's rank for the first time, "I am not afraid."

Rashid nodded; then, smiled, as if Gaius' answer pleased. "Nor I, Centurion Gaius Linneus, but for a different reason. You seek to protect the ones you love and to give your death meaning. All I love and knew is gone, fodder for these creatures' bloodlust. My death means nothing to anyone living except in the manner of its ending. I long for a noble death, one with meaning. Is this too Roman of me?"

This time, Gaius smiled. "Close enough, Rashid. We can use the confusion of battle to slip away. We will ride swift horses and lead two more each. We will use no saddle to save weight. We will ride them into the ground to gain us time. We will carry little food and eat in the saddle." He stared at Rashid, forcing the Berber to look him in the eye so he could read the truth. "Are you certain Nergal will turn away from the city and follow us?" he demanded. If the amulet spoke to Rashid as he claimed, he should know the answer, but even after days of being near him, Gaius still didn't know if he fully trusted the Berber.

"The sigil draws him. He knows it is ancient magic and the only thing that can imprison him. He will seek to destroy the amulet and its wielder. He will follow."

Rashid's eyes neither blinked nor quavered, and his voice remained even. Gaius believed him.

"What of the creatures?"

"Some he will retain to act as his tools. The others … I do not know. The city may yet fall."

Gaius had already accepted that possibility, even its inevitability. "You need rest. It is a long journey to Hamad Rus, and we must ride swiftly."

Rashid nodded and climbed down the stairs. He moved slowly and his steps were weary. The stone of the amulet drained Rashid's body of life, but Gaius needed to learn all he could of Nergal, and only the amulet, through Rashid, could provide the answers. He hoped the Berber lived long enough to reach Hamad Rus. In spite of their differences, he liked the Berber prince. *Another death to add to my mounting tally*, he thought grimly.

Gaius glanced one more time at the spiraling ebony storm growing closer by the hour. He could hear the high keening on the wind, the creatures eager for blood to offer to their ancient god. He didn't need to estimate the approaching army's speed. He knew they would arrive that night after the moon had set. Darkness was their milieu.

The remainder of the day, he stalked the fort like a specter, appearing suddenly and vanishing just as quickly. He spoke with the apprehensive officers to reassure them that his tactics would work. They did not believe him, but obeyed anyway. The *milites*, the common soldiers, didn't understand what was happening. The odd preparations for battle and the presence of the conscripted native population confused them, but they saw their officers obey and moved swiftly to each task assigned to them. He thanked good Roman discipline for that. He instructed the weapons master to school the recruits and the civilian conscripts in the proper use of their weapons. They were eager but lacked confidence in their ability. He decided to improve their odds.

He sought out Antonius Cossus, whom most of the men knew. He found the wizened veteran sharpening his swords, both his gladius and his longer spatha, to a razor-sharp edge. Two finely honed acilii lay beside him. He worked methodically but without haste, knowing a legionnaire's keen-edged weapon was his best chance for survival. He had endured his imprisonment with the indifference of one used to such hardships. To him, jail had been just another conflict he had survived.

"Antonius," Gaius said in greeting, "I am need of a tesserarius. Would the job suit you?"

Antonius stopped his preparations and glanced up at Gaius. "Aye, the extra pay would suit me, for as many hours or days as I might draw it."

His straightforward manner was a relief to Gaius after dealing with so many whose words danced around the truth, such as Praefectus Calidus. "Are you afraid?" he asked, repeating the question Rashid had posed to him.

Antonius shrugged and resumed running the honing stone along the blade's edge with long, even stokes. "What is death to a legionnaire? A long life or a quick death; a man can choose neither. The gods mete out their judgment as befitting their whimsy. What will my duties be, Centurion?"

"I want you to round up ever triarii in this garrison whom you believe trustworthy and skilled. I want one veteran for every twenty raw recruits and conscripts, if we have that many. They must act as their charges' anchor and pull from them their maximum effort. Rough or gentle, I want the recruits ready by the setting of the moon. They will answer to you and Tesserarius Marcellus alone."

He smiled. "Me, a tesserarius. That will turn a few heads in this place. Aye, I accept your promotion, Centurion. I know a few men capable of doing the job, if they are sober."

"See that they. You can start now."

As Gaius walked away, Antonius said, "You honor me, sir."

"I make of you a target, Tesserarius. The creatures retain enough of their former memories to recognize a leader from a follower."

"A Roman legionnaire is always a target. What does it matter who the enemy is?"

That problem solved, he visited the *valetudunarium*, the infirmary, to see how Marcellus fared. He needed his tesserarius' experience and strong sword arm with him. He was appalled to find over thirty men inside the room lying on cots. He called the medicus to him.

"Physician, what is wrong with these men?"

The doctor, a tall, thin man of at least fifty years of age with a fringe of white hair rimming his baldpate, set down a bowl filled with blood and laid a bloody lancet beside it. His toga smelled of herbs and astringents used to clean instruments. "One has a broken leg, but it is healing nicely. Two suffer from heat strokes. Most suffer minor stomach ailments, dysentery, or maladies of the humors. I feed them rhubarb, horse heal, and licorice root and for their stomachs, egg yolks for dysentery, and bleed them for their misaligned humors." He pointed to Marcellus. "This man has an unusual injury. I drained the pus and sewed the wound. I applied a poultice of gentian to draw out the poison and yarrow to help heal the wound." He continued with a smug look on his face. "I have read the works of the Greek Galen and practice as he does."

Gaius' face grew redder as his ire increased. "If they must shit, let them shit on the wall facing the enemy with a sword in their hands. Queasy stomachs or loose bowels do not concern me, physician." He jabbed his finger in the medicus' face. "Bleed no more men. There will be blood enough within these walls before this night is through."

The physician was aghast. "But they ...."

Gaius stopped him and pointed to Marcellus, lying in the corner of the room watching the proceedings with amused interest. "That man suffered an injury delivered by the enemy. Attend to him. Send these shirkers and malingerers back to their duties. We need every man at his post." He addressed the men in the room. "If the enemy overwhelms us, your fate will be far worse than any you could ever conceive. Lying here in this room will not save you. There will be no quarter given. I can spare no one to protect you. Rome needs you. Your comrades need you."

Marcellus threw back his blanket and rose from his bed. He wobbled slightly as he stood a moment to catch his balance. Gaius winced at forcing his tesserarius out of his sickbed. Marcellus was silent as he laced his sandals. Then he faced the others. "I will be in the armory preparing for war. Join me if you love your country, your comrades, or your title as legionnaires of Rome."

Gaius placed his hand on Marcellus' should as he passed. He noticed the flax thread suturing his would. The flesh around it was still sickly yellow. Of them all, he wished Marcellus could remain in the infirmary, but now his example would serve him well. The others, shamed by Marcellus' call to arms, looked at one another and began dressing to join him. They did not like Gaius' appellation of malingerer or shirker, deserved or not. Such a label followed a legionnaire throughout the legion, through every posting. The physician stared at them dumfounded and in disbelief.

"See, medicus, your treatments have been miraculous. Now, prepare yourself for the coming battle. There will be few wounded, but their wounds will be grave."

His eyes seethed with resentment at his ill treatment, but he held his tongue and nodded his head. "Yes, Centurion."

Somewhere in the long day, Gaius took a few minutes to eat. The food was of better quality and more plentiful than any he had eaten in weeks, but he didn't taste it. He ate as he worked, wiping his hands on his tunic when he finished. When he saw any group of soldiers resting, he verbally berated them. They were tired, he knew, but better tired than dead. If they won the battle tonight, the survivors could rest tomorrow.

He tested all the archers, both the Legion sagittarii and the civilians, to determine their most effective ranges, and then placed them into three ranks according to strength and skill. They were his second line of defense, the siege engines being his first line. Crossbows were more effective inside the fort. These, he kept in reserve for when the creatures breached the walls, for he knew eventually they would breach them. He had seen the warrens beneath the mountain. Given enough time and the cover of their self-generated dark cloak, they could claw their way through the five-foot thick limestone walls, if Nergal didn't tear it down first.

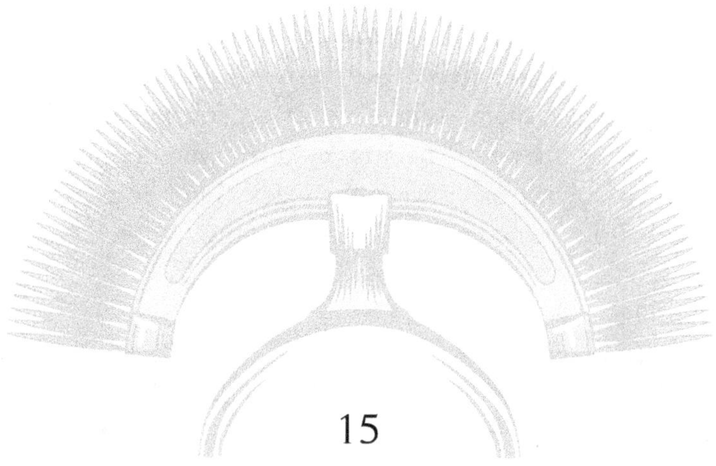

15

Just after sunset, Gaius ordered the fires lit, sealing the defenders to their fate inside Castra-Flacco. They were as ready as they could ever be, but it would not be enough.

The earth-shaking, subterranean passage of Nergal now jarred the ground, as if from a continuous earthquake. The waters of the thermae sloshed over the sides. The pounding of Nergal's tentacles against the stone became the beating of a hundred tympani drums, the high keening of the wraiths a chorus of a thousand trumpets. Despite the raging dust storm looming over the city, no wind stirred the air, as still and as calm as the sea before a tempest.

However, the lack of wind didn't prevent the arrival of the stench of a thousand abattoirs from descending on the fort. The reek of rotting flesh and putrid blood disheartened the soldiers manning their posts, but there was no defense against it.

Gaius waved to Marcellus to his right, and then to Dracus on his left. Neither man was fit to fight, but both refused to allow another man to take their place. Men stood by the onagers and ballistas, awaiting his command to fire. Three ranks of archers lined the parade ground. Clay jars held hundreds of arrows for each archer to reload quickly. Fires blazed beside them to ignite their arrows.

In the distance, the screams of those who had refused to enter the fort or flee the city, began, as the mass of shadows descended on them. Gaius steeled himself to their cries, convincing himself he could have done nothing to save them. When the air began to grow chilly and the shadows deepened, he knew the attack was imminent. Suddenly, as if a tapestry ripped down from a wall, the black cloud evaporated, spilling shadows across the moonless sand. The shadows writhed like a nest of vipers.

"Ready!" he yelled.

The wraiths appeared from the darkness, unfolding from the night, a wall of black creatures so deep he could not count their number. When they were within range of the catapults, he signaled the optio in charge. Men ignited the oil-soaked cloth-covered rocks cradled in the spoon-like depressions of the heavy timber throwing arms. The artillerymen hammered out the firing pins, releasing the tightly wound ropes tensioning the arms. The arms slammed into the padded frames with a resounding thud that reverberated through the night. Even as their blazing payloads arced high through the air, men turned the windlasses preparing the onagers for their next projectile.

The projectiles traveled a distance of 300 yards, landing among the advancing horde of creatures, and bouncing a path of flaming destruction through their tightly massed ranks. Seeing the results, a cheer went up from the onlookers. It quickly faded as the gaps filled with more of the creatures as quickly as water rushes to fill a void in a pail.

The onagers were effective but slow to reload. They continued to punch holes in the attackers, while Gaius readied the ballistae. At 200 hundred yards, they hurled their bolts through the lines of wraiths like the thrust of a flaming sword. More scores of the creatures fell with each bolt, exploding into black dust, and yet Gaius could detect no reduction in their number. At 100 yards, the sagittarii loosed their arrows, firing as quickly as they could notch another arrow in their bows. Now, the leading edges of the Inyosh army slowly withered. For the first time, Gaius sensed hesitation in their attack.

That indecisive lull lasted only for a few minutes, long enough to give the defenders heart, but not long enough to turn the tide of battle.

A commotion at the rear of their ranks sent a surge of creatures forward, forcing the others closer to the walls of the fort. The flames around the bases of the other three walls held them at bay, but they began to infiltrate the gaps Gaius had left in the Southern wall of flame to entice them into range of the arrows. The creatures that survived the flights of flaming projectiles met scores of hurled spears and javelins, each a tiny speck of burning light falling among the enemy.

They withered under the barrage. The flames of the arrows, javelins, and spears illuminated the battlefield. Buildings and tents of the city of Marzuq became burning pyres, forcing the flood of shadows to part. They milled about, daunted by the fires and the flaming projectiles. For millennia, no one had opposed the creatures. Now, they had encountered the Roman Legion and felt doubt.

Then, the earth shuddered as if a mountain had fallen. Buildings collapsed. The walls of the castra shook. Deep cracks appeared in the stressed stone, running along the top of the wall and down the sides. The shaking wall tossed men from it like a dog shedding ringing water from its fur. Those who landed inside the fort suffered broken bones. A few died. Those who fell outside the wall disappeared into the black cloud of death encircling the fort. A tremendous keening rent the night. Most manning the walls saw only the wraiths pausing. Gaius, whom the amulet had touched, saw their features through their dark shrouds, saw their blood-demon eyes turn and stare south in fear. He saw their deadly maws open obscenely wide as they wailed to greet their god. Nergal had arrived.

The ground beyond the edge of the city erupted as if birthing a volcano. Sand, soil, and rock flew through the air, but instead of hot lava, a cold ebony blackness spilled from the crater and flowed through the city, crashing against the wall of the fort. Something else rose from the newly opened pit, a gigantic parody of a human with an elongated head with tentacles surrounding the enormous maw. Twin red slits gazed over the city as if searching. When Nergal's gaze focused on the fort, Gaius felt as if the creature stared directly at him. He wasn't. Instead, the eyes darted to an azure glow growing steadily brighter atop the wall – Rashid.

The ground trembled as Nergal surged forward on his massive tangle of lower tentacles. His upper tentacles snapped out to pluck roofs from buildings tumble walls. Gaius felt the familiar tingling in his chest as the amulet's power grew in intensity under Rashid's chanting. An azure wall of energy exploded from the amulet and swept through the fort. Every weapon and every piece of iron burst into blue flames. The edge of the azure wall touched the front ranks of the dark army. They tried to flee before it, but it traveled deep into their formation before dissipating, leaving nothing behind. The creatures it touched vanished.

The brilliant glow of the stone in the amulet faded. Rashid swooned and collapsed atop the wall. That the affected weapons continued to glow offered the only evidence that he still lived.

The creatures, more frightened of their god to their rear than the enemy in front of them, scampered up the stone walls, their claws digging into the solid rock for purchase. Gaius' men met them at the top of the wall with swords, spears, and pikes all doused with burning oil and suffused with the blue glow of ancient magic. The few that evaded a flaming death launched themselves on the nearest soldiers, enveloping them in their ebony cloaks, but they, too, met death on the swords of his second line of defense.

A runner raced up to him across the top of the wall out of breath. "The creatures are gaining ground on eastern end of the wall. Sesquiplecarus Armis asks you send men to his aid."

Gaius saw a swarm of black shapes pouring over the wall near Dracus. He motioned a reserve squad of twenty tirones waiting on the ground below the wall and watched newly appointed Tesserarius Antonius Cossus lead them up the steps. They spread out along the wall to reinforce Dracus Armis' beleaguered squads. The half-trained recruits performed well. Antonius moved among them, barking orders and slashing at wraiths with his blazing sword. They held the wall, but at great cost. Half of Antonius' men disappeared within minutes, taken by an ebony wall of creatures.

Dracus went down with two of the creatures on him. One, he killed with a thrust of his glowing gladius, but the other ripped into his chest with its claws and yanked out his still beating heart. A flaming crossbow bolt fired by one of the archers stationed on a roof adjacent to the wall passed through the heart and the wraith, exploding it. Young Dracus' heart fell to the ground beside his body. More bolts erupted from the rooftop and swept the wall clean of creatures. Antonius quickly assumed command and rallied the men, but for every creature they dispatched, a dozen more scampered up the wall.

Nergal continued his rampage, shattering buildings like clay pots, and flinging debris that rained down on the men on the walls. Gaius had clay pots of his own. He signaled the onagers to hurl their urns filled with flaming embers. Each onager fired five urns at a time. The urns broke apart upon impact, sending hundreds of shards slicing through the ranks of creatures like flaming shrapnel. To his dismay, the urns that struck Nergal bounced off and broke apart on the ground, setting more buildings aflame.

"Send jugs of oil!" he yelled at the loaders.

A barrage of jugs of oil fed the blazes higher. Now, a line of burning buildings formed a flaming barricade. Gaius hoped it slowed the creature long enough to rally his disheartened troops.

Nergal spoke. His voice was the deep, sonorous trumpeting of a thousand war elephants that shook the ground. Gaius covered his ears with his hands, but could not shut out the powerful voice. Gaius sensed words in the horrifying sound, alien and unintelligible, but a language nevertheless. Whatever the command, the creatures responded to their master. Thousand of them, a sea of black, hurled themselves into the flaming city, using their dying bodies to smother the flames and clear a path for their god. With the fire extinguished, they resumed their assault on the fort. Though greatly reduced in number at the whim of their god, they still out numbered the garrison. Singly, and then in small groups, they evaded the defenders atop the wall and dropped into the fort, quickly spreading out to cause destruction.

He watched several of the creatures overwhelm the guards stationed outside Praefectus Calidus' apartments and enter. Seconds later, the agonized screams of the Praefectus split the night. Gaius hoped they developed a venereal disease from Titilus Calidus' disease-ridden body.

Nergal drew nearer the fort with each ponderous step. Gaius knew they could not stop him. Wraiths surged over the walls in a dozen spots. He ordered the squads he had assigned to protect the interior of the fort to engage the wraiths, but when the fires died, they would overwhelm the fort. If Rashid's plan was to work, they had to leave now. He left a young optio in charge and went to Rashid. The Berber appeared dangerously weak, leaning against the wall for support. He saw Gaius approaching and struggled to stand, tottering as if he would fall.

"It is time, Roman. Your part in this battle has run its course. If you wish to save these men, we must lure Nergal back south away from the city."

Gaius knew Rashid was right; nevertheless, abandoning his command left a vile taste in his mouth. The word coward haunted his thoughts.

"I know, Berber," he snapped. "Let us do it before I change my mind."

He motioned for Marcellus. Marcellus raced to his side.

"It is time to leave."

"I know. Nine horses await us beyond the stables near the rear gate."

"Nine?" Gaius said in surprise.

"I will accompany you to this last fight. The battle here will be won or lost by individual soldiers fighting for their lives and not by the commands of an officer. Tesserarius Antonius or any of the optios can serve as well as me. If what we do draws some of the enemy away, they stand a chance. If no one goes, we all die."

Gaius nodded. "Very well, Tesserarius. We ride."

Two soldiers stood beside the rear gate holding nine unsaddled horse, Apollo among them. Gaius would save his war steed for the last leg of the journey. He would not use him up and discard him as he had his legionnaires. The three men slipped satchels of food and filled water skins over their shoulders, and mounted their horses' back, blankets only. They each held the reins of their two spare mounts in their hands.

"Open the gates," Gaius called to the guards. "Close them when we exit."

As soon as the gates swung open, Rashid sent a burst of azure flame ahead of them. Only a few creatures barred their passage, but those few disintegrated. Gaius glanced back to see the gates close once again. Burning timbers tossed from the wall barred the gate. He kicked his horse in its flanks and headed it south toward Hamad Rus.

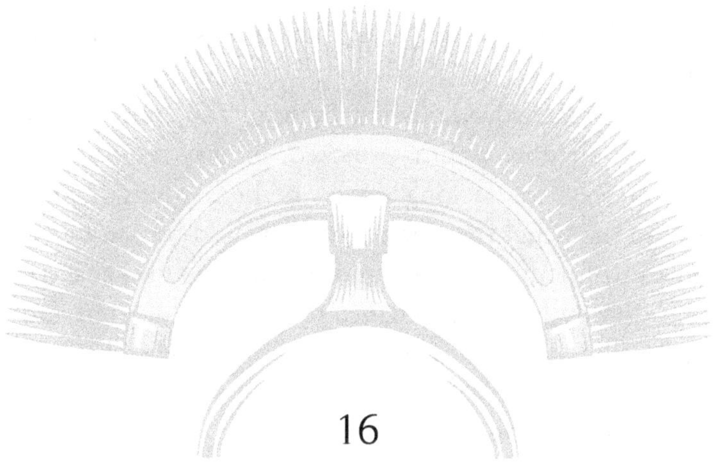

16

At dawn, they stopped long enough to rest the horses and drink wine laced with honey to fortify them for the journey; then, mounted their horses and rode south. Gaius held no thoughts of victory or of glory. Death seemed a certain and just reward for a leader who had three times sacrificed men under his command. He could honor them best by helping the Berber return Nergal to its eternal tomb. He tried not to dwell on Marzuq and Castra-Flacco or if the dawn found the men he had left behind alive or dead. Rashid assured him that Nergal followed them. He had no choice but to believe the Berber. They had saved the fort that unwinnable battle at least.

They rode into the afternoon until their mounts began stumbling in the sand, and then mounted their second horse. The leagues passed but he paid them no heed. His mind, rather than lingering on any one thought, refused to consider any thoughts for fear they would lead to doubts about his purpose. If his purpose was false, then he had sacrificed his men needlessly. He rode in a daze.

They couldn't stop for sleep, though it felt like days since Gaius had last closed his eyes. Each idle minute allowed Nergal to gain ground on them. Rashid could sense the creature's presence, as Nergal could sense his. They moved just slightly faster than the creature could travel underground. They would arrive in Hamad Rus barely minutes before the creature.

As night approached, Gaius felt none of the apprehension he had once felt. If the shadow wraiths attacked, he was certain Rashid could repel them, at least for as long as the Berber's strength held out. He held tightly to the belief that the creatures would not assault them, that they would wait for their master to deal with the humans. That would give them a slightly improved chance to reach the warren and perform their task. After that, it didn't matter. He could never return to Rome. Death in the desert was preferable to a dishonorable end at the hands of Emperor Marcus Aurelius.

That Marcellus showed little curiosity about what he and Rashid intended to do surprised Gaius. The veteran had fought the creatures, knew firsthand of their abilities, and yet showed no fear. Marcellus offered him his complete trust, never doubting him. Such was the loyalty of a true Roman Legionnaire. Gaius hoped he did not lead Marcellus to his death, but knew the likelihood high.

They rode through the night and the next day with only brief stops for rest and water. Before dusk, they switched to their last mounts. Apollo was eager for the weight of his master upon his back. He had refused to trail Gaius on his leash as Gaius used up the other two horses, instead running beside him. Gaius wished the horse wasn't so trusting. It would make their parting less painful for both of them

Even before Hamad Rus came into view, Gaius felt the chill of the dead city reaching out to him, a frigid hand inside his body squeezing the strength from his heart and the determination from his soul; while outside, the sun continued to bake his skin as it gasped out its last searing breath nightfall. He didn't know if he was the only member of the party to feel the death lying in wait for them in that dire city, but Apollo did. The horse whinnied and struggled to free the bit from his mouth. Never in their long history together had the warhorse shied away from a battle.

The distant low rumble coming from the city became a ground-shaking roar as they approached. A cloud of dust hung in the air, obscuring the heart of the city. A foul, fetid odor like the bowels of hell assaulted them. Rashid raised the scarf around his neck and wrapped it across his face to cover his nose. Gaius fought down the bile rising in his throat and forced Apollo forward.

"We need not enter the accursed city where the Inyosh dance to welcome their god's return," he called loudly so that Marcellus could hear him over the din. "It is to the cavern we must ride."

Marcellus nodded and prodded his horse. The horse reared and tried to throw him. Marcellus fought the horse, pulling sharply on his reins, but it would go no farther. He stared at Gaius for instruction. Gaius suspected the horses sensed the evil surrounding them, and that their animal intelligence shouted for them to flee. He wished he could listen to the same voice in his head.

"We will set the horses free here and continue on foot."

Gaius slid off Apollo's back. The horse nuzzled his side as if in apology. Gaius rubbed the horse's snout, and then removed the blanket and bridle. He buried his face in the horse's neck, inhaling the familiar tang of sweat. "Run free, my old friend," he whispered.

Apollo snickered and raced away. He stopped at the top of a dune and waited until Marcellus and Rashid had freed their mounts. Then, he led the other horses over the dune and out of sight of Hamad Rus. The loss of his horse saddened Gaius more than the deaths of his men. Apollo had been his constant friend and companion for fifteen years, longer than he had known any of the men under his command, longer than he had known his wife. During that period, he had spent more time in the company of Apollo than he had his family. Gaius hoped that Apollo survived. Someone should come through the ordeal alive, and it seemed unlikely that he would.

As he stood at the entrance to the cavern, staring into its inky black depths, Gaius hesitated. The stench of death was strong, and he swore he could hear the screams of his dying men echoing from within the solid rock. He had hoped to find the cavern blocked by the landslide, but as Rashid had predicted, the creatures had cleared the entrance of rubble.

"It will be dark soon," Marcellus noted, staring at the sky. His ancient eyes squinted as he looked up at the sun, drinking in its radiance, as if its strength could help dispel the darkness within the mountain.

"It matters not," Gaius reminded him. "We journey into perpetual night."

Beside him, Rashid mumbled quietly with closed eyes. The amulet began to glow softly. The azure light looked pure and holy. He opened his eyes and stared at Gaius.

"The amulet will guide our steps to the dark tower, but I fear we may have to return in darkness."

Gaius understood the meaning behind the Berber's words. He intended to leave the amulet to ward Nergal's prison after they lured the creature inside. If they survived, they would have no torches, no burning oil to guide them through the warren of dark tunnels.

He nodded. "It seems I have always stumbled blindly in darkness. One more such journey will make little difference."

He glanced to the north. Less than a league away, the sand undulated like water from the prow of a boat with the hissing of a thousand serpents. Nergal was almost upon them. Taking his last breath of fresh air, he followed Rashid into the tunnel.

They met no resistance. He feared that more than fighting his way inside. The creatures were too busy either worshipping their dark god, or luring them deeper inside the black abyss to offer them as sacrifice. Gaius tried not to gaze at the discarded pieces of armor and weaponry scattered throughout the tunnel, refused to dwell on the soldier who wore the armor or carried the sword. If, as Rashid thought, the souls of the dead became wraiths, it was his responsibility and duty, perhaps his last, to free their tortured souls.

As they delved deeper into the mountain, the amulet shone more brightly. Its light bathed the walls of the tunnel in soft cerulean radiance and dispelled the gloom. Soon, tremors beneath their feet became stronger and more rhythmic – Nergal was on his way.

Marcellus held his sword in a two-fisted death grip. His gaze darted around the tunnel in agonized wariness. Though he could not see them, his veteran senses told him the enemy neared. Gaius realized Marcellus vacillated between doing his duty and fleeing for his life. Gaius feared that if the wizened old soldier fled, he would follow. He had faced fierce enemies from many lands, but he had never before challenged a nightmare.

The journey seemed to take forever. Each step became a laborious affair, as tired, aching muscles began to clamor for attention. He longed to sit and rest, but feared whatever act of providence had given them clear passage into the warren would end. In his sleep-deprived mind, Gaius began to believe the creatures had rearranged the tunnels since his last ignoble visit, creating a maze for the sole purpose of trapping them beneath the earth. Though certain each step brought him inexorably closer to his doom, he yearned for an end to the situation and a chance for either a long sleep or death.

Rashid was near collapse. His pace faltered. Beads of perspiration dotted his forehead, and his face was pallid and strained. The amulet drained his strength, using him. In spite of his declining condition, he held the amulet tightly in both hands, staring into it as if reading a map of the warren in its azure glow, guiding them unerringly through the maze of tunnels. To Gaius, he appeared even gaunter than just a day earlier. *If he dies*, Gaius thought, *I will be trapped here in the dark with wraiths all around me.* He shuddered at the idea.

"We must rest," he said.

Rashid stared at him with lids half closed. His lips were thin and blanched and his voice was weak, as he replied, "No, we must continue. We draw near."

"It will serve no purpose to arrive at our destination too exhausted to complete our task. We must rest and replenish our depleted energy." He pulled a wineskin from his belt and handed it to Rashid. "Here is wine fortified with honey. It will quench our thirst and soothe our anxieties." When Rashid didn't accept the wine, he shook the skin in Rashid's face. "Drink. Do not be a fool."

Finally, Rashid nodded and took the skin from Gaius' hand. He turned it up, drank deeply, and handed it back, smiling weakly.

"Thank you. You are right. My desire to see an end to this nightmare has blinded me. My yearning for vengeance has overshadowed our true purpose, to end Nergal's hold on this land."

Gaius sat down with his back against the wall of the tunnel. A spark, dark and foreboding, leaped between his flesh and the blood-soaked rock. It seemed as if the very malevolence, the centuries of death and sacrifice of the shades of the Inyosh, had imbued the stone with the taint of their horrific master. The stone drained the willpower to continue from his body like the blood-sucking, hands-width-long leeches of the *Pomptinos Ager*, the vast marshland along the coast where the Tiber meets the sea. His mind instantly filled with dark images of rituals and sacrifices to timeless Nergal spanning eons.

Loathsome creatures more reptilian than human offered up captured apelike hominids, using their long claws to disembowel their captives and tossing their bodies into deep chasms coursing with glowing lava. In another scene, goat-faced creatures stood on an icy frozen plain watching their high priest sacrifice a squirming human on an altar made of ice. He fell forward to break contact with the stone, and the images vanished.

Rashid looked at him with sympathy in his drained eyes. "You felt it? Such abhorrent images have inundated my mind since we first entered the cavern. Nergal senses the amulet and seeks to force me to turn back."

Gaius had felt only an instant's flash of the horrors, and his flesh felt unclean. He wanted to rip it from his body. "How do you stand it?"

He grimaced. "I conjure an image of my wife and children as I last saw them. It gives me strength."

Gaius realized that if Rashid's premise that the dead became wraiths, the Berber's family and kin would be in the cavern opposing him. He wondered if he could carry such a heavy burden. He glanced at Marcellus to offer him wine and saw that the old soldier struggled to breath. He had fallen to his knees, holding his infected arm to his chest. The wound had re-festered. The swelling had split the sutures and viscous, stomach-wrenching, malodorous pus suppurated from the wound, staining the cloth binding it a sickly yellow.

"Why did you not inform me your wound had worsened?" he demanded.

"I would not hold you back."

Instead of berating Marcellus, he pushed the wine skin into Marcellus' hands. "Her. You need strength."

The veteran stared at the wine skin and shook his head. "You and the Berber share it. It is wasted on me, I fear. It appears the creatures can kill in many ways. This slow death is an ignoble way to die. I would use my sword and strike one last blow against these creatures." He paused. "I can but wonder if dying in such a manner at the hands of these inhuman creatures will bind my shade to them, making me one of them. That ignominy I could not endure. Better to die fighting than wasting away from within."

Gaius offered Marcellus the only comfort he could. "Your service to the Legion and to me has been exemplary. If we succeed in this mad venture, your soul will join those of your loved ones."

Marcellus chuckled. "Loved ones. I do not remember the faces of my parents nor can I remember any act of kindness they bestowed upon me. I have neither loved nor been loved by anyone. I have had many women, but I do not remember their names, if ever I knew them, and I am sure they do not remember me out of the hundreds or thousands of faces that have crossed the brothel thresholds. My only love has been the Legion. I have led the life I wanted and will regret nothing if only I can strike one last blow before going into oblivion."

"Spoken like a true legionnaire," Gaius said. "We will prevail."

"When you say it, Centurion, I want to believe."

"Death is but one step in a long journey," Rashid said.

"Spoken by a man who has not tasted death," Marcellus replied. "It is much the same as a man proclaiming he does not like dog meat having never tasted it."

"Perhaps, but without the promise of an existence beyond death, why would life be worth the pain it causes."

"Save your philosophies for later," Gaius said. "Rest now."

"Later does not have the same meaning it once had," Marcellus quipped. "Now, later may mean our last day on earth."

The increased earthquakes all too soon forced them to resume their journey. Nergal did not rest. If they did not reach the pit before him, he would bring the entire mountain down on them. Gaius forced himself to keep his feet moving though his legs ached with each weary step. *Soon, no more steps.* He was not fool enough to believe he would ever leave the warren. Any aches or pains he felt would soon end. He would have peace. *Unless I become that which I abhor most – wraith.*

They arrived at the entrance into the open chamber with the pit. Gaius half-hoped to find it still blocked, but the resolute creatures had cleared the ceiling collapse of debris. The way into the cavern was open. The rock and soil bore the marks of their claws. The crushed helmet of the soldier caught in the collapse lay gleaming in the azure light cast by the amulet. Of his body, there was no sign. A smoky haze hung over the cavern floor, hiding from view the bones of the dead. Gaius wondered if the dead of Marzuq and Fort Flacco were already among the bones littering the floor of the cavern.

The stench of death permeated the air, making each breath a challenge. Even to one used to the reek of the aftermath of a battle where rotting corpses littered the battlefield and the soil oozed blood with each step, entering the cavern was difficult. A sudden surge of panic begged him to flee before death or madness struck. He glanced at Rashid, saw the stoicism with which the Berber prince faced their end, and fought down the terror in his soul.

The base of the truncated cone of the half-collapsed tower rose near the center of the cavern, its crumpled base shrouded in smoke haze. By a trick of the azure light, it seemed to float on a gray cloud. The horrific statue, the altar of the wraiths, was shattered and thankfully unrecognizable. Boulders from the fallen tower and slabs of stone from the ceiling lay scattered about the cavern, covering much of the carnage. Gaius' gaze moved inextricably to the center of the cavern and the great yawning chasm dominating the cavern like a gateway to Hades. It drew him as a magnet draws iron. Invisible fingers of energy enveloped him. He fought the overwhelming urge to fling himself down into the dark abyss. Then, he felt Rashid's hand on his shoulder, drawing him back to the land of the living.

"Do not let it entrance you," Rashid warned. "That way lies death."

Gaius nodded and took a deep breath to calm his jangling nerves. "Is there any way that does not end so?"

Rashid did not reply. Gaius already knew the answer.

The tremors had increased in intensity as they approached the cavern, a steady drumming and thundering of rock cracking from the stress of Nergal's heavy strides. Now, the solid stone directly beneath his feet echoed the movement of the nether god returning to his lair, drawn by the arcane power of the amulet. Whatever gods or mysterious creatures had created the strange stone in eons past; its potency had remained undiminished over the millennia. It burned so brightly that Gaius had to avert his gaze to avoid blinding by its opulent luminescence.

Rashid stood suffused by its arcane power, glowing from within. At that moment, Gaius felt a spark of hope. The magic that withered the Berber's body, as it drew upon his flesh and blood for nourishment, enveloped it in a coat of azure armor. He held the amulet like a sword aimed at the very heart of the evil despoiling the land – Nergal.

Around them, the tunnels filled with the disquieting yammering, as the Inyosh gathered to watch their dark master deal with the frail human interlopers, unable themselves to approach the amulet's azure conflagration. Gaius had difficulty remaining on his feet, as the ground groaned and swayed in agony at Nergal's approach.

Ancient words spilled from Rashid's mouth, sending icy chills racing through Gaius' marrow. That such words issued from a human throat filled him with dread. Their meaning still eluded him, but now the words seemed more familiar, as if by concentrating, he could repeat them. The words and phrases were multi-dimensional, existing in many planes of existence at once, in many times. He knew that if misused, their power could unravel the threads that bound the fabric of time and space together. The world would cease to be.

The force of their creator's fashioning quickly became evident. The amulet erupted with power, sending tendrils of light lancing from Rashid's fingers. The azure glow enveloped Rashid's arm, searing his flesh, but he refused to relinquish his grip on the ancient talisman. His drone of alien words continued unabated. The power within the stone that had healed

Rashid now drew deeply from the Berber's body. He seemed to shrivel before Gaius' eyes, becoming almost transparent, as if he stood in many different places and many times at once. The light intensified, burned into the substance of the rock, sending tendrils of arcane energy racing throughout the mountain.

Marcellus faced away from the pit and the Berber, keeping watch on the unseen enemy lurking like shadow rats within the tunnels. He ignored the fever that wracked his body and the agony of his infected arm. He held his sword in his good arm ready to defend Gaius and Rashid. He was once more a Roman Legionnaire, duty bound to protect his comrades and his Centurion. The grizzled veteran would fulfill his obligation until his last gasping breath.

Gaius could not wrest his gaze from the Berber, though the light burned his eyes until they wept. Rashid stood, his right hand grasping the amulet extended into the air, as if a Roman statue carved from the finest marble, the heroic figure made manifest in flesh.

With a final shudder that rocked the entire cavern, Nergal completed his journey back to his lair. A cloud of dust that carried with it the odor of ancient unholy tombs billowed from the abyss and settled over them.

Rashid's glazed eyes fell on Gaius. Gaius could distinguish the cavern's far wall through the Berber's translucent body. He was but a shadow cast by his body from some other place and time. He lowered the amulet until it touched Gaius' sword. Power leapt from the amulet to the steel blade. The eldritch power of the amulet pulsed through the hand gripping the sword. Gaius fought to keep his fingers laced around the sword's hilt, as power flooded his body until he felt as if it would burst from his pores.

"Go now," Rashid said, his voice as much in Gaius' mind as in his ears.

Did the Berber sense how badly he wanted to run away? Gaius gritted his teeth and clenched his jaw, but he did not move. "No, I came this far, prince of the Berbers. I will remain by your side."

Rashid smiled and shook his head. "I was born for this task. I cannot defeat the creature; only imprison it. You must make the world aware of the danger it faces."

Before Gaius could reply, a roar so loud it rattled the cavern's ceiling erupted from the pit, sending a cascade of dust and rock falling from the ceiling over them. The debris bounced off the azure glow surrounding them as if it were a shield.

"Go!" Rashid repeated more forcefully. "Live, Roman!"

Gaius stared at Rashid, refusing to leave. It took all his willpower to keep his feet planted in the dirt beside the Berber. He had never deserted a comrade in battle. He would not desert the Berber. They had started the battle together. They would end it together. Then, he felt Marcellus tugging at his sleeve.

Marcellus' single eye, ever watchful, darted between Gaius and the dark openings surrounding the chamber. "He is right, Centurion. We cannot add to this battle. It has passed beyond the realm of mortal men. Let the Berber complete his task."

Rashid had already dismissed them from his consciousness. He stared down into the dark depths of the pit, willing the azure light to penetrate its depths. Waves of cerulean light poured over the lip of the pit and washed down its sides. Marcellus was right. His sword was useless. Reluctantly, Gaius followed Marcellus away from the pit. He stopped at the edge of the cavern and looked back at Rashid.

Tentacles as large as the bole of an oak tree rose from the pit. They danced around Rashid, now completely cloaked in indigo, as if fearing to touch him and with cause. Each time the light touched the creature's flesh, the flesh bubbled and smoked. Nergal exploded in rage. The tentacles thrashed around wildly, smashing the base of the collapsed tower, hurling boulders through the air, and scattering the piles of skeletons littering the floor of the cavern until fragments of bone and bone dust fell like rain. The ground shook and cracked. The ceiling groaned under his Titan assault.

Finally, one of the tentacles reached out and grasped Rashid. The air around him exploded in lances of azure power. The reek of seared corrupt flesh filled the chamber, an odor so acrid it ate away at the stone. Still, the Berber's litany did not diminish. The glow surrounding him intensified until it became a brilliant blaze as bright as the sun. With a howl of rage, the creature released him. Rashid fell at the edge of the pit. Only the power flowing through and around him sustained his broken body.

He looked toward Gaius and smiled; then, flung the amulet with his last remaining strength toward him. It arced through the air. Gaius caught it with one hand. Its glow did not diminish. He stared at the amulet for a moment; then, looked back at Rashid. Rashid's body, thoroughly infused with the arcane power of the amulet, glowed as brightly as the amulet itself. His eyes glowed azure, his flesh cerulean. Cobalt droplets poured from his pores like sweat. His pale sapphire lips trembled and moved.

"I see now," he said. "*I* am the power that will bind Nergal to his prison. Keep the amulet safe in case the world had need of it again. Listen to it. It will teach you its secrets."

The floor of the cavern trembled violently as the creature pounded on the walls of the pit. The edge split and cracked; then, crumbled and slid into the chasm. Gaius caught one last glimpse of Rashid; now glowing so intensely that to look at him was akin to staring into the blazing sun. A soundless explosion of azure light spilled from the pit and bathed the walls of the cavern. It swept through and past Gaius and Marcellus. The Inyosh, caught in its beam, wailed as one before exploding in a burst of ash. With the sound of snapping tree branches, sections of the ceiling broke away and began falling. Gaius knew the time to leave had arrived.

With his glowing sword in one hand and the amulet clutched in the other, he and Marcellus retraced their steps to the outside world. Only once did a wraith attack. His sword reduced it to ash. The remainder of the creatures swarmed to their god. Gaius hoped every creature in Tripolitania joined them. Their defeat must be in one fell swoop. Behind them, the battle continued. The glow grew in intensity as it permeated the rock, sanctifying it. The ground shuddered and danced. The deep, resonant groans of dying rock mixed with the high keening and wailing of frightened and dying creatures.

By the time he and Marcellus reached the fresh air of the entrance, the mountain's collapse upon itself was inevitable. Barely noticing that his sword no longer glowed, he turned his back on the caverns and walked into the desert away from the city of Hamad Rus. The ground rocked and the landscape tilted, throwing him and Marcellus to the ground. A great, billowing cloud of red dust erupted from the city, hiding the city from view. When it had dissipated, the city of Hamad Rus, having survived for millennia, was no more. Only a sand-filled depression remained where the city had once stood.

Behind them, the bluff continued to shake itself to pieces. The cavern entrances were gone, hidden by tons of rock. The sides of the bluff cracked open, bathing the surrounding desert with azure light. With the roar of a gigantic wounded beast, the top of the bluff collapsed into itself. A column of blue light stabbed toward the heavens through a cloud of dust. As Gaius watched, it slowly faded and the rumblings silenced. Nergal was trapped within.

Night had fallen while they were in the cavern, but Gaius no longer feared the darkness. The light generated by Rashid's sacrifice had cleansed the cavern and tunnels of the dark god's minions. The souls of the dead were now free. The Berber, not the amulet, had been the key necessary to seal Nergal in his tomb. Gaius wondered if Rashid had suspected this all along.

Marcellus flexed his injured arm. Wonder bathed the old legionnaire's features as he examined it, now mostly healed of its arcane infection. He smiled. "A needle and a little thread and it will as good as new." He glanced at the bluff. "The Berber was true to his word. He did it." He offered Gaius a pensive look. "What now?"

Rashid's explosion of light had done more than cleanse the cavern of its evil presence. Gaius felt no pain from his leg or from his cancerous stomach. He knew he never would again. The living entity within the amulet's stone had sliced the cancer from his body with aqua light. Like Marcellus' arm, the torn and scarred muscle of his thigh had knitted itself whole. Unsure if the amulet had made him complete as a reward or because it needed him hale and hearty to act as host, he nevertheless welcomed the relief and his reprieve from a sure and painful death.

He quickly assessed their situation. They had no food or water, no horses, and they were several days march from any village or spring. He had thought their fates sealed upon his decision to accompany Rashid into the cavern. That they had survived surprised him and left him searching for options. He had not envisioned an afterwards.

"We rest, old friend," he said and lay back on the ground, allowing the sand to cushion his body. Healed he may be, but his muscles ached from exhaustion and his mind reeled from lack of sleep and horrid memories.

As he laid there, his eyes closed in deep thought, remembering his wife and son, a distant whinnying drifted to his ears. He looked up to see Apollo galloping toward them, his fear of the dead city of Hamad Rus now gone. Behind him came the other two horses. The sight lightened his heart. Apollo had survived the ordeal. With horses, they could reach the oasis where they had found the remains of the Berber camp. The Andalusian warhorse knew the way. From there … That part he still pondered.

"Perhaps the gods favor us," Marcellus remarked with a broad grin. "We will not have to walk."

"It is better if the gods ignore us," Gaius replied, as he stood and shook the sand from his tunic. "Man worships gods thinking they listen to our prayers. I think perhaps they only tolerate us." He stared at Marcellus. "Some gods should be forgotten."

"What of Rashid's request? Do we not report what we have witnessed?"

That question had run through Gaius' mind as well. In spite of his usual devotion to duty, his answer surprised him. "And who would believe us? If any survived at Marzuq, no one will believe the story they tell. Certainly, they will pay no heed to the ravings of the natives. Rome worships many gods but believes in none." He paused. The thought running through his mind was alien to him, but he knew it did not come from the amulet. It was alien only to his nature.

"I am through with armies and empires, Marcellus. I have given my life to duty and honor and have nothing to show for it. It has cost me much I hold dear. The amulet has given me a new chance at life. I will use it. I will make my way home to my wife and my son and take them to some distant land beyond the reach of Emperor Marcus Aurelius and the Roman Empire. There, I will try hard to forget what happened here and live my life ignorant of gods and monsters. What of you, Marcellus?"

"My desire to waste away in Tuscany has vanished." He sighed. "It was but a dream anyway. If you allow me, I would accompany you to the new land you seek. I place myself in your service, Centurion." He paused. "I will keep my sword handy. I fear the world has not heard the last of this foul beast."

"May that time come long after our span of years has passed," Gaius replied.

"Aye, Centurion. I am too old and weary for another such battle."

"Perhaps, you should start calling me Gaius, my friend. Centurion I am no longer."

Marcellus moved to stand beside him. "Aye, Gaius."

Apollo rushed up, stopped in front of Gaius, and nudged his side. Gaius laid his head on Apollo's neck and patted his nose, inhaling the horse's familiar musky scent. "Take me home, old friend."

He dropped the amulet into the leather pouch on his belt. It no longer glowed, but he detected a lustier sheen to its brilliance and perhaps a kernel of brightness deep within. In his new home, he would have no statues of gods in whom he no longer believed, but he would keep a reminder of the man who had saved them all.

"Rest in peace, Rashid," he said. In truth, he did not know if the Berber had died imprisoning Nergal, or if he, like the ancient god, possessed eternal life and even now battled the monster. He hoped a better end for Rashid.

He climbed up on Apollo's back. He kicked the horse in the flanks and placed the ruins of Hamad Rus at his back. As he rode, he hoped he only imagined the ground tremble beneath the horse's feet.

Glossary of Roman Terms

Roman Legion Composition – 160 CE

Contubernium – a tent group of 8 legionnaires
Centuria – 10 contubernium, or about 80 men
Maniple – 2 centuriae or 160 men
Cohort – 3 maniples or 540 men
Legion – 10 cohorts or 5,400 men

Roman Legion Ranks – 160 CE

Emperor – Ruler of Roman Empire, protector of Pax Romana
Praetor – Regional Governor
Imperator – Commander of a Legion
Legate – Second in command of a legion
Praefectus castrorum – Commander of a fort
Tribune – Third in command of a legion
Centurion – Captain of a cohort
Optio – Lieutenant
Tesserarius – Sergeant
Sesquiplecarus – Corporal
Decanus – Private
Milite – common soldier
Tirone – raw recruit
Munifex – untrained workers
Triarii – veterans
Evocati – re-enlisted veterans
Immunes – specialists, cooks, paymasters, musicians
Sagittarii – bowmen
Medici – doctors
Auxilia – non-legion soldiers
Cornicen – bugler

Roman Legionnaire Uniform

Amillae – Gold ceremonial Manica issued for awards
Balteus – belt for sword, dagger, etc.
Braccae – Trousers
Caligae – metal-shod leather sandals
Cingulum – shoulder sash, sometimes for sword
Focale – neck scarf, usually red
Galea – metal helmet, officers wore a transverse plume on top
Greaves – metal leg protector
Lorca hamata – chain mail armor worn over tunic
Manica – metal arm protector
Paludamentum – cape, usually red
Subligaria – underwear
Torc – gold necklace given for valor

Weaponry

Arcus – long bow
Aclis – javelin
Gladius – short sword
Hasta – spear
Onager – a catapult that hurls large rocks.
Puglia – dagger
Spatha – heavy sword
Sputum – shield
Siege Engines – Ballista, a catapult like a large crossbow that fires arrows.

Legion Terminology

Balnea or thermae – Roman bath
Capsarii – bath slave
Castra – fort

Cornu – horn
Flagrum – short, leather whip with metal pieces braided into lashes
Fustuarium – jail
Lictor – soldier assigned to use the flagellum
Lime – A line of forts
Lupanarium – brothel
Papilia – leather tent
Puella – prostitute
Querquetulanae – spirits residing in oak wood
Strigil – curved bone tool for scraping the skin in a bath
Valetudunarium – hospital

Glossary of Berber Terms

Aduar – village
Aguram – tomb
Akuzzi – gas passed from the anus
Amazigh – Berber people
Azarqis – blue
Chott – salt flats
Erg – sand dune sea
Hamada – rocky plain
Iharz – amulet, medallion
Imalayka – angel
Serir – gravel plains
Tabyni – darkness
Tamdda – vulture
Tamzawit – Dust devil
Tamazight – Berber language
Tignut – dust storm
Wadi – dry valley

About the Author

James E. Gurley, a 66-year old retired chef, lives on Dauphin Island, Alabama with his wife, Kim, and two cats. He writes horror, science fiction, and military fiction novels when he's not playing guitar or keyboards for local blues/rock bands.

www.jamesgurley.com